A Second Story

J. A. Collignon

A | Arrowmount Press

Book cover art and design by Tessa Brenan, @roguecorner on Twitter.

Interior maps and illustrations by J.A. Collignon

Print ISBN: 978-1-7388682-0-9

Ebook ISBN: 978-1-7388682-1-6

A | ARROWMOUNT PRESS

For those of us who wander willingly into other realms

CONTENTS

Tua Outreach
Dunnaloch Pass
Antovers
Prelun
ENSGÁRD
Dunvale
Tórduu
Ardnablane
Glasrock
Blackshell Reach
Malgárd
NERIAN EMPIRE
Northdenn
Falenroch
Underthall
Chârteau
Grenne
ALIEWETH
Deliar
Crestborne
Narveil
Claymore
Ironcoast
Basingrove
Tage's Reach
BLACKSHELL FOREST
Silver Creek
BRENEM
Feycross
Keat
Tanju
EMPIRE
Boarsrest
PRALON
Hutton
Notton
Riverspoke
ARROWMOUNT
Quhar
NARAKAMI
Lilleby
Kenmar
Mosfell
Wolf's Peck
Ryefeld
Taimen
Almsir
Talimar
ZIDIEN
Rath
Meadon
Caspasian Sea
Caspasian Isles
RAVAR

1. Town Gate
2. Stables
3. Arrowmount Books
4. May's Cafe
5. Cobb's Down-By-The-Beach
6. Old'n Narrow
7. Lighthouse
8. Alderidge's
9. Town Centre
10. The Bronze Bee
11. Eldar's Wall
12. Port

PART ONE
Wildflowers

1

DANCING WILDFLOWER REVERIES

Wildflowers danced happily in the sunshine, their brilliantly colored heads ducking and swaying throughout the meadow. Arileas Damaris sat surrounded by his other party members, wondering, not for the first time, what he had gotten himself into.

"Ari, you're lost in the clouds," said a charming, honey smooth voice from behind him. Coming out of his reverie, Ari jumped as a man plopped down on the grass beside him and propped himself up amidst the flowers on one elbow. The man shook his shaggy, curling black hair away from his face and turned his ocean-blue eyes on Ari.

Finnean Goldmark.

From the billowing shirt that lay casually open, revealing a curling patch of black hair on his chest, down to neat leather trousers that cut off just under his knees and the casual pose he struck, Finnean oozed confidence and a natural charisma that enchanted Ari.

Rays of sunshine cast a soft glow against his golden skin, highlighting the unshaved stubble on his angular jaw. A smile spread lazily across Finn's face. It was unfair how beautiful this man was.

It felt as though Ari was staring straight into the sun, and he couldn't stop.

"Arileas," said Finn in a sing-song tone, waving a hand in front of Ari's eyes. Iluinn's mercy, had he been staring?

Ari laughed awkwardly and dropped his gaze away from Finn's intoxicating smirk. "Finnean."

"I've been calling your name for minutes now. I never thought that you, the infamously focused Arileas Damaris, would get so distracted by a view. The flowers, of course," he added as Ari's cheeks blushed pink. So he *had* been staring. *Gods.*

Finnean laughed, the sound full and hearty and totally carefree. That's what Ari liked best about being around him. From the moment the man had strolled into the bar back in Feycross and joined their party, even if they were neck deep in a bloodbath of trolls, fighting a hag, or drinking subpar ale in a rundown tavern, he had an uncanny ability to find the bit of joy in any moment.

"Alright, my lord," teased Ari playfully, flicking a bit of grass at him. Finn was the son of some lord in a far-off kingdom — though, thankfully, he was not a lord himself, which probably would have made him even more insufferable. Any poke at his familial status caused a playfully affronted smile to appear on his face, the single dimple by his mouth pulling at Ari's heart.

Finn shifted forward to grab a bundle of wildflowers, plucking them free. He cast a look around at the meadow and their fellow party members that were scattered about, twiddling the flowers between his fingers absently. A small crease appeared between his eyebrows, as though thinking something through.

A short time ago, their group had been barely acquaintances that had arrived in a tavern, gathered together by a king to do a job. Over the past couple weeks, though, they had settled into something more akin to friendship. Finn and Ari had become nearly inseparable, which continued to surprise Ari every day. In Feycross, Ari had rolled his eyes when this charming, beautiful man sat down with them. Ari believed that Finn thought rather highly of himself, and Ari had had spent too much of his life around people who were just like that.

But, as quickly as that opinion had formed, Finn showed time and time again that he was more kind and thoughtful underneath all that shiny, smiling exterior. His energy drew Ari in constantly. Ari's heart tumbled fast into an affection deeper than he ever thought he could feel, truth be told.

"I love flowers," said Ari, watching those in Finn's fingers dance. "They remind me of the meadows near my home."

"What was your home like?"

Ari shot Finn a look. He knew perfectly well what Ari's childhood had been like — the man had coaxed most of Ari's life story out of him one night after the party had come across a sensational stash of alcohol. Ari had lived under a tyrannical mother that ran her household exactly how she wanted, down to the shining white marble halls that remained silent as the stone themselves. As head cleric to the church their family belonged to, it was expected of Ari and his siblings to follow suit. The others did, but Ari had had other plans.

Plans that involved a near obsession with wizardry as a boy, which got him tossed from their household by his mother's personal guard as soon as he was old enough to live on his own.

"I mean the landscape," said Finn, motioning to the flowers around. "The hills. The flowers."

Ari nodded, letting the memory of the hills fill his mind. "They were wondrous. Rolling hills coated in long grass and wildflowers in the summer with snow-topped mountains framing it all in the distance. There were beautiful streams all throughout the woods that surrounded them, perfect for swimming and hiding from responsibilities. In the winter, they were often untouched by anyone but me." Ari let out a long breath and smiled, looking down at his hands. "It felt like my own little world."

"That sounds absolutely glorious."

"It was," sighed Ari. "This meadow is only a fraction of the size of what those hills were, but it does have its own beauty to it."

Finnean sat up, bits of flowers and grass clinging to his clothing as though he was a magnet. Without hesitation, he reached over and threaded the tiny bundle of wildflowers he had been fiddling with through one of Ari's braids, right above his long, pointed left ear.

"There," said Finn quietly, almost to himself. "Now you've got a bit of that beauty to carry with you."

Ari choked on his next question, words dying on his lips, and simply stared at the man in front of him. Was Finn purposefully letting his hand linger by Ari's hair, or was it just Ari's imagination?

One of the other party members cracked a joke from behind them, but Ari's brain was too loud with the sound of his own heartbeat to hear. Finn laughed and turned his attention away from Ari, running his hands over his shirt, brushing off all the bits of the meadow as he stood, leaving Ari's side.

Ari's fingers tingled, wondering what it would feel like to thread them through Finn's hair.

Come on, Ari, he chided himself, peering out at the sea of wildflowers once again. *He may be rather handsome, and have the prettiest eyes I've ever... oh, gods, I'm fully gone, aren't I?*

Arileas sank onto his elbows and dropped his head back, letting the mix of loose hair, braids, and flowers fall behind him in a curtain of white. He closed his eyes against the sun and let his traitorous heart beat for the man, knowing it was probably hopeless.

Probably.

2

UNTRACEABLE TRACES

Finnean

Night fell around the party slowly, like ink spreading through water. Low murmuring came from three of the party members — Soren, Brennyn, and Prim — who were seated around the fire. Soren's wings, out in a relaxed position behind him, shone in the moonlight, the black feathers turning slightly purple. He gestured toward the flames, playing with the sparks that danced toward him, turning them into tiny illusory fairies to dance around the others.

Prim, their tiny barbarian that packed more than your average punch, poked the fire with a stick to keep the flames and sparks roaring, an amused smile on her face.

"Damaris, are you taking next watch?" Klea walked back into the clearing from the end of her rounds, rolling her muscular orcish shoulders beneath the weight of her armor that she started to undo. Finn perked up slightly at the sound of Ari's name, his eyes immediately falling on the white-haired elf that was seated a little way off against a tree, reading a book. How he could read in the dark was beyond Finn.

"I can," Ari answered, standing up.

Finn was on his feet before he could stop himself, his heart too eager to spend more time with Ari alone. "I'll join you."

He flinched inwardly at himself, knowing he should've stayed quiet by the others. Ari didn't need him chasing his heels, and Finn for one did not need his stupidly, suddenly romantic heart to latch on so fiercely to someone he knew he wasn't going to be around for long.

"If you wanted privacy with your boyfriend, you could've just asked," teased Brennyn, tapping an arrow they were fletching against their forehead, winking at Finn. Finn felt his face heat up, thankful that the sky was darkening to hide it. Was it really that obvious that he liked Ari so much?

He hoped not, because if Ari knew, then it would make what he had to do even worse.

"Do you think that we'll get to Boarsrest by tomorrow?"

Finn blinked a few times. It took him slightly too long to realize what Ari had said, his mind getting caught on the moonlight shining on Ari's hair, reminding him of starlight. He cleared his throat and fingered the hilt of one of his daggers. "Oh. Uh. I don't know, maybe? I haven't been out this way before."

"I am getting tired of chasing this man around the realm," said Ari with a sigh, sending an arrow straight to Finn's heart.

As a party, they had been assembled with one purpose back in Feycross: to hunt down the notorious royal assassin called the Shade. They had been collectively hired by the King of Zidien, King Zoren, to bring about this assassin's demise. Finn, being who he was, had wiggled his way onto the team without much effort or error. His skills with his daggers were as yet unmatched in the party, and he was rather good at sneaking.

"I wonder what King Zoren would do if the Shade was never caught," mused Finn, flicking his dagger out to toss it around between his fingers.

Ari chuckled darkly. "Probably throw some kind of tantrum that would end with someone being sentenced to death."

"Good ol' Zoren really does love his death sentences, doesn't he?"

"Hopefully it will not come to that," said Ari, peering around the forest with a watchful eye before turning to look directly at Finn. "Do you really think the Shade has made his way to Boarsrest? It seems almost... to obvious."

Finn snorted. "You're not wrong. What kind of assassin goes around leaving traces thick enough for us to follow? Even I wouldn't do that."

"That's why I'm suspicious. Maybe he's leading us off in a completely different direction." Ari tripped over a protruding root on the ground that he missed in the low light, swearing under his breath. Finn reached out in a snap to catch him, the two of them coming to a stop for a second. Finn willed his fingers to let go of Ari before he lingered too long, like he had with the wildflowers.

"But Boarsrest is the only lead we have, of course." Finn smiled, ducking beneath a low hanging branch. "This Shade — he seems so pompous, doesn't he? With all these rumors of his glory. Before I left home, there was something new going around about him killing the King of Alieweth's right hand with a look alone, like that's possible. And another about cleaving through a duke at his own dinner table without anyone else noticing. I don't believe any of it."

"Some of it is real," said Ari with a shake of his head, as though he too didn't believe most of the stories. "I was present when the duke's body was found. It wasn't at the dinner table, that was a court rumor flying out of hand. He was killed in his own locked chambers before the feast, when he was visiting King Zoren. He was found mostly naked, halfway through changing, with his hands still trapped inside of his shirt."

Finn and Ari snorted in laughter, scaring a few birds out of a nearby tree.

"I shouldn't laugh," chortled Ari. "The man's dead, for godssake."

"Who found him?"

"His manservant. The poor lad had to be given a double shot of brandy before he calmed down after finding his master in such an intimate way."

"Tell me," said Finn with a careful glance at Ari, "was the duke found with the Shade's trademark left on him?"

"Thumbprint of blood, right on the man's cheek. I won't tell you which one."

Finn let out a snort. "Like leaving a lip paint stain on a lover. Brazen man. I wonder why he does that?"

"We can ask him when we catch up to him," said Ari.

Finn knocked his shoulder amiably into Ari's, shooting him a sideways smile. The two of them continued in companionable silence for a while beneath the trees. Nothing moved in the forest except for them and the occasional bird, though truth be told, they wouldn't have noticed anything unless it walked right in front of them.

"What are you going to do when all of this is done?"

"I'm not sure," answered Finn, reaching up and pulling a bundle of leaves off a tree to fiddle with, pocketing his dagger. "Do you have a comfortable home to go back to? What, with you being a king's man?"

"A place to live, yes, but I wouldn't call it comfortable, or a home," said Ari, shooting Finn a glance that made him laugh. "Zoren gave me one when I came under his employ, but it doesn't really feel like mine. I have very little to go back to."

"What do you mean?"

Ari cringed slightly, and Finn worried he had pressed a sore spot. "It might have been an incredibly stupid choice, but I let the king know that this was my last job for him. Once this is done, I'm..." Ari let out a long sigh, as though the weight of the situation he was in had just increased. "I didn't really have anything in mind, actually. I quit."

Finn slowed in his walking, his mouth hanging open. From the moment he met Ari, Finn knew that he loved decision making and keeping everything orderly and planned out, so things went well. "That doesn't seem like you at all."

"I know," said Ari, his voice pitching up an octave as he laughed nervously. "I hated it there, absolutely detested working for a king. I didn't realize it until he called me in for this job, but it was exactly like working under my mother. You had to be ready at all times to drop everything and do what they asked, exactly as they asked, or else."

"After this job is done, you're going to return to the kingdom?"

"I figured I might do some travelling on my own," said Ari. "Maybe search the realm to see if I can find a place where I feel like I could really... settle in. It's been so long since I've felt like I belong — I don't think I've ever felt that way."

Finn *hmmed* under his breath, slightly surprised by the elf. "I like that idea. Travelling the realm on your own terms. Perhaps I'll visit the coast, or venture down south, see what the sands have to offer."

"You don't have a job or a life to go back to?"

Not after this, he thought to himself. "Not one that is worth caring for. I'm sure that my employer won't mind if he never saw me again."

Ari chuckled before he tripped again on a tree root, this time falling to one knee before Finn could catch him. "I think we could both use a break, then," he said as Finn helped him back up.

"My dear elf, you hit the nail on the head. We could all do with a break, somewhere far away from these godsforsaken forests with all their hidden roots."

"Maybe you and I will find something to do, once the Shade is in irons or in the grave."

The two of them rounded the camp a few times, talking of nothing, filling the night with their voices. A beam of moonlight cut through the clearing and hit both Finn and Ari as they returned to the others a while later, startling Finn slightly. He reached out a hand to stop Ari as he noticed something dangling by his ear.

"What?"

Finn gazed at Ari for a moment, unable to form the words. He had kept the flowers in his hair. *Perhaps he had forgotten they were even there in the first place,* said a voice in Finn's head. Against his better judgement, he reached toward the elf and gently touched the bundle that had come dislodged.

"You've still got the flowers."

Ari lifted his own fingers up to the bundle, their two hands getting tangled. The bundle of wildflowers that Finn had weaved there earlier fell to the ground as bits of Ari's braid came undone.

Finn bent to retrieve them at the same moment Ari crouched down. He recoiled from Finn, as though their proximity was too much for him. Hiding a small wince, Finn threaded the flowers back into place.

"I didn't mean to knock them free," he said quietly. "They belong there."

They froze, staring at each other in the moonlight. Finn couldn't help but let his fingers linger along Ari's skin, brushing softly down. He was making it so much worse on himself. Ari was impossible to stay away from.

Ari shivered away from his touch at the same moment Finn became aware of the sounds of crackling fire behind them. The scent of roasting meat drifted over, reminding Finn of where they were.

He shot to his feet. *Stupid, traitorous heart,* thought Finn to himself, knowing full well nothing could ever come of this. Not in this life.

By the warm light of the fire, Brennyn and Soren were in the middle of an intense card game of Knights as Prim sharpened her greatsword nearby. Klea was already dozing with her head propped up on her bag, scimitar clutched in her arms like a prized possession.

Finn settled down by his things, trying to get the memory of Ari's skin off his fingertips. The party settled in for the night, each of them taking watch in turns, poking at the fire to keep it lit. Finn knew he should be sleeping, but his brain wouldn't stop whirring as he lay there staring up at the stars.

After this job, he would never — could never — see any of these party members again. He tried to empty his mind, turning over to stare at the fire, before shifting the other way to look at the shapes of his sleeping party members in the moonlight.

His hand travelled to the bundle of small spheres he kept tucked in an inner pocket of his trousers, his fingers rolling over each one to ensure they were still there.

One more job.

3

A Life of Murder and Mayhem

Arileas

"**G**ET DOWN!"

The other party members ducked on cue as Arileas stepped out from behind a tree and pointed furiously, a bead of light shooting toward the wolven. It exploded in a furious ball of fire, hitting the beast with a searing blast of heat. The wolven gnashed its teeth and let out a wail of pain as flames licked across its fur. Prim and Klea peppered it with blows, bringing it down in seconds.

Chaos roiled around the meadow as the pack of beasts attacked from all sides. Having had very little warning before the creatures burst through the trees and into the meadow where they were sleeping, most of the party had no armor on.

He shot flames and lightning toward whatever had fur and teeth, hands slicing through the air as fast as he could cast. Yells and shouts from the rest of the party filled the air. Blood began to seep between the trampled and ruined wildflowers, soaking the bottom of Ari's boots. Heart pounding, panic clawing up his throat to mix with the taste of iron on the air, Ari tried to stay calm as he breathed through his mouth, tracking the beasts around them.

Klea's scimitar swung mercilessly into the body of the nearest creature, a snarl on her already bloody face. Soren and Prim surrounded another, bringing it down with a mix of metal and glowing, radiant magic. Brennyn backed up, attempting to gain distance enough to shoot their bow, aiming at another of the pack.

And Finn —

Where was he?

Sucking in a sharp breath, Ari ducked back around a tree, sneaking over to the next. He launched another ball of fire at a beast, its wails of pain echoing through the clearing. Ari knew that he was not the strongest of the party, so he preferred to keep a distance, preparing spells to shoot off when the moment came, acting as backup for the others.

A gasp of pain sounded and Soren dropped in a flurry of feathers, unconscious.

Standing in front of him, dagger raised in his fist, was Finnean.

What?

Ari felt the world stop as Finn's eyes found his, blue depths sharp in the second they locked eyes.

"You son of a bitch," hissed Ari.

Finn spun away as Ari lifted his fingers, aiming for an attack. The man brought his blade down and through the body of one of the last wolven, blood spurting across his face and chest. With a shout of encouragement, Brennyn spun into view, moving close to Finn without fear. They hadn't seen what Ari had.

A beast stepped into Ari's line of sight, causing Ari to lunge to the side trying to keep Finn and Brennyn in view, but when he could see clearly once more, Brennyn lay crumpled on the ground too. *Shit.*

Prim turned then, noticing something was off. She advanced on Finn, a snarl on her face. "What's happening here, Goldmark?"

"Slight change of plans," called Finn. "My name isn't actually Goldmark. Though, I won't lie, I do like it a hell of a lot more than my real one. Has a better ring to it."

Prim brought her sword down in a hard blow, which Finn barely managed to side swipe with his two daggers, throwing Prim off balance. Finn used his height over her to his advantage as he got in her face, slashing viciously with his blades. They were moving in such a whirlwind that Ari couldn't get a clean shot off on Finn.

"Who are you really?" growled Prim.

"My name is Finnean Shademark," Finn answered, sidestepping her, "or better known as the Shade."

Shock ricocheted through Ari at the same time that Prim's face twitched in surprise, her sword hesitating ever so slightly, a half-formed word on her lips. Finn brought the butt of his dagger down against her temple and she dropped to the trampled wildflowers.

Ari felt as though he was on fire. He ducked back behind the tree and sank back on his heels, breathing hard. What was happening? Was he hallucinating? Or was Finn, the man who had joked and become friends with everyone in the party truly attacking them — using the name of the assassin they were hunting?

A heartbeat later, Klea let out a yelp of pain as she too went down. Ari stood, trying to make as little noise as possible, desperately trying to think of a way that this could all make sense.

"So."

Ari spun, finding a blade at his throat, sticky with blood. A strong arm pinned him back against the tree, bark digging into his shoulders through the thin linen of his shirt. Ari froze and sucked in a breath.

"Finnean," he said carefully, acutely aware of the way Finn was pressed into him, bodies almost flat against one another.

Ari's fingers twitched at his side, drawing energy together and holding until the right moment. He had the slimmest chance of beating Finn to the punch — the man was exceptionally fast with those daggers. Which, now that he thought about it, made perfect sense.

The Shade was too.

Their chests heaved, the only sound in the silence of the meadow their ragged breath, both waiting for the other to move first.

The dagger held still against Ari's throat. It wasn't enough to pierce his skin, but if Ari so much as moved wrong he knew the edge would cut. Finn's expression was still as stone, something that Ari had never seen on his beautiful face before.

Then, as though he had peeled off a mask, Finn's eyebrow twitched, and a smirk broke across his face. Ari didn't know if that was more terrifying than the mask, this look of familiarity on a face that he thought he knew. A low chuckle began to shake in Finn's chest. Ari could feel it through his body, all along the spots where Finn was pressed into him, pinning him in place.

"I've got to admit," said Finn, panting slightly. "I've been wanting to put you in this kind of position for a while now."

"Oh?"

It was all Ari could choke out.

"I wanted to see how you could handle yourself with a blade pressed to your throat." Finn's eyes flicked down to Ari's hand, where magic held steady, waiting to be released, before coming back up to rest on Ari's face.

"Though, I did imagine it going a bit differently."

"How exactly did you imagine it going?" Ari snapped, an insane bout of sarcastic bravery encompassing him. He swallowed, feeling the blade nick his throat, the warmth of blood start to drip down his neck.

"Hmm," said Finn, looking Ari's face up and down, letting his smirk curl into a smile. "Something like this."

A tight burst of panic shot through Ari as Finn twisted his dagger away from Ari's throat, expecting it to plunge into his chest. He raised his fingers, the spell coalescing, before Finn stabbed the tree next to Ari's head. With his other hand, he grasped Ari's face and pulled it to his, kissing him as though he was drowning and Ari was air.

The spell vanished from Ari's fingertips, replaced by pure shock.

Finn tasted like sunlight and blood — which Ari promptly forgot as the kiss and the entire situation caused his brain to malfunction.

When they pulled apart, Finn kept Ari's head in his hands and gazed at him. His expression flickered sadly before Finn shook his head. "I'm more sorry for this than you know."

Before Ari could react, Finn dashed the butt of his second dagger into Ari's temple.

He dropped like a stone.

4

THREE MAGIC BEADS

Finnean

Ari's eyes closed and his body slumped forward into Finn's arms. Finn laid him down gently, trying all the while to fight back the enormous weight of guilt settling on his shoulders. *This is wrong,* said a small voice in his head that sounded irritatingly like his own, over and over. He hesitated before crouching down, pressing his fingers into Ari's throat, double checking that Ari's pulse still pounded, strong and true.

"Why now?" he hissed to himself. "Why do I gain a conscience *now*?"

All his life, he had been trained to do one thing and one thing only: kill at the behest of King Tenan, exactly how he ordered it. Tenan preferred to keep an outward order to his kingdom that ran with an undercurrent of blood and deceit. To do that, Tenan needed his assassin, as the king preferred his enemies to die without a sound, leaving barely a trace. The mystery and terror behind the name of the Shade let Tenan hold power over the entire realm through fear and the unknown.

Finn trained as a boy into adulthood, becoming someone who could disappear in the shadows and who got the job done without error — and he was *good at that*. The Shade became well known by name, but not by face, thankfully. King Tenan liked to keep his best kept secrets, well, secret.

Finn hadn't let himself become attached. Not when the king could have him kill anyone at any time or in any place. That he had learned early on. For the longest time, Finn hadn't cared one way or the other. He rarely felt anything as the Shade.

But now this man, this gorgeous elf, threatened to unspool him. Emotions roiled up to the surface that he hadn't felt in years — maybe at all in his entire life. Finn was choked with it.

He didn't want to let go of him.

Get the job done, said a second voice in his head that sounded too much like King Tenan's. One last job. One last time he would be beholden to the name of the Shade. Then he could run wherever he wanted, as far as he wanted.

Finn forced himself to let go and stand, the warmth of Ari's skin lingering on his fingertips. He pushed aside his emotions, tamping them as far down as he could.

He withdrew the bundle of small spheres from his pocket, fingering them carefully as he walked away from Ari and back to the other unconscious party members. A dull throb of remorse thudded through him. He had really come to like these people over the past few weeks. It was the first time he felt as though he was part of something, rather than just someone that lurked in the shadows, watching.

Before he left his kingdom, Finn had begun devising the plan that now lay in the palm of his hand. He cleared his throat and blinked down, refocusing on his mission here. One last one, then he was free. What had

Ollie said to do?

"One small crush of a finger, and you'll have about thirty seconds to get as far away from those as you can."

"How does it work?"

"It's a concentrated modify memory-like spell," Ollie had answered, carefully reaching over the old, stained and chipped wooden counter to place three perfectly round dark blue beads in his open palm. "Something I cooked up for — well, that's beside the point."

Finn had nodded curtly, rolling the beads around with his thumb. Whatever Ollie had been doing was her business. "Will these be enough?"

"You'll have enough firepower with these to take out about twenty people in a thirty-foot radius. All you need to do before hand is imagine exactly what you want them to think happened, picture it clearly in your mind, and the enchantment should take effect."

Finn wasn't one to dwell on *should* because they made the certainty of freedom feel less solid than he liked, so he had quickly pushed the possibility of failure from his mind.

Standing in the forest, Finn pulled a different shape out of his other pocket — a flat, cream colored disk so thin it resembled a piece of parchment. He was not overly familiar with magic, so he had needed as much help as he could get.

"The magic in that will take hold the moment it dissolves in blood," Ollie had said, looking far too pleased at the thought. "Your blood. That's what seals it. Blood and intention. You do not need to be a magic user to manipulate it."

"How long will it last?" he had asked, taking the thin material in hand.

"Oh, enough time," said Ollie, which had made Finn wonder briefly if she knew what he was planning to do, despite how little information he had given. "Twenty-four hours, easy."

Twenty-four hours. Twenty-four hours that this beast in front of him would look like his dead, bisected body. Twenty-four hours for the others to burn it, as he knew they would — it was the burial custom in the Brenem Empire — before he would be officially free.

He used the edge of his dagger to draw blood from his thumb, the one he so often left imprinted behind on victims. With a glance around to choose a fitting creature, he pressed the disk into the crimson liquid on the beast's fur, picturing exactly what he wanted to happen. When he placed the disk, nothing happened for a moment, causing Finn's heart to launch into his throat with panic. *What if this fails? What if the magic is faulty? What* — then, the creature transformed.

In a matter of seconds, Finn was looking down at his exact double, right down to the clothing he was currently wearing, blood stained and torn.

Except *that* Finn was very obviously dead.

Finnean suppressed the rising nausea in his throat as he leaned over, sliding a ring off his thumb, one that would be used to prove his death to the king. The party would need something physical after all, to prove they had killed him. The ring on his thumb had King Tenan's insignia marked on the inside, and his father's house on the face. Once they looked close enough, any king would be able to identify the Shade's ring without fail.

He cast one last look back at the tree where he had left Ari, unconscious. *You can't just leave him there,* he thought to himself. *Not like that.*

Before Finn crushed the memory beads, he walked over, picking some of the remaining wildflowers that had not been trampled and draped them over the dagger he left stuck in the tree.

Why, he wasn't entirely sure. He knew Ari wouldn't remember their last moments together the way he would. Maybe it was his own, new-found sentimentality coming back to haunt him.

One last time, he let himself look down at Ari, wondering what their life could have been if they met differently. If he hadn't been the Shade, if Ari hadn't been part of the party that hunted him...

Don't dwell, snapped Tenan's voice in Finn's head, shocking him out of his fantasies and pushing him back to the clearing, leaving Ari and the dream they could have had behind.

That was not Finn's reality. This was. The magic in his hand was his ticket to freedom.

Finn closed his eyes as he stood in the forest, holding two of the three small spheres, picturing in his mind how the fight should have gone after he had taken out Soren.

Klea and Prim would have come up to flank him, faces contorted with fury as they found out who he was. The two of them would have taken him down after a tense fight — two of them with large weapons would have been too much for him and his daggers. Then, wolven would have snuck in behind, taking Klea and Prim by surprise, followed by Brennyn not far off.

He painted the scene in his mind, layer by layer. Memories were fickle things. Easily malleable, changeable.

As Finn pictured himself falling, body cleaved almost in two, he crushed the spheres like Ollie had instructed, letting their pieces fall amidst the muck of blood and crushed wildflowers, a soft shimmering magic emitting from them as the enchantment started to take hold.

With one last look at the party, at what he had done to secure his freedom, Finnean Shademark turned and ran as fast as he could.

Finn travelled west, taking the same route that the party had been heading. He hadn't lied to Ari when he said he wanted to travel this way when the job was done — it was why he had decided to place the threads off in this direction through the empire anyway. Whenever the opportunity came to flip the script on the party and find his freedom, he would simply keep on this track, no matter where he was. West was a hazy destination set in his mind, without any real reason, if he was being entirely honest. Perhaps it was because it was far enough away from his home that he wouldn't have to think about it any longer. Perhaps it was simply because it was a direction, and he needed a plan to follow to keep himself sane in his new freedom.

And free he now was.

It was an entirely strange feeling that he was still not becoming all together comfortable with, being free and alone. Finn had been alone emotionally and mentally his whole life — but not physically. Yes, he worked alone in the shadows, but when he was in kingdoms and palaces, there was always noise. There were always servants, courtiers, people breathing down his neck wherever he went.

Walking in the forest, aimlessly headed west for no reason other than it was the inkling of a plan in his brain, he found himself feeling more desperately alone than he ever had.

He hadn't expected to feel lonely when he was free. He had expected to feel elated, relieved, joyous — but as of yet, he hadn't felt a single emotion like that. Maybe it was because he was used to travelling with the party, or he was realizing how little he liked being actively alone.

Every morning he woke up, he would turn automatically as though expecting to see one of his party members next to him sleeping, the shape of Klea's broad back as she snored lightly, or the flash of black feathers as Soren tended to breakfast. And when he remembered he was entirely alone, he would feel this ache of emptiness in his chest that would keep him pinned to the ground for a little too long, staring up at the sky.

It was always worse when he woke up expecting to see Ari near him.

Or when he was walking through the forest, as he was now, and turned his head to look over his shoulder, a half-formed sentence on his lips as though some kind of torturer had taken over his subconsciousness.

He made it to Boarsrest in good time, feeling the knot in his chest relax slightly with the sound and sight of people. The villagers cast him looks over their shoulders, some nodding in greeting, as he walked through the scant buildings. The dirt roads coalesced into a small meeting point, where the largest cluster of buildings were placed all facing the center, which Finn supposed was an imitation of a town center or city square.

And that was it.

This was the tiniest place he had ever laid eyes on. He was looking at on the entire village, too, from where he stood, turning slowly on his heel.

He sagged slightly with a sigh and peered at the worn, cracked signs around him until he found one that said, quite simply, INN.

Where there was an inn, there was food, drink, and a bed. The simplest things a man could ever need.

5

PYRES AND DAGGERS

Arileas

When Ari awoke to the sounds of people talking and the press of feathered hands to his chest, he blinked up at a dagger lodged into a tree above him, wrapped with a bundle of wildflowers.

"We got him," said Soren, coming into view, grinning wildly. He stood and extended a feathered arm down to Ari.

Ari blinked a few times. A throbbing pain shuddered through his temple, causing him to wince as he sat up. How *had* he been knocked out? "Did we?"

"Come and see for yourself."

His legs wobbled slightly as he stood, rounding the tree to find the carnage of wolven bodies. The memories of the fight began to surface in pieces. Hazy images of wolven attacking his party members flashed in his mind, clouded slightly from the pounding in his head.

"You okay?" Soren was there suddenly, steadying Ari as he swayed where he stood.

"I..." Ari dragged a hand over his face, feeling as though his mind

27

was trying to scrape through hardened mud to put thoughts together. His face felt swollen and off, as though whatever had knocked him out had also punched him in the mouth. For some reason, he could taste something slightly citrusy, though the last thing he could remember eating was the meat that Brennyn had prepared last night over the fire.

Soren patted his shoulder gently, grief mingling with something that looked like relief flashing across his bird features. "Maybe you don't want to see this. You can take my word for it, we got him."

"I don't understand," said Ari slowly, looking at the wolven. "Got who?"

Soren grimaced and pointed at a shape amidst the dead wolven as the memories finally surfaced in Ari's mind. They slid into place slowly, as though the memories didn't quite believe themselves. He took a careful step toward the shape, his mouth filling with an overwhelming burn of iron and stomach acid.

Flashes of Finn taking down Soren, then turning to find both Klea and Prim behind him, weapons raised. Flashes of metal and weapons and blood, and finally —

Ari's heart gave a hard pang of grief, taking in the body in front of him. Or, rather, he should say *pieces* of a body. He didn't want to believe his eyes, couldn't wrap his mind around what he was seeing. It was as though someone was yelling at him that this wasn't real, this was not what happened. But here was the hard proof, in the shape of a nearly bisected body with the most beautiful face Ari had seen.

Finnean Goldmark.

No.

Finnean Shade*mark. The Shade.*

Pure, burning anger at Finn's betrayal seared through the rest of the fog in Ari's mind. How could he? How could he have come into their party and lied over and over in his actions, in his words, in his eager enjoyment in being a part of the party that was meant to take him down?

And now he lay in pieces.

Nausea rose in Ari's stomach. He turned, putting his back to the man who had burrowed a deep groove into his heart and mind over the past few weeks.

Ari peered around at the others as they talked through Finn's betrayal and their supposed subsequent win. Klea clapped Brennyn on the shoulder, squeezing as Brennyn sniffed hard, wiping tears off their face before standing up straighter and setting their jaw.

They bent down to the body and slid a ring off of Finn's thumb, peering at it with a scoff. "The proof was right in front of us. It has the royal seal on it — King Tenan's seal."

"It'll be enough for King Zoren," said Prim with a soft grimace, taking the ring from Brennyn and pocketing it. "Proof the job was done. I'm not carrying pieces of him back to the kingdom."

They all believed this unerringly. And why shouldn't they? There was no evidence to the contrary as to what happened, except for the nagging feeling in the back of Ari's mind that kept pushing him to see something that he couldn't quite pinpoint.

The evidence was right there.

So why couldn't Ari believe it?

The party watched Finn's body burn for a little while on a pyre they had quickly built, surrounded by the corpses of the wolven, until the heat and the smell became unbearable. Then, quietly, they gathered their things, getting ready for a journey.

"Where are you all travelling from here?" asked Ari, adjusting the strap on his bag to rest more comfortably on his shoulder. The others turned to him, equal looks of soft confusion on their faces.

Prim took a few steps forward and placed a gentle hand on his forearm. "Why do I get the sense that you're not going to be following us back to the kingdom?"

"I..." Ari shook his head slowly. "I don't have anything back there. This was my last job for His Majesty, and Finn —"

He cut off; the name painful in his throat as a swell of conflicting emotions warred in his gut. Ari still couldn't entirely wrap his mind around the circumstances, but he couldn't disbelieve what his own eyes were seeing as they drifted back to the pyre and the burning bodies.

Prim cleared her throat and smiled up at him softly. "Well, no matter what you do, Arileas. If you ever make it back home, don't be a stranger."

The others nodded around her. Ari's heart ached gently as he took them all in. He hadn't expected to feel this way when leaving them all. But for the few short weeks they had been together, they'd become his only friends.

"You're all heading right back?"

Klea shrugged lightly. "Who's to say what we find on our way back? We expected to be on this quest for a fair bit of time, didn't we?"

"We can always see if there are any places hiring for little jobs. Never hurts to gain a bit more coin," added Soren. "Other than what we're going to get from this job. You sure you don't want to stick with us for a bit?"

"I'm going to..." Ari shook his head, a small, sad laugh escaping him. "I don't know what I'm going to do. I'll send word to you with where I will be to collect my portion of the earnings. But for now... As you said, Klea, who's to say what I will find."

They all said their goodbyes, and quicker than Ari thought, he found himself alone in the destroyed meadow, still staring at the fire. He sucked in a steadying breath and immediately regretted it as the smell of burning fur and flesh overwhelmed him. He turned on his heel in the direction the party had been going before Finn —

Before Finn.

Ari hesitated, his eyes catching on the bundle of untouched wildflowers still pinned to the tree, swaying gently in the breeze. A weird feeling of hope bloomed in his chest. Sometimes life was funny like that. Showing you beauty in a moment of pure and deep heartbreak.

He walked over and plucked the dagger free, slid it into his belt, and weaved the flowers into one of his braids, before he headed off west.

6

NOTHING MORE THAN DREAMS

Arileas

Arileas traveled for over a week on his own, moving at his own pace through the day and finding odd places to tuck himself at night to stay safe. It was a lot lonelier travelling on your own, but at least no one bothered him when he read in the evening.

Without Finn, though, everything felt wrong.

Ari pushed at his thoughts every night, trying to understand why his mind felt so off. He still had the dagger in his belt, and the now-dried flowers twined in his braids.

The further he pushed his memories, the odder dreams he had. Sometimes he would wake up with the strangest taste of blood on his lips, or he would find himself standing in a field of wildflowers, a figure off in the distance with their back to him. One where he felt Finn's hand on his face, lips pressed against his with a hunger he hadn't seen in the man before, plagued him regularly.

But by day, those images in Ari's mind were nothing more than dreams, fading into the fog that refused to let go of his brain.

Finnean betrayed us, he reminded himself. *He turned on us in an attempt to... flee? Save himself? Kill us all and... what?*

When he finally reached a town, he wasn't really surprised to find himself in Boarsrest. He didn't have a plan as to where he was headed, but it felt right, letting his feet take him this way.

Boarsrest itself was nothing more than a couple dirt roads shooting along a clearing with a few trees here and there, ramshackle buildings, a well-used inn, and a stable that housed one sad looking horse. The people moving about the tiny village looked just about as dusty as the surrounding buildings, but the few who saw him nodded amiably as he passed.

Ari let out a long sigh. Their party, if they had ever reached this village, would have immediately known that the Shade would never have stepped foot here. It was far too small and quiet. Any newcomer would stand out too much.

Doesn't matter. The Shade won't ever step foot in this tiny village anyway. Ari pushed the deep, churning grief in his chest down, and walked toward the inn. The moment he stepped over the threshold, he felt himself relaxing as the soft noise of people talking washed over him. He hadn't noticed how much he missed the sound of life around him.

"Hiya," called a warm, bright voice from behind the bar. A tall half-orc woman with purplish-grey skin waved him over. "You look as though you need a drink, a wash, or a bed."

"All three," said Ari, handing her a gold piece. "For at least a night."

The woman led Ari to a room before leaving him to wash up in the communal bathroom, scraping at the dirt from the road from his skin. The water was ice cold and smelled slightly of stagnant pond water, but it was better than nothing. Ari scraped his hair back, planning to weave it into a fresh braid, and dislodged something there.

The bundle of flowers fell free.

He looked at them for a moment, laying sad and crumpled on the dirt-covered floor before picking them up. With a sigh, he left them on the ledge of the washing basin and took one last look at himself in the mirror. The face that stared back looked haggard and worn from the days of travelling, but what concerned Ari most were the dark blue circles under his eyes. He mustn't have been resting as much as he thought. Hopefully a proper bed tonight would help.

He dropped his gaze and finished braiding his hair back before returning to the bar below.

"Here." The half-orc woman slid a large tankard of ale over to Ari as he walked up. "Some of my best brew."

"Thank you." He took a long draw of the golden liquid, feeling it settle in his stomach pleasantly.

The woman nodded before waving at another patron, who just entered the bar. "I'm Ayla, and welcome to my inn. What brings you to Boarsrest? Not many folks from those kingdoms by the coast make it up here often."

Ari chuckled. "Let's just say I'm seeing where the road takes me. I've been stuck in the same place for a long time, doing the same kinds of things, and I met someone recently who... who showed me a bit of a different outlook on life."

Taking out a fresh tankard to fill with ale, Ayla slid the cup over to a different patron down the bar. Ari kept his eyes down on his own tankard before taking a long pull.

"Whoever they were, they sound pretty smart," she answered.

"You could say that."

"Ah." Ayla leaned against the bar and nodded solemnly, eyes tracing

Ari's face. "I'm sorry."

Ari took another deep gulp of his ale, feeling slightly unmoored. "I don't know if I am sorry for the loss. Should I be? Should I care that he lit up my days, only to turn it all on me in the end? I... I don't even remember those last minutes clearly. It's like something is messing with my head."

"Grief's a smarmy bastard." Ayla handed him a bowl of gnarled, shiny brown lumps that had flakes of salt on top. "It can play tricks on the mind. Have some pretzels. You look like the ale is hitting you hard."

"It's just ale."

"My brew is a bit stronger than most."

Ari took a few and threw them into his mouth. They were surprisingly good, buttery and the perfect level of salty. He leaned his chin on his hand and finished both the bowl of pretzels and ale, watching Ayla go about her business. Patrons came and went occasionally. After a while, Ari's eyes began to droop and itch. He didn't want to accidentally knock anything over by dropping his head onto the bar, so he stood up and left a couple coins on the counter.

Ayla eyed him from the other end of the bar. "You feeling alright?"

Ari nodded, yawning. "The pretzels helped."

"Let me know if you need anything else. I'm always here." Ayla waved him off toward the stairs leading toward rooms upstairs.

Ari dodged a few of the other patrons and wound his way toward the stairs. The front door to the inn swung open, letting in a brief burst of sunlight, drawing his eye as he glanced over his shoulder, foot poised over the bottom stair.

Ari stopped in his tracks, feeling as though his stomach had plunged into his feet.

"*Finnean?*"

7

AYLA'S ALE

Finnean

Finn felt as though he had walked into a wall. Or perhaps had tumbled into another realm on accident. It was entirely possible that he had. He couldn't think of any other possibility wherein he had walked into the small, dingy inn where he had been staying for a few days trying to gather his willpower to head on toward somewhere unknown and see Arileas Damaris at the foot of the stairs.

Finn's heart thudded painfully as he took Ari in — everything from his neatly braided hair that was pulled back from his sharp, elegant face, down to the dark blue of his worn travelling shirt that was still, despite the weeks on the road, buttoned up properly and cleaner than any single person's clothing in this inn. Along Ari's belt, hung an incredibly familiar dagger.

Oh.

Oh.

What in all of Ravar is he doing here?

And why was the look on his face enough to make Finn want to fall to his knees?

"Finnean?" Ari breathed, that one word sounding so perfectly painful and wonderful at once. Something in his purple eyes fluttered.

"Ari," answered Finn, feeling entirely dazed and undone. Oh, oh gods, Ari was here. He was *here* — Finn cast his eyes around the bar in a panic looking for the other party members, feeling as though everything he had done up to this point was nothing more than a thin, flimsy spectacle. He *knew* that he shouldn't have trusted magic. "You — you're here."

Ari closed the space between them and punched Finn with everything he had. Instant, red hot pain flooded through his skull. He tasted blood and sputtered, taking a half step back from Ari as he held his throbbing nose.

"Try not to bloody my floors too badly," called Ayla from behind the bar.

"I deserved that," said Finn, blinking through the pain radiating through his head. Gods, getting punched was something that he did *not* enjoy. He carefully touched his nose, making sure it wasn't broken.

"What's happening here, Finnean?" Ari's eyes tracked every inch of Finn's face with an unreadable expression. "You died. You — you're the Sh—"

Finn launched into movement. Ari cut off mid word as Finn grabbed his arms and drew him to a table in the corner of the bar, depositing him in a chair. Finn shot looks around, making sure that the other patrons weren't listening. Most of them were chuckling into their ale at the display, turning back to their own business.

"What in the nine hells are you thinking, saying that name out loud?" he hissed at Ari.

Ari shoved him off and moved to stand, but Finn barred him in. His purple eyes stared daggers into Finn, but slowly, Ari sat back. Finn glanced around again.

"Where are the others?"

Ari snorted and shook his head, looking down at his hands.

Finn tried again. "How are you here right now, and not a week's travel back toward Zidien?"

"Why was our entire party convinced that we were burning your body?"

Finn sucked in a slow breath. Was he going to have to do this? Here, in this bar? Again, Finn looked around, feeling as though he was going to jump out of his skin. Where were the others? If Ari was here, then the others had to be.

His leg started to jump, and he desperately wanted something to fiddle with, but the only thing he had was his dagger. The first night he was here, he had made the mistake of drawing it to flip between his fingers, as he usually did. Ayla had nearly kicked him out for it. The inn had a no weapons policy, apparently.

Ari sagged slightly, something soft skating over his brow as he looked at Finn.

Finn dropped his gaze and cleared his throat. He was having the hardest time looking at Ari. Every time he did, he burned with guilt at what he had done. Swallowing hard, he dragged his chair close enough that their knees could touch. Could, but didn't.

He lowered his voice so that just Ari could hear. "First, what do you remember?"

"The truth," Ari breathed. His cheeks went slightly pink when Finn looked back up at him. "You, knocking out our party. You, being the... him. And you kissing me."

Finn's own gaze flickered down to Ari's lips, the memory raw in his mind. "Right. The magic didn't work. Where are the others? Preparing to jump out and kill me, after you get the whole story?"

"They're heading home."

Finn blinked. "What?"

"*They* believe they killed you. And I did too, until I saw you walking in that door. Though... the memory felt wrong." Ari shook his head as though trying to clear it. "Why?"

Finn felt his mouth twitch into a sad smile and pitched his voice slightly lower, so that Ari had to lean forward to hear him. "It's as I told you, mostly. I wanted out. I wanted a life where I could do what I wanted. When King Zoren's proclamation and demand for my death came through, it was my ticket out."

"You decided to fake your death."

"It made the most sense. But if the spheres didn't work on you, then how am I to know that they will hold on the others? I knew I shouldn't have trusted magic."

Ari let out a long sigh. "It could be a simple logistics issue. Magic is always fickle. Wh— did you say spheres?"

"I had a contact in the kingdom who gave me some kind of memory spheres," said Finn quickly and quietly. "Doesn't matter now, if they didn't work."

"I think they did," said Ari, looking slightly interested, as though this magic was something he hadn't come across before. "The others didn't waver, from what I saw. I was further away from them, so maybe that affected it?"

Finn looked down at his hands. That made sense. Ollie had said the range was about thirty-foot radius, didn't she? The others would still think they had killed him. And soon, they would be bringing that proof back to King Zoren, sealing the Shade's death and Finn's freedom.

Hopefully.

Silence fell between them, Finn's knee bobbing up and down cease-lessly. Ayla brought over two tankards of ale and looked curiously at the two of them, an eyebrow raised before she walked back behind the bar.

"Here," said Ari, digging in his pocket before withdrawing a bit of fabric, handing it to Finn. "Your nose is still bleeding."

Finn chuckled, accepting and twisting it a few times over in his fingers before holding it to his nose. Of course, Arileas Damaris would have a *handkerchief* on him, even after weeks of adventuring. "You have a better arm than I thought, with you hiding behind trees all the time."

"It's always safer at a distance."

"Sometimes." Finn eyed Ari warily, acutely aware of how close their knees were. "Why did you come here, Ari?"

"I didn't want to go back to the kingdom," said Ari. "You made me realize that maybe there was more of the world to see, and so I wanted to... see it, I guess."

They fell into silence again before Ari let out a long sigh, dropping his voice to a murmur as he leaned in closer to Finn. "Are you going to explain more, or just leave me sitting here wondering while the man I thought we burned on a pyre a week ago dabs at his bloody nose?"

8

ANYWHERE AND EVERYWHERE

Arileas

Emotions warred inside of Ari as he sat with Finn, who looked rather pathetic as he dabbed at his nose carefully. Every ounce of anger that Ari hadn't realized he'd been harboring toward this man had exploded out of him the second his fist connected with his face.

But that didn't stop the mingling of grief and a sense of relief from rampaging all throughout his chest.

Finn dropped his hands from his face, a thumb rubbing absently at a now-bare finger where his old signet ring used to sit.

"Right. I guess I have nothing left to hide since you're... well, you're here."

Ari raised an eyebrow and waited.

Finn cleared his throat and cast one last paranoid look around the bar, before he started, keeping his voice low. "As the royal assassin, Tenan liked to use me for his nastier jobs. The ones he wanted done quick and quiet. He wasn't a pleasant man to work for, let me tell you."

"Kings rarely are," said Ari softly. King Tenan, to Ari's knowledge, had amassed a brutal reputation over the length of his reign of Pralon. He had garnered a lasting peace, but at what cost?

Finn took a sip from his tankard and continued. "From when I was a boy, I trained to be... who I was. And I became good at it, quickly. So good, in fact, I became his number one man, and found myself with a healthily mysterious reputation.

"Over the years, I got too good. Tenan became more and more pushy with jobs. He went too far, and suddenly I was the one gaining the ire of nearby kingdoms in his name." Finn began to twist the bloodied handkerchief in his hands. "I was alone, Ari. Living in shadows. I knew everyone and no one — because no matter who they were, I was still me, and the king could have me kill anyone. Which he did.

"And then he had me go after a duke visiting his brother, the king, and that king got offended. Now here we are."

Ari took all this in with a slow nod. "So you cooked up some scheme to get away from it all."

"It was a good plan," said Finn, shooting Ari a look. "I wanted to be able to control my own life."

Ari shifted in his chair. He knew he should be furious at Finn, betrayed by what he had done — but right then, all he could see was the man he had come to really, really like being around.

"Why did you always leave those thumbprints on your victims' faces?"

Finn let out a sputtering laugh. "It was a mistake, on my first proper job as a kid. I left the mark because I was sloppy. But, it kind of took off as a bit of a mystery and, well, I thought, hey. Why not leave a mark, if no one knows who I am?"

A slow, shuddering laugh escaped Ari's chest. "Brazen."

"Brave. And smart. Kind of like a calling card."

"Why did you kiss me?"

The question was out of Ari's lips before he could stop it.

Finn looked at him for a long moment, his blue eyes piercing. "I never thought that I would get attached to anyone. I hadn't, for so long, so what was the harm in joining an adventuring party? And yet, there you were."

"That's not an answer."

"Ari..." Finn shook his head and looked down at his hands. "If I could, I would go back and change everything so that you and I could have met in a town where I was nothing but a baker's boy and you were some scholar. And maybe then we could have fallen for each other like people are supposed to. I kissed you because I *wanted* to. I wanted to maybe live in a fantasy for a moment."

This overwhelmed Ari entirely. He grabbed hold of his tankard, desperate to hold onto anything physical and real.

"So now what? You've successfully gone through with your plan. The party is heading home, proof in hand. Finnean Shademark is soon to be a free man."

"Am I free?" Finn looked at Ari sharply, desperately, searching for something there. Ari could hear the question through that gaze: *are you going to keep my secret?*

Slowly, gently, Ari nodded.

Finn sighed and visibly relaxed. "I don't know what's next. I didn't realize how unusual travelling alone would be, after being around people for my whole life. I kept looking over my shoulder, expecting you to be there. I guess from here, I will travel wherever I want to. Find odd jobs, see where the adventure takes me." Finn bit his lip. Then, as though he couldn't help himself, he blurted, "Come with me."

Ari blinked, wondering if he had heard him correctly. "What?"

"I know it might sound ridiculous, but please, Ari. Come with me. Let's see the realm together."

"Why would you possibly want me with you?" Ari let out a startled laugh. Never in a million years would he have dreamed that Finnean was asking him to go *with him.* "And who's to say that I would even go, after what you've done?"

He knew it was a lie the second it left his lips.

He didn't know exactly when he had, but Ari had completely forgiven Finn for what he had done. There was no space for a grudge when someone simply wanted to live, free.

Finn looked at him, incredulous. "Why would I want you with me? I thought I answered that back when I had you pinned to that tree. I like you, you silly wizard." The chair creaked under Finn as he leaned forward, repeating a little breathlessly, "I like you. Possibly too much for my own good."

Ari shook his head and began to laugh. It started down in his core and worked its way upward, taking him over as though a spell had been cast on him. Finn's face furrowed and he sat back, a crease forming between his eyebrows with slight worry.

Before Ari could talk himself out of it, he pushed up out of his chair and toward Finn's. He braced himself on the arms, pinning Finn in, and leaned down close enough that their lips were inches apart.

"If I didn't know better, I would say that there's something in this ale," breathed Finn. He looked down briefly to Ari's hands on either side of him, locking him in. "Is this what it felt like to have a blade at your throat? I know what those hands can do with magic."

"Oh, shut up."

Ari kissed the man fiercely, tasting the remnants of ale on his lips. He sank down, feeling Finn's hands skate up over his shirt and up around his neck, fingers finding their way to Ari's braided hair.

When they finally separated, Ari's hair fell in tendrils around his face, and he had to catch his breath.

"No more secrets between us," he said. "I don't want to wake up and have you gone again, alright?"

Finn's face split into an uncontrollable grin, oceanic-blue eyes glittering. His hand toyed at Ari's waist band, sending heat into his cheeks. "No more secrets."

"Finnean."

"I see you've still got my dagger. We're going to need that, where we're going."

Ari laughed softly and let his forehead fall to Finn's. "And where is that?"

Finn took Ari's chin in hand, eyes smoldering. Suddenly Ari felt as though Finn was the one braced over him, pinning him in. "Anywhere and everywhere."

PART TWO

Salty Sea Air

9

A LOVE AFFAIR WITH BOOKS

Finnean

Finnean breathed in the salty sea air as they drew nearer to the shores of Arrowmount, the sun glittering off the nearby ocean like a pile of gold. He beamed as a deep relaxing joy spreading through his chest. The seaside town looked like a jewel nestled along the beach, with all its red roofs and shining, sunbathed cobblestone streets. There was even a lighthouse whose top windows shone blindingly in the sun, drawing him to its shores.

Arrowmount was a charming town that ferried much of the Empire's trade from its shores. Neither Finn or Ari had been to it, but through their travels around the empire in the last eight months, they spotted it on a map right by the sea, and decided it was perfect for a vacation together.

The sight was more welcoming than any Finn had seen in the past few months as they moved continuously around the empire to remain untraceable by King Zoren.

Ari and Finn were allowing themselves to stay in Arrowmount for a few weeks, actually letting themselves relax into a vacation, rather than treating this town like the others they had been to. If a job happened to fall into their lap, they may take it on, but there was no need to worry. Finn had been dreaming of sleeping in a proper bed — and finding one by the sea was simply an added bonus.

Finn swayed back and forth along with the beautiful chestnut horse beneath him. He reached up to a tree nearby and grabbed a fresh bundle of leaves, throwing the one he had long since twisted into pulp aside, and began anew. His shirt billowed open to catch the slight sea breeze that reached them up here in between the trees. They rode on until the tree line ended and the hills began to taper down into slow, gentle slopes filled with long grass and flowers.

Finn's hair had grown down to his shoulders and curled around his neck, which now tickled with sweat. Under him in saddle bags, gold and jewels they had collected from months spent doing odd jobs around the empire jingled pleasantly. A soft orchestra of seafaring birds and the clopping of their horses' hooves filled the air.

He laughed, delighted.

"What, darling?" Ari looked over his shoulder from atop his white horse, walking pleasantly beside Finn on the road. Ari's impeccable white hair flowed down his back, loose from any braids, with flowers threaded here and there in little splashes of color.

"Oh, nothing," answered Finn, reaching out across the space between them to lace his fingers through Ari's. "I am so completely and incandescently happy, and it's all down to you, you know that? It feels like I'm living in a dream."

Ari laughed, the warm sound singing straight to Finn's heart.

Finn squeezed Ari's fingers before letting go and kicking his horse into a canter. "Let's go swim in the ocean."

The two of them led their horses down toward the salt-stained grey stone walls that surrounded Arrowmount and left them at the stable sitting right outside the gate. Ari and Finn walked arm in arm to the open gate, both guards stationed there waving them through without so much as a second glance.

Finn gloried in the way that the cobblestones clacked under his feet reassuringly, mingling with the warbled chatter of townsfolk and the call of seabirds above.

Lively multicolored flags hung strung between the buildings on every street, weaving from rooftop to balcony to any place that the locals could find to tie them. Finn saw some tied amongst plant pots and window shutters, and even one tied to a laundry line. Along the street level, townsfolk meandered about, people of all kinds striding happily in the sunshine.

Finn nodded to a stately half-orc woman who had a fruit stall they passed by, featuring the brightest most delicious looking fruit he had ever seen.

He tossed her a silver and winked, the coin glinting in the sun. "One of your choicest treats, my dear madame."

She snorted and caught the coin deftly out of the air before she tossed him back a perfectly ripe mango. Using one of his daggers, Finn sliced the fruit and handed Ari half. The mango was perfectly ripe, and the second his dagger cut through the flesh, his mouth began to water.

"Where, by chance, does this town post it's news and job listings?"

The fruit seller gestured off down the street. "In our town center, you can't miss it. Posted on a board there."

Finn gave her a nod of thanks and bit into the mango, juices bursting down his chin. He closed his eyes briefly, savoring the sweetness. Ari chuckled and led him on.

They passed through the town center and briefly checked the notice board as they had gotten into the habit of doing in every town they passed. The Kingdom of Zidien had yet to release any statement in regard to the Shade's death — to the general populous' knowledge, the assassin was still alive and breathing and killing. And so, Ari and Finn stayed on the run, looking over their shoulder for any sign that the king was on their tail.

"Nothing," sighed Finn, letting a few papers that advertised a sale on fish that had passed a few days ago and a reminder to keep the streets of Arrowmount clean fall back into place. He shook his head, turning away from the board. It was nothing new, and they were in a beautiful place together. What more could he want?

Ari linked his fingers with Finn's and squeezed before they continued on through the town, slowly winding down toward the sea.

"Gods, this could be the most beautiful thing I have ever seen," Ari breathed, coming to a stop in the road. Finn *hmmed* appreciatively, finishing off the sublime mango before looking around and throwing the skin to a nearby dog.

"I know you don't mean me, but it's nice to hear appreciation every once and a while."

"Look up, Finnean."

Finn did, wiping mango juice from his lips with the back of his hand. He found himself in front of a rather shambling storefront with a worn sign that read ARROWMOUNT BOOKS in faded writing.

"This is a bookstore."

"I am aware," said Ari.

"You have four books hanging off your hip alone in that holster, and last time I checked, another five in your saddle bags back with the horses."

"Plus, my Bag of Space that contains my entire personal library. You didn't think I would leave home without access to all of my books, did you?" Ari shot him a sideways look before lifting a small, familiar bag from his satchel. It was a dark maroon and looked as though it could fit a couple mangoes inside.

Finn blinked at him. "That's what you carry in that bag?"

"How do you think I manage to read so many different books?"

"Honestly, love, I thought you were rereading them," said Finn, looking at the bookstore a little bit closer.

The two-story building leaned out toward the street as though it was peering down at the shoppers below. The front facade was chipped and peeling in places, the salty sea air having wrecked complete havoc on it. He supposed it had once been a bright blue, but he couldn't be sure, since it was now a dingy, grimy-grey. Ghosts of books were visible through the two thick, grime covered windows on the front that flanked the old, chipped wooden door.

"This place is falling apart, Ari."

"Yes, well, it is a bookstore," said Ari simply, grabbing hold of Finn's hand and drawing him to the door.

"You've dragged me into so many of these stores," said Finn playfully. He couldn't really care less about how many bookstores Ari took him to and would happily go to each one in the empire if it meant he got to see Arileas' face of pure joy each time. "What's so different about this one?"

"It's a bookstore by the sea," said Ari, a look of anticipatory glee on his face as he pulled the door open. His expression fell slightly as he took in the dank, musty space, but his eyes still glittered at the prospect of browsing. "You never know what treasures you're going to find in a place like this."

Finn could almost taste the layer of dust clinging to the back of his throat in the humid, trapped air inside. He waved Ari on ahead of him, his love vanishing into the many-roomed shop to unearth whatever treasures he could. Finn let out a low whistle as he stood in the first room, taking in the sheer number of books around him.

They were double stacked floor to ceiling along the empty spots on the walls, triple stacked haphazardly on shelves, and shoved pell-mell into crates under the front windows. Half of the spines weren't facing the correct way, unreadable in the stacks hundreds deep. A small, crumbling front desk was shoved against another wall, half-hidden by the overwhelming amount of books on and around it.

Finn slipped into the next room, sidestepping more stacks of books, eyes travelling along the shelves and walls. There was no organization to the place at all — history was jammed in with romance, old alchemy texts and children's books stacked into another shelf alongside something that looked like a recipe book for deadly potions. How anyone found anything was beyond Finn.

Though, if anyone could find a method to the madness, it would be Ari.

"Ari?" he called after a few minutes. Finn walked by a staircase that led up to a second floor, which was corded off and nearly inaccessible due to the tomes lining both sides of it.

He frowned, peering up into the dusty darkness above, wondering what was up there.

"Over here, darling."

Finn found Ari standing in front of a rather grizzled old dwarf with grey hair that sprouted every which way on the top of his head. The dwarf looked extremely harassed. And Ari, of course, had two books tucked under his arm protectively.

"I was just speaking to Mr. Dew here," said Ari, turning to look over his shoulder with an expression that said *Oh gods, please help me.* "This charming store in his."

"I would never have guessed," answered Finn dryly.

"Eh," the dwarf grunted, waving Ari back a few steps. "The place is a dump; anyone can see it. I didn't expect patrons today, not when my shop girl is out. I am not built for this people-talking thing. Now, get out, if you don't mind. I have things to do."

Finn scrunched his nose at the shop owner's incredible rudeness before turning on a bit of his charm, smiling at the old dwarf. "If you don't mind, sir, my partner and I were perusing your wondrous book selection. Truly, I've never seen anything like it before." *Not really a lie,* he thought to himself. "We'll be out of your hair shortly."

Dew made a dismissive sound in the back of his throat and didn't turn around, waving at him irritated.

"Kind man," said Finn to Ari under his breath as the man disappeared amidst the books. "We should ask him out to dinner."

"Let's not stay for long," said Ari, looking around at the books with a concerned look on his face. "I'm nearly done, either way."

The two of them made their way through the rest of the store, finding the back part of it entirely blocked off with rope. Finn would have missed the room completely if Ari hadn't been poking around a stack of books nearby that obscured most of the entrance.

Ari carefully toed aside a fallen stack nearby as they poked their heads in to snoop around. Finn recoiled slightly as the smell of mold and old water assaulted his nose.

This room was void of books, with the bones of broken shelves that sagged all along the walls. The wood was so rotted and swollen it looked black. The entire back half of the ceiling and wall had crumbled in large pieces that looked as though they too were rotted through with water damage.

"How awful," commented Ari. "I hope no books were harmed in whatever caused that."

Finn threaded his arm through Ari's and took the two books from his hands to peer down at them. One was a slightly water-stained red clothbound, and the other a dark, royal blue that had the shape of a bird pressed into the cover. "These look wondrous. Let's go see if there is some sunlight somewhere, or if we have wandered into a different realm in here."

10

MAY'S CAFE

Finnean

Y ou'll have to excuse my love," said Finn to the half-elven woman that had guided them to their table. She eyed Ari interestedly as she set down two glasses of water. "He has a love affair with books so strong that I simply cannot deny him the pleasures of reading at lunch with me."

The woman jingled slightly as she moved. Countless tiny beads and bells strung into her reddish-brown hair that spiraled in thick curls down her back tinkled against one another. She had a soft pink scarf tied around her head to keep her hair out of her face except for a few curling bangs, accentuating her pointed ears and glittering cheeks. Flowers bloomed out of her soft green dress pockets, thin vines curling up the bodice of her pastel corset. Delicate jewelry of all kinds decorated her neck and hands.

"No worries at all," she said, smiling at him warmly. "I love it when people are so enthralled in their books that they can't stop reading, even to order food. I'm May, by the way. Welcome to my cafe."

Ari was currently nose deep in his book — not reading, though it looked like he was. Strands of his hair drifted around him and over the pages as he leafed through the book, the breeze teasing them aloft.

Finn had slowly learned the intricacies of how Arileas treated a new book, whether used or newly printed. First, he always thumbed through it tenderly, looking at the pages fly by, feeling them under his thumb for quality or just for the pleasure of it, Finn wasn't entirely sure. Then Ari would flip through again, slower, eyeing each page for imprints left from previous owners. Finally, once that was done, he would lean into the book and read, a look of soft delight on his face.

"Apologies," said Ari, peering up to smile at her. "There is something about books that I cannot stay away from."

"Just like me and my plants." May smiled back. "What can I get you both?"

Ari placed a careful finger in his book to hold his page. "I would love to try anything you recommend from your menu and one of those sparkling blue drinks that I saw you making when we arrived."

"Good choice. It's one of my newer creations." She looked at Finn. "And I take that you'll order something slightly stronger — black coffee, iced?"

Finn tilted his head up at her and grinned. "Do you have a knack for guessing what your customers will have, or is it just me?"

"You become rather skilled at reading people, doing what I do," she answered with a wink. "I'll bring those out right away."

She reached toward a low hanging plant that had begun to snake its way over her shoulder, teasing it up over the rafters above with a gentle wave of a finger before walking inside her cafe.

The cafe was a slightly down from the bookstore, closer to the sea, and cast in greenery. Plants of all kinds flourished around the trellises and rafters, curling up the walls and winding around windowsills. Their table was wrought iron with a few real, green vines snaking through the curvatures, lazily waving in the breeze.

A few other patrons sat inside and out, sipping at drinks or nibbling at food as they gazed out at the sea. Ari set his book down on the table and laid a hand over the worn, red cover, smiling at Finn.

Finn set his own hand on the table and moved it until his pinky touched Ari's, gently linked them together. "This place is glorious."

"I know. It's an absolutely wonderful spot to vacation."

After May brought out their drinks — Ari's a gloriously fizzing blue number with purple ice, Finn's iced coffee perfectly sweetened with what he suspected was caramel — the two of them settled in comfortably. Finn gazed at the sliver of sea peeking through at the end of the street. It glittered gold in the late afternoon light, the soft sound of waves lapping gently at the shores.

As Ari took a sip from his drink, his face lit up with pleasant surprise. "It has the most interesting feeling, like sparkling magic at the back of my throat before it smoothes right out. You've got to try it."

Finn took a sip of the blue fizzy drink and let out a laugh at the sensation that ran down his throat. "That's oddly refreshing."

May came back out to chat with various customers that cycled through, leaning on the backs of chairs and refilling drinks. Ari's eyes tracked her movements before settling back on Finn with a soft, dreamy smile.

"So, you two just passing through Arrowmount, or are you here to stay a while?" May moved back toward their table chiming softly, smiling down at them.

"Visiting," answered Finn. "I'm Finn, and this is my partner, Arileas."

"It's an absolute pleasure to have you, for however long you'll stay."

May twirled a finger absently toward the edge of Ari's drink. Tiny white flowers bloomed around the base of the glass in the pools of condensation, their teeny bulbs curling toward her.

"Where'd'you hail from?" Piped up a voice from behind them. They turned to see an elderly fiendling from a nearby table. His dark blue horns curled around multiple times toward the back of his neck, and the wrinkles around his eyes gave him the impression of being always on the verge of a smile. His mouth was mostly hidden by a gloriously thick white moustache and beard that pointed down toward his chest. He lowered his coffee mug, peering over thin wire spectacles with a glitter in his eye. "Pull up a chair, May."

"We've been all over," said Finn as May slid gently into a neighboring chair.

"We met up in an old inn that was mostly falling apart, remember?" Ari smiled at Finn. "Started in Feycross back with an adventuring party. Since then, we kind of went our own way."

"Ah, a classic love story," rumbled the old fiendling.

"Connected eyes over a drawn dagger and all that." Finn winked at Ari as Chervil chuckled.

"It's been years since I've properly met adventurers around these parts. Most don't stop by, or if they do, they run in and out with supplies before we really learn they were here. The name's Chervil," he said, waving an old, gnarled blue hand toward the end of the cobblestone street where the lighthouse stood picturesque against the sea. "I run the old lighthouse at the end of Fetterly Place."

"Have you two lived here long?" Finn leaned forward, looking curiously between May and Chervil.

Chervil nodded. "My entire life. All my family has ever done is run that lighthouse. Once you have a bit of the sea in your blood, you'll never be satisfied until you come back to its shores, I say."

"It was actually Chervil here that convinced me to move to Arrowmount," said May, winking at him. The longer she sat with them, the more the plants all around the cafe entrance crept toward her like she was the sun. The flower buds from around Ari's drink had slithered toward her along the pools of condensation on the table's surface and wrapped themselves around her wrists and up her fingers. "It was a long time ago, but back then I had only a little wagon of wares that I would cart around, making tea for those who asked. There was something so perfectly enchanting about this place, though, and here I am all these years later."

"I bet everyone here loves it," said Ari, looking out at the sun filled street wistfully.

"You'll find your nay-sayers in any town," said Chervil. "Take ol' Dew for example. He's never once been happy here. Back when I was a lad, the shop was run by a wonderful woman who ran it up until my granddaughter was about eight years old."

"Starla Waters used to have that door open all the time, propped up by a small potted plant that looked as though it was on its last legs every time I saw it," added May with a laugh. "She made sure that there was music and laughter no matter the season."

"When Dew bought the place, we all expected him to keep it up, as she had for so long. He did, for a bit, but..."

Ari made a sad sound in the back of his throat. "How sad. Bookstores should be the life of a town."

Chervil barked out a laugh. "You'd get along with my granddaughter. She works there and tries to keep the place from falling completely into disrepair."

The conversation meandered off from the bookstore and to the town itself before Chervil stood, using the back of Ari's chair to hoist himself up. Ari and Finn stood as well, leaving a small mound of coin on the table for their drinks and food. The old fiendling towered over them both.

"Where would you say is the best to stay for the night?" Finn asked Chervil as they walked away from the cafe, waving goodbye to May.

"If you're just staying for the night, you'll want some inn by the entrance of town. But if you're planning on staying a little longer," Chervil eyed the two of them carefully, "then you'll want Cobb's." He pointed a gnarled thumb down where he was heading. "Best views of the ocean, next to the lighthouse of course."

They bid farewell to the man and watched him amble down the road, his long dark blue tail swaying behind him. Finn shook his head, smiling bemusedly after him.

"Should we get a room, then?"

Ari looked up and down the street before lacing his fingers with Finn's. "Cobb's it is."

11

PROSPECTS AND DREAMS

Arileas

As the sun dipped closer to the horizon, coloring the sky a brilliant mix of orange and pinks, both Ari and Finn found their way to the beach with a blanket and bottle of mead from Cobb's stores. They were only a couple minutes away from their room at Cobb's Down-By-The-Beach, which was an utterly perfect place to vacation over the next few weeks.

A sense of deep, profound relaxation settled over Ari as the sand tickled between his bare toes. They found a spot a little way up from the water to watch the brilliantly orange and pink sunset.

After travelling for as long as he had with Finnean, Ari had come to realize how much he longed for rest. Perhaps even finding a place where they could settle into, somewhere they could call their own. Even though he loved adventuring with Finn — it was his favorite thing to do, besides read — the constant moving and unknown was draining. And, it wasn't exactly the *adventuring* part that he loved. It added more pain and stress than he ever wanted in his life.

He loved adventuring because it was with *Finn.*

Finn oozed life and happiness everywhere he went. He expected so little of Ari, as long as he was honest with him. He was everything opposite to the life that Ari had grown up with: he was kind, gentle, and never berated him for making a mistake. Finn might tease and joke, but there was always good humor and forgiveness at the foundation of it.

Where Finn dreamed, Ari kept him pinned mostly down to earth and gave him realistic paths to get to those dreams.

And, Finn helped Ari dream.

Perhaps when they finally heard word that King Zoren had declared the Shade dead, they could ease back on the constant travel. Though they had amassed a fair bit of wealth from the odd jobs they had done, Ari would do just about anything to slow down a little bit.

Though, Ari wasn't entirely sure that the king would ever release such a statement now. It had been roughly eight months since he and Finn had left the inn in Boarsrest. Much longer than any party needed to return to the kingdom and claim their prize, offering up proof of the Shade's death. More often now Ari found his thoughts drifting to the possibility that whatever magic Finn had used was truly faulty — not just on him but on the entire party — and they were still being actively hunted.

Which is why they stayed on the move. They couldn't risk the possibility that their old party was still out there hunting Finn, or perhaps that another party had set out as well, on the king's orders.

Finn sat back on their blanket and gestured at Ari with the sealed mead bottle, breaking him from his momentarily anxious thoughts. Finn's golden face was tinged maroon from the few drinks that he had had at dinner, a relaxed smile stretched across his face. Ari pointed a single finger at the bottle of mead, sending the cork flying out with a gentle pop. Finn snatched it out of the air with his free hand before taking a long swallow.

"You know, my love," he said, throwing an arm behind his head and handing Ari the bottle as he laid back, "I could get used to a place like this. Maybe our next bit of adventuring will be to venture up the coast and keep the sand between our toes."

Ari *hmmed* in response, taking a sip of the mead with a smile. It was full and thick, coating his throat with sweet spiced honey. Paired with the waves rolling in and out near them, he was almost put in a trance as the alcohol hit his stomach.

"One day, I'm going to buy you a library three times as big as that bag," mused Finn, pleasantly drunk now. "That way, you can have every single book in the world, if you wanted it."

"It's impossible to have a library that large, darling." Ari smiled down at Finn and brushed one of his curls off his forehead. "My bag is a little pocket of space between the realms. Most bags like this are not measurable in size."

"We'll have a castle to sit atop it," said Finn, not a care in the world. "What kind of rooms would you want in the castle?"

"One full of plants," he answered, thinking of May's Cafe.

"Plants," nodded Finn. "And an entire chamber filled to the brim with pillows and mattresses."

"An entire chamber? The whole thing, bed?"

"That is what luxury is, my dear Arileas." Finn took a long drag from the bottle again before gesturing out oat the sky with it, bits of the rich liquid sloshing out onto his shirt. "The ridiculous and the amazing."

"What would you like besides books, plants, and beds?"

"I don't need anything but that room full of luxury and you," said Finn. "Soon, my love, we will find our castle."

"You like the life of adventuring too much."

"Being heroic is quite taxing on one's body. I believe that at some point, I will have to stop. Maybe right now, because the sand is quite comfortable. Have you noticed how comfortable it is?"

Ari leaned down and kissed Finn, the taste of honey mead on his lips. "Your stone fortress will have thick walls of the most beautiful stone, with dungeons full of gold and treasure, fit for a king. Or rather, one Finnean Shademark, because you want more than any king could. I know you too well."

"You *do* know me too well," confirmed Finn. He grinned at Ari, reaching out and pulling at a lock of Ari's long hair. He began to twist and play with it absently. "I love that you don't mind I'm an absolute menace when I'm drunk. Am I drunk?"

"You are."

"Good. Being drunk by the sea with the love of my life is a glorious thing. You know, our castle should be…"

Ari let Finn rattle on about their potential future, the castle and their life becoming grander and filled with increasingly ridiculous things. Finn liked to muse and spin tales of a future he never thought he'd actually have, a pure dreamer.

He turned his attention to the lighthouse in the distance, watching the arcane beam of light cascade over the water, signaling to sailors far off in the distance. A few remaining seabirds called from above, their cries mixing with the sound of the waves.

Finn reached up and sloppily placed his hand on Ari's cheek. Ari smiled softly as Finn yawned, fading fast. "You're wonderful, you know that? You deserve it all. You deserve to wander a library fit for kings, Arileas Damaris."

His warm hand slipped off Ari's cheek, leaving a ghost of a palm behind.

As Finn fell into a soft slumber next to him, Ari's mind wandered through rows and rows of books tucked tight into shelves.

12
A LITTLE BROWN TAIL

Arileas

Warm morning sunlight dappled in through the window next to their bed, bringing with it the scent of warm salty sea. It slid in between the slatted wooden shutters, striping across their tangled forms.

Ari squinted and yawned, feeling the weight of Finn next to him on the bed and his leg thrown over Ari's, heavy and reassuring. Ari poked a toe into the man's calf, eliciting a grunt.

"Finn?"

The man groaned before rolling over and off of Ari. Finn had been deeply asleep by the time Ari had carried him up to bed, all the stars shining above them. It took Ari a good fifteen minutes to roll everything up and carry him back — thanks to the use of magic, of course — but he didn't mind at all. Finn was incredibly adorable when he was asleep. Although he did sometimes drool.

Instead of waking him fully, Ari let Finn snore his way back into slumber, watching his bare, golden skinned back rise and fall among the sheets. Ari smiled, the soft morning light playing in Finn's curls. Knowing Finn, he'd be sleeping the drinks off for a while, so Ari rolled out of bed and dressed.

Peeking through the blinds as he pulled on his trousers, the sight of the ocean and adjacent cobbled street sent an immediate thrill down his spine.

The fresh salty air filled his lungs as he stepped out, pulling his hair back into one thick braid as he walked. He lifted his face up toward the colorful triangular flags that adorned the space between buildings on either side of Fetterly Place, letting a smile break across his face as the sun warmed him head to toe.

The town already bustled with life as he walked over the cobblestones toward May's cafe. Townsfolk milled about, their slightly sleepy faces peering at the fronts of shops that were opening for the day. Amidst the townsfolk, shop owners appeared, along with delivery people and workers going about their daily tasks.

Ari ducked into May's, a bit of greenery snagging on his hair as he walked inside. He grabbed a tea and a perfectly golden sticky bun before finding himself outside again, carrying his breakfast. He worked his way up the length of Fetterly Place and moved on through the core of Arrowmount itself, on the hunt for a good spot to eat.

He passed by merchants setting up their carts of various wares — a cart with trinkets and oddities caught his eye as the owner unfurled a hand painted sign with MAGIC GOODS written on it. It sat beside another cart that was full to the brim with fresh vegetables and fruits. The half-orc woman that Finn had purchased a mango from stood behind it, screwing a small canopy in place above her.

Arrowmount was full of haphazardly placed buildings, some that leaned toward the streets, some that pulled back as they stacked up further toward the clouds. Beams of dark wood crossed across light plaster on some, and others were made of stones and rock. Throughout the whole of the town ran the dark cobblestones, connecting every street whether they were so slim carts could barely pass through or as wide as open as Fetterly Place.

Life bustled around him in shades of color. A brilliant blue water elemental threw open the top windows to her building as Ari passed, shaking out a massive multi-squared blanket. A large grey goliath in a soft blue apron ferried their cart chock-full of wares that tinkled in hundreds of variously sized glass bottles, nodding to Ari as they passed. Various scents of baking bread, the sharp tang of metal, and the occasional waft of salty sea air followed Ari as he wound his way through the bustling streets.

Soon, buildings fell away as Ari passed a lone guard stationed at the town gates who waved him through. He found himself walking off the main road around the town boundaries, knees pushing aside tall green grasses and wildflowers. The fresh scent of greenery filled his nose and he had to fight back a sneeze as pollen kicked up into the air. Heavy, draping trees lined the hillside, casting large swaths of it in cool shade. Bees and butterflies floated through it lazily, the air singing with their soft sound.

Ari climbed up the small hill until Arrowmount stretched out below him, framed by the sea beyond. Wildflowers tickled his neck as he sank down to the ground to enjoy his breakfast.

Citrusy sweetness popped on his tongue as he sipped the tea May had brewed for him which paired perfectly with the light doughy cinnamon taste of the sticky bun. Ari leaned back against the bark of a tree and chewed, gazing out at the scenic vista around him. The town glowed in the morning sun as the heat of an early summer day began to swell around him. Rich, red roofs greeted him, between which he could just see the multicolored flags fluttering in the breeze, catching his eye again and again. A tiny cottage peeking through the line of trees facing Arrowmount, which Ari hadn't noticed before. A tiny bit of smoke trailed up to the sky from a chimney he couldn't see.

A small shape began bobbing toward him through the high grass, the tip of a brown tail visible tickling the undersides of the wildflowers as it made its way up the hill.

"Hello," said Ari, extending his hand out to a tiny brown cat as she appeared by his knee, looking up at him with a slight frown. He extended a hand out for her to sniff. She was a brown tabby with a shock of white along her belly and bright yellow eyes that shone like lamplights from her dainty face. Her small triangular pink nose sniffed at the air toward him, working up from his boots to his outstretched fingers, tail flicking back and forth before she decided he was satisfactory.

"You're a lovely little girl," Ari cooed at her, scratching her between the ears. Her eyes closed in pleasure as she leaned into his hand. The cat stepped up onto his lap and curled there, pinning him in place.

Once he finished his breakfast and tea, he continued to pet her for a long while before whispering an apology and setting her down on the grass once again.

"My love will be waking soon," he said to her as she stared indignantly at him, letting out the tiniest meow. "I have to get back to town. You can join me, if you like."

He pushed himself to his feet and dusted his hands off, ridding them of sugary sticky bun crumbs and cat hair before heading back toward the entrance of town. As he walked, the little brown tail skirted through the wildflowers along behind him.

13

THE LIFE OF THE TOWN

Arileas

Ari returned his tea mug to May's and meandered about Fetterly Place. The little brown cat disappeared at some point as he stopped to gaze into yet another window, probably growing tired of his ambling around. He turned on his heel to look for her one last time before continuing on his way, smiling at the persnickety nature of cats.

Soft movement in a nearby window caught his eye, pulling him to a stop.

Arrowmount Books loomed in front of him, its crumbling and faded facade a gloomy cloud against the bright blue sky above. Ari frowned at the shop, wondering what the movement had been, since the windows looked the same as the day before: books barely visible through the layers of grime. Perhaps he had imagined the movement.

It wouldn't hurt to investigate, though. Not when there were books involved.

He took the few steps to the door and entered the dim interior. He blinked a couple of times to let his eyes adjust and cleared his throat against the taste of dust and old books clogging the air.

"Hello!"

Ari jumped at the bright and cheery voice, totally at odds with yesterday's visit. He turned toward the front desk and found an absolutely beaming young fiendling staring back at him, her curved horns poking out of a cascading waterfall of green hair, hands full of books. The young woman rose up on the tips of her toes with a burst of excitement and set the books down on the desk in front of her before shooting toward Ari. Her long green tail swept deftly behind her to catch and steady the stacks of books as she passed.

"Good morning! Welcome to Arrowmount Books." She beamed at him some more, her smile so large that Ari couldn't help but smile back. The fiendling wore a calf-length, light pink patterned dress that floated elegantly around her like some of the gowns Ari had seen on royalty back at court, with a brown corset overtop that had what looked like a couple thin pockets sewed into it that held a few pens. Her skirt, too, had a multitude of pockets, into which she placed a book off the top of a nearby stack, not even glancing at the title. "I'm Sage."

"Ah, you must be Chervil's granddaughter."

Sage smiled. "You've met Granddad?"

"I'm Arileas Damaris," said Ari, reaching out a hand to shake. "I arrived in town yesterday along with my partner."

"Oh! Are they coming in too?" Sage glanced over Ari's shoulder, standing up on her tiptoes again.

"No, he's busy sleeping off too much of a good night," Ari answered. "Something about wine and sea air got to him. We came by yesterday."

"Ah." Sage cringed slightly. "You happened across Mr. Dew, didn't you?" She shook her head solemnly and looked surreptitiously around the shop as though expecting Dew to pop out from behind a stack of books. "He's a nice man, though he doesn't often treat people very kindly. He loves the store, I know he does, deep down, but..."

Her voice faded away as she half-heartedly lifted a shoulder, looking around the shop at the grime covered windows and the thick layer of dust on the books.

"You must have so much to do around here, helping, though. And with that back room being damaged I'm sure your space is incredibly limited."

Sage nodded, her eyes getting larger. "I was here when it happened. It was an absolute catastrophe, Mr. Damaris. All of those books, lost! The carnage."

"Arileas or Ari is fine, Sage." Ari moved over to the stack of books that Sage had toppled onto the counter, picking up the top one. "I can't imagine, it looks like water came through."

"It was during a really bad storm a few months back. We still haven't been able to fix up the walls, but at least it didn't get the whole shop."

Ari glanced down at a few of the titles in his hands. These, unlike the ones he had purchased the day before, were brand new. "Do you get shipments in from printers around, too?"

"Sometimes," Sage answered, adjusting a few books on the tightly packed shelves. "They're not as frequent as I would like, because I can't help myself when it comes to new stories. There's a press here in Arrow-mount that publishes a few books a year, but it is super small, so we have to outsource directly to Pralon. Is there anything in particular I can help you find?"

"I don't really know why I came in here, actually. It was as though the store called to me."

Sage laughed. "I know how you feel, Mr. Damaris. I am quite the same. I love this place so, so much, though it's not what it used to be. Ms. Waters used to keep it absolutely spotless — we even had a display in the front that was just for kids to look through and borrow books from if we wanted!"

The beginnings of a library, thought Ari, the idea nestling itself into his mind. He could picture it, a tiny little Sage pouring excitedly over books in the front. "Your grandfather mentioned that Ms. Waters was quite the life of the town."

"That's what a bookstore should be," said Sage, sighing. "No matter where you are, the bookstore should be the heart of the town. This is where stories live and breathe — well, where they should breathe." She frowned, drawing a finger along the shelf nearby choked in dust.

"Exactly." Ari took a step forward and shook the book he was holding excitedly. "Especially in a little seaside town like this."

"This place needs a person like you to run it, Mr. Damaris. Someone to bring life into it again." Sage shook her head sadly. "Mr. Dew... well, he... you know. What do you and your partner do? Do you run a bookstore somewhere? You seem like the type."

Ari chuckled, trying to ignore the small thrill that shot through his heart at the thought of running a bookstore. "My partner and I, we're adventurers of a sort, I guess you could say? We're on the road a lot, we do odd jobs here and there."

Sage let out a squeak. Her eyes had expanded to the size of saucers and a brilliant smile broke across her face. She lunged forward and grabbed Ari's arm in a vice grip. "Oh. My. Gods. An actual live adventurer! In our store!" She did a little happy dance, her tail curling up behind her. "I've heard of people meeting adventurers, but I have never been able to meet some myself. I have always said, if I had the chance, I would sit down and talk for hours with them — with someone who had actually done it, been out there and *seen* the world."

Ari thought back to the pack of wolven, memory charms, and kissing up against a tree with a knife to his throat and shook his head amiably. "It's not as exciting as it is in books."

Sage looked at him starry eyed for a moment before she came back to herself, taking a tentative step back and letting go of Ari's arm. "Sorry — Granddad is always telling me I need to think before I get too excited, or I might scare people away."

"Nonsense, you aren't scaring me away at all. I admire your joy and zest for adventure. In fact, I think you and my partner would get along quite well. Finnean loves telling stories."

Sage grinned before turning to pick up the stack of brand-new books from the front desk. "Bring him around the shop! I'm in every day for the rest of the week, if you're sticking around for a while. Besides, the books need someone other than me to love them."

Ari smiled and turned to look around the shop. He *was* here after all. He *hmmed* under his breath as he scanned the shelves, taking a couple here and there, straightening them out. The touch of pages under his fingers sent soft, soothing energy up his arms and into his spine. As he moved slowly around the front room, he felt his shoulders drop, relaxing into the familiar motions of being in one of his favorite kind of places.

"What did you find?" Sage slid a stack of books off the front desk as he came up, a book in hand. She laughed, the sound bubbly and bright as she read the title. "Oh! I absolutely loved this one. It's filled with the best kind of adventure — mixed with the most heart wrenching romance I think I have ever read. Plus, there are dragons, which are my *favorite*."

"We have kindred souls, Sage." Ari slid coins across the desk to pay for the book. "Dragons are my favorite too. I'd love to actually see one one day."

"You know," said Sage, drawing out her words as she slid the money over to her side. She looked at him meaningfully. "I might be able to convince Mr. Dew to sell this place, you know. If there was someone... looking."

"We're just visiting, Sage. And what would adventurers do in a bookstore?"

She sighed. "Yeah, you're probably right. Still."

He shook his head and waved his book toward her. "Thanks for your time and conversation, Sage."

"Come back any time, Mr. Damaris. I hope to see you at the lighthouse for a tour at some point — I know Granddad would love to show you around."

As he exited the shop, he turned and looked once more at the chipped, sad facade of the shop. *Mr. Dew should consider selling the place,* he thought. It could really do with a nice coat of paint to brighten it all up, and a new sign, maybe. A fresh start for the store, for the town.

14

FREEDOM OF ADVENTURE

Finnean

B y the time Finn woke up, sunlight beamed directly through the window slats and into his eyes. He groaned and threw an arm over his head, blocking it out. The world tilted to the side as a throbbing headache thudded painfully through his entire skull.

"Ari?" he grumbled into his arm, hoping that Ari was nearby to hand him a coffee or something magical to get rid of his raging hangover. Finn knew that there was a potion in his bag nearby, but the thought of moving anything more than a finger right then sent preemptive nausea shuddering through him.

Silence greeted him.

He sighed and steeled himself, slowly turning his body toward the edge of the bed to slide out as easily as he could without triggering a particularly nasty throb of his head or lurch of his stomach. He groaned the entire way to a sitting position, gritting his teeth, feeling as though he had aged forty years over night.

I am a well and true idiot, he thought to himself, bending slowly to fish around on the ground for his bag. He squeezed his eyes shut and held his breath against the rising nausea, pulling the familiar leather satchel up onto bed with him. He should never have suggested the bottle of mead when they went down to the beach. But he had been a little tipsy at dinner, drunk on Ari and the sea, and at the time it was a great idea.

His fingers searched in the bag until they came up with a smooth vial of potion, which he unstoppered and drank without hesitation. The familiar, awful, too-thick sludge burned down his throat, tasting like brine and overcooked eggs, but it was the best hangover remedy one could find in the Brenem Empire.

He grimaced and waited a few minutes as the little miracle of magic got to work. It was a powerful little concoction, and one of two kinds that Ari and he carried around regularly. The other one, a health elixir, would've probably helped a hangover after a while, but Finn had never found a faster working potion than the disgusting sludge ones.

As the Shade, he had only ever worried about poisons and powders that aided in his work — it had taken him joining their adventuring party to find out that things like healing elixirs even existed. He smiled down at a small vial of bright red liquid that was visible in his bag, remembering when Ari had tossed the contents of one down Finn's throat in a desperate move, hoping that it would be enough to keep Finn from the brink.

They should never have messed with that hag.

Once the pounding in his head had subsided, Finn ran his body through a cold bath as best he could in their small bathroom, standing half-naked in front of the basin inside. When he finally surfaced, peering at himself in the mirror, he laughed. He would never have allowed himself to look this disheveled at court. He had a brief flash of looking into a mirror, seeing his perfectly styled clothing and a grin that could cut as good as the knives at his belt before he stood up, his bare chest and dripping face taking the vision's place.

Two different lives. Both were his, but the Finn in both felt like entirely different people.

He ran a hand through his wet, unruly curls and tried to make them sit normally, smiling as bits of sand fell free between his fingers. *I wonder if Ari had had trouble with me last night.*

As he dressed in a light billowing shirt and simple trousers, he found a large bruise along his elbow. He vaguely remembered hitting a doorframe, and a softly hissed curse and apology under Ari's breath. Chuckling, he tied his curls at the nape of his neck and slid his daggers into their place along his belt and stepped outside.

Finn headed down the road in pursuit of hot coffee and breakfast. He let a hand fall familiarly onto the hilt of one dagger, thumbing the iron and gold filigree along the pommel over and over, more out of habit than anything else.

The heat of the day greeted him along with a soft sea breeze that did nothing to cool the sweat that began to bead down his lower back.

Today, the town felt about as busy as yesterday, the movement of people carrying with them the feeling of an easy vacation town. Finn smiled at everyone he passed, nodding occasionally. He winked at a small, red dragonkin girl that bounced from foot to foot beside her mother. She squealed and waved back with both her hands, one with a book clutched tight in her fist. Her mother chuckled and smiled affectionately down at her.

Taking a deep breath, his lungs expanded with the delicious sea air. He stopped and turned to peer down the street at the ocean. Bubbling joy prickled up his spine as he took in the glittering waves with the sounds of happy townsfolk all around him, feeling as though he was floating.

You know, he thought to himself as he turned on his heel and headed toward May's cafe, *this town is rather charming.*

As he arrived at the cafe, two elderly gnomes stood up from the table and waved to May, leaving a sparkle of coins behind. The two women toddled hand in hand toward the beach, leaning on each other as though they knew neither would let them fall. It was a kind of trust and love that Finn rarely saw, so sweet and tender that it stopped him in his tracks.

"Finn," said May, appearing suddenly at the table, coins disappearing into her apron. "You coming in for a bite?"

"Yes, definitely." He grinned at her, shaking away the odd feeling of detachment that had gripped him at the sight of the two gnomes.

"They're adorable, aren't they?" May pointed with her chin at the retreating gnomish couple, gathering their plates. "Della and Neema. They've been living here together longer than most of us on Fetterly Place — they've been here longer than both Lord Wymarc and the lord that was stationed here before him. That's what love should be, don't you think? Aging together, finding a place where the two of you belong and are truly happy."

Finn chuckled, feeling slightly unmoored at the thought. He hadn't ever thought about *growing old* before. "If you can find something that rare, definitely. It sounds like a wonderful dream."

May led him inside. "I've seen the way you and your partner look at each other. It might be a more approachable dream than you think. Coffee?"

"Please. Have you seen him, by the way?" Finn settled onto a stool along the countertop bar that ran along the left side of the cafe.

"He stopped by earlier today, before heading off into Arrowmount to explore a bit. Did you have a bit of a lie in?"

"Too good of a night," said Finn with a self-deprecating wince, turning to look at the cafe. "Something about mead and the beach felt romantic in the moment."

May hummed and turned to a large coffee machine behind the bar and began to create.

Alongside the long, sprawling bar and counter that was filled with everything that Finn could conceptualize one would need to run about ten cafes, the cafe itself was a quaint, cozy space filled to the brim with plants. A shelf ran around the upper rim of the cafe, filled with a variety of plants so lush that the air inside the cafe was thick with the scent of growing things and freshly brewed coffee.

It took Finn a few minutes to realize there was someone else inside the cafe, watching him over a mug of something that steamed in thick flourishes around their spectacles. They tilted the mug toward Finn in greeting, revealing a flat, snout-like nose covered in soft, brown fur, and long flopping ears that hung out from under a rather jaunty looking hat. The giantkin winked once before they turned their sparkling, bright eyes to their paper to read.

"Here you go, handsome." May cut into Finn's meandering thoughts and observances of her shop. He turned back toward the counter as she slid a mug of stone-black coffee across it. He was instantly consumed with the aroma of rich, almost salty coffee — as though she had infused it with some of the sea lingering in the air. "Careful you don't burn your tongue, it's piping. Food will be up in a moment."

"This is glorious," sighed Finn, taking a long sniff of the steaming liquid.

May chuckled happily as she bustled by a small stove, the greasy deliciousness of butter filling the air.

Finn spent a delightful half-hour in May's listening to the town outside mingle with the sea rushing softly in the distance, the popping and sizzling of May's stove and coffee maker as she served the occasional customer the perfect soundtrack to his breakfast.

Before long, though, Ari walked by — the flash of white hair unmistakable in the sunshine.

"That's my cue," said Finn, placing a few coins on the table. "Thank you for that delicious breakfast May, I feel like a new man."

"It's more along the lines of a late lunch now, lad," said a deep, smooth voice from above Finn's shoulder. He startled and looked up, a hand drifting to his dagger, before he realized it was just the giantkin from the corner. They had been so silent; how did Finn not notice them get up? Maybe his reflexes were getting dull. They glanced down at Finn's hand, and gave Finn a look of almost pitying kindness. Finn flinched slightly back, dropping his hand. Instead of saying anything, they simply smiled and folded their paper over their arm, nodded genially to May before exiting the cafe.

Finn blinked, slightly off put by the mysterious being's behavior, before exiting the cafe and heading off after Ari, casting a glance around for the giantkin. They were already a way down the street, tall frame noticeable above the rest.

Odd. People usually didn't act so casually around daggers and knives.

A flash of white brought Finn back to the present. "Ari!"

His love stopped and turned on the cobbles, a smile spreading across his face. Finn half ran up to him, drinking in the beautiful elf before him. Ari was absolutely resplendent in the sunshine. Of course, he already had a book in his hands.

"Good afternoon," said Ari dryly, placing a kiss on Finn's cheek. "Did you sleep alright?"

"Like a drunk rock. Thank the gods for those hangover potions."

Ari linked his arm in Finn's and turned them down the street toward the beach. "We might have to order in more if you're going to continue drinking wine on the beach."

"It was simply in celebration of us finally arriving at the seaside!" Finn nudged Ari in the side. "I heard you were already at May's."

"I took a tea and a delicious bun up out of town and met a curious little cat," said Ari, gesturing toward the rooftops of Arrowmount. "There is a lovely field full of wildflowers and trees that has a picturesque view of the town and the sea."

"Perhaps we can venture up there with one of your new books and read? Or rather, you can read and I can watch you enjoy the book."

Ari shot him a sideways look. "You might actually enjoy the books if you gave them a try."

"I know I would. You have excellent taste. But when it comes to books, I prefer to watch you take them in. It's almost as if I can read the whole story as it happens on your face. I love how you lose yourself to a story."

Ari turned slightly pink and smiled. "I met Chervil's granddaughter. She's the one manning the bookstore today — she's the complete antithesis to Dew's curmudgeonly nature."

"Oh?"

"I think you'd like her a lot. Loves adventures."

"She's an adventurer at heart?"

"Heart, mind, body, soul — mark my words, that girl will be heading off on an adventure the second she can."

"Do you remember being like that?"

Ari turned to glance into the window of a curiosity shop nearby. "I don't think I was ever that excited for an adventure, except when I was leaving home."

"I loved the idea of what being an adventurer would give," said Finn, nodding along. "I wanted out, I wanted freedom."

Ari looked at Finn contemplatively before they continued on past the shop. "We both wanted a different reality than we had, didn't we?"

"A different future, one that we had control of." Finn grinned at Ari before kissing him in the sunshine. He tasted slightly salty, like the air around them had already left its mark. "The freedom of adventure. There's nothing like it."

"Sage will be more than happy to talk your ear off, darling."

15
ELDAR'S WALL

A handful of days later, Ari and Finn found themselves leaning against the bar of Cobb's Down-By-The-Beach, looking at the owner himself.

"We're looking to explore a bit more of Arrowmount," said Finn, leaning against the bar. Bertie Cobb stood behind it atop a stool, drying a rather large tankard. "What would you say is the best way to experience the town? Learn a bit more about it?"

"Hmm," grunted Cobb, setting down the glass and leaning forward on the bar, his thin wiry arms flexing as he gripped the top. He teetered slightly on the stool but didn't look bothered. "You'll be best checking out a few spots while you're here. Something like the lighthouse, you'll not want to miss that — and some of the old part of the town."

Ari raised his eyebrows. "There's an old part?"

"'Course, you're standing in it," Cobb chuckled. "This town used to be quite a fair bit smaller. In fact, Fetterly Place was the center of town from the beginning. Most of our buildings along this strip have been rebuilt and held up to protect against the elements many times over, but a lot of what we have is still the old part. Have someone show you 'round."

Cobb hopped off his stool with a soft *hup-pah* and ducked behind the bar before climbing back up and plunking down a few clean glasses, ready to be filled. "If you get the chance, head on over to the Bronze Bee."

Finn glanced sideways at Ari. "The Bronze Bee? What's that?"

"Trust me." Cobb smiled mischievously at them. "You'll have to go see for yourselves."

Ari led Finn out onto the street, leaving the cozy interior of the inn. "Who should we ask?"

"Sage, of course," said Ari immediately. "I'm sure she'd be happy to be a guide. Let's see if she's at the shop."

They found Sage dusting shelves inside Arrowmount Books, a slight dreamy look in her eyes. Her hand passed over the same spot about five times, her focus elsewhere, before she realized she wasn't alone.

"Oh! Hello Mr. Damaris, welcome back!" She beamed, her tail swishing behind her. "And you must be Mr. Damaris' partner."

"Finn." Finn extended his hand and shook Sage's with a warm smile on his face. "Ari's told me all about you."

"I hope only good things, Mr. Finn."

Finn chuckled. "I *have* heard a bit about your adventuring soul."

Sage's cheeks turned slightly darker green as she blushed gently, her face brightening even more. "I was hoping that you would come by to chat about it. I've never actually met people who've adventured in real life before!"

"Are you working much longer, Sage?" asked Ari. "We have half a mind to explore this little town with someone who would know it's secrets and stories best."

Sage turned to glance at the shop before shrugging. "I wasn't supposed to come in today at all, but I didn't have much else to do, so I figured I would try and tackle some of the cleaning this place desperately needs. I'm not really making a dent, though, am I?"

"This shop needs a bit more than a dusting, I think."

"And I think I was daydreaming a bit," said Sage, shaking her head at herself. "It is so easy to get lost in a good daydream in a bookshop, though, isn't it?"

They found themselves standing back out on the cobblestones of Fetterly Place as Sage tucked a book inside one of her dress pockets and waved to Mr. Dew, the old dwarf, who she had unearthed from the depths of the shop to deposit at the front desk. He frowned deeply as they left.

"Where to first?" Sage straightened her back and tossed her hair over her shoulder.

"Cobb told us about the older part of Arrowmount? And he also said to visit the Bronze Bee, whatever that is."

Sage nodded. "If you want to really get the Arrowmount experience, then that's the place to go. First, though, I think..." Sage tapped her lip a couple times, thinking, before her eyes lit up. "Ah, I know just the place to start."

She led them up and out of the town, toward the hills where Ari had enjoyed breakfast on their second day in town. She hiked up her skirts so they wouldn't get caught along the lengths of the long grass and wildflowers and marched off, ignoring the bees and butterflies as they fluttered away from her.

"From up here, you can get a good view of the town," said Sage, motioning with one hand at the vista.

"But you do miss out on most of my favorite bit of history," she continued, walking up the hill a bit. She headed in an upward arc, angled toward the sea. "Over here are some of the last remaining ruins of Eldar's Wall."

Sage brought them round a copse of trees to a rolling section of hill where, after a bit of searching, she found the beginning of a stone pile. "It doesn't look like much from here, but if you follow it down far enough, it feels like you're walking through the past. There are also remnants of a guard station they used in the war."

"War?" Finn scrunched his face in confusion. "There hasn't been war this far into the Brenem Empire for centuries."

"Exactly." Sage nodded sincerely. "Eldar's Wall was built to protect Arrowmount during the Centurion."

Ari let out a low whistle, crouching down next to a piece of centuries-old stone. The Centurion had been a war hundreds and hundreds of years ago, between gods and men that had ravaged much of the continent. Ari couldn't really name the feeling that overwhelmed him as he placed a hand on something that had been around since an event that had become nearly mythological in their world.

Sage walked a little further and hopped up onto the stone with a flourish of blue skirts. "This wall is what kept Arrowmount and its people from falling to enemy forces. The soldiers built it when they heard of incoming danger and found themselves battling for their lives atop and around it."

They fell silent for a while, staring out at the swaths of nature around them. An occasional breeze rustled through the trees along the hill and flowed through the sea of long grass around them. It was difficult to imagine a battle waging here, in such a peaceful place.

"The man who helmed building the wall was named Eldar the Bold," continued Sage, leading them on down the length of the wall through the long grass and flowers. "He gathered the soldiers here — they weren't trained in battle, but they were all that Arrowmount had — and told them how he planned to keep the town safe. He's quoted in one of our history books saying, 'we will not let them take us, for if we do, they will surely cause grief like none other.' And he wasn't wrong. If the enemy forces had taken Arrowmount, they would have had access to our port and would have been able to attack the empire's armies from two sides, which would have given them the upper hand.

"And there," she pointed a little further up the hill, between a copse of leaning trees, "is the foundation of one of the guard stations they built. From that point, Eldar dove into battle from a topmost window, sword swinging, and cut down a dozen men."

Sage continued to regale them with stories of the Centurion and Eldar's Wall, weaving in a romantic storyline of a princess who had come to see the wall that saved the empire and fell in love with Eldar himself. The length of crumbled stone stretched down toward the sea like an ancient sea serpent.

Finn whistled low, turning on his heel to look back up to where they had come. "All those people laying down their lives to save the town. Makes you forget about yourself for a little bit, in the grand scheme of things."

"It's all very romantic and heroic," sighed Sage, a dreamy look on her face. "If I was the princess who came here, I would have fallen in love with Eldar the moment I laid eyes on him. No — I would have fallen for him long before that. As soon as I heard of his heroism, even his name itself. Eldar the Bold."

"Heroes," chuckled Ari. "Our history and world are full of them."

"Without them, we wouldn't have an empire to traipse about in, my love," said Finn, pulling Ari in by his waist and placing a kiss on his cheek. "Then where would we be?"

Sage sighed dreamily. "You two are like heroes from the stories, but better, because you're *here* right now. Imagine, fighting on this very wall," she hopped up onto the stone once again and dropped into an imitation of a fighting stance before flailing about with her arm as though fighting an imaginary foe, "and battling for not only your home, but your heart."

"We're just lowly adventurers, Sage," said Finn. "I don't think that counts as heroism."

"Tell me you haven't saved someone from an evil creature."

Finn shot a humored glance toward Ari as Ari let out a snort. "We've fought many creatures, but the idea of evil and good is quite relative and grey in the real world."

"Oh, I'm not so sure," said Finn. "What about those trolls? They were definitely evil, my love. If we hadn't taken them down, then what would have become of that village nearby?"

"See?" Sage poked her finger into the air. "You *are* heroes."

Finn took over the role of storyteller as they walked the length of the wall down to the sea. He told Sage stories of their adventures, embellishing here and there — because, as real adventurers know, the truth behind is rather less heroic and wonderful as stories make them sound.

They sat on the edge of the stone wall and dipped their toes into the cool waters lapping along the shoreline. Ari couldn't help but smile as they settled on the stretch of the wall, listening to Finn talk. He leaned back against the sunbaked stone, squishy moss and sand grit under his hands.

He hadn't felt this comfortable and this at ease in a really long time. As he tossed his head back and closed his eyes, listening to the animated melody of Finn's voice pockmarked every so often with Sage's excited one, he cast his mind back, trying to remember ever feeling this way.

Being constantly on the move kept them churning from place to place, barely stopping anywhere before they were off again. Even though they'd only been here a few days, though, Arrowmount had dug itself into Ari's skin and bones.

It feels like home.

The thought brushed his mind unbidden, causing his heart to pang painfully in his chest. He sucked in a deep breath and pushed the thought down, trying not to think about what making a life, making a *home* here would be like.

From here, the two of them would probably travel up the coast, angling along toward Feycross or perhaps more east, even further, up to Alieweth. It would be an okay adventure, he mused, but something deep in his chest wished that they wouldn't leave this little seaside town. Hopefully, King Zoren wouldn't come calling and they could stay until they had their fill of the sun and the sea.

Hopefully.

16

THE BRONZE BEE

Arileas

Sage looped her arm around Ari's as she led them back into Arrowmount. "I'm glad you asked me to play tour guide," she sighed wistfully. "I like you two too much. I wish you were staying for longer, and not just *visiting*."

Finn and Ari shared a look of amusement.

"You just want to milk us for more of our stories," said Finn, winking.

Laughing, she guided them through an alleyway so narrow that Ari's shoulders brushed against either side of it. They wound around aged, salt-stained and chipped away wood and stone until the alley opened up to a small area of ancient buildings that leaned on one another.

Sage threw out her arms in a wide gesture and did a small spin as they arrived in the tiny courtyard. "Welcome to one of the oldest parts of Arrowmount."

A few people milled around, nodding to Sage as they squeezed off down other alley ways or the way that the three of them had come. She led Ari and Finn to a doorway that had what looked like a lumpy, aged carving in the door. There was no sign above any of the buildings, leaving what was behind the doors a complete mystery.

"Most of these buildings have been turned into apartments over the years," explained Sage. "Most, but not this one. This place is the same as it's always been."

Ari frowned at the door, which looked as though it had been built at an angle amidst the stone and realized what the carving was.

A bee.

"Welcome to the Bronze Bee," said Sage, pushing the door open. Both Finn and Ari had to duck a fair bit under the doorjamb as they entered the dark interior after her.

Ari's eyes adjusted, snapping the interior into focus. The Bronze Bee was a pub, squished into the tiniest space he could imagine. The ceilings were so low that the top of his head brushed along parts of wood as they walked in, causing him to hunch instinctively.

Everything was tightly packed with furniture; Ari couldn't imagine how claustrophobic it would be in here if a crowd came in. Thankfully, it was only them and a lone gnome sitting at the bar, sipping at an enormous tankard. They lifted the tankard in greeting as Sage weaved her way around the tables and chairs. Their tankard settled onto the bar with a hard *thunk*.

"Need a refill already, Delvin?" The rough, high-pitched voice proceeded the person as a figure shoved a stool into place behind the bar and climbed up. The tiniest gnarled gnome appeared with a jaunty kind of hat perched on her head. She blinked at the other gnome, hand halfway outstretched toward Delvin's tankard before turning toward the three of them.

"Oh! My mistake, I didn't hear ya enter." She hopped off the stool and came scurrying out from around the bar, a smile on her wrinkled face.

"Welcome to the Bronze Bee. What can I get ya?"

"A round of Arrowmount's finest," answered Sage. "Tae, this is Mr. Arileas Damaris and his partner, Finn."

"Pleasure to meet ya, I'm Taena, owner and purveyor of this here establishment. Welcome to the Bronze Bee," said Tae warmly, reaching up to shake both of their hands, "the oldest pub you'll find in Arrowmount, and possibly all of the Brenem Empire! Once, I'll have you know, that Eldar the Bold himself walked through that very door to enjoy the Bee's infamous brew."

"Wow," said Finn, nodding around at the place. "You're saying this place is centuries old? That hardly seems real."

"I know it's hard to wrap your noggin' round. Looks only a couple decades old, eh?" Tae led them to one of the larger tables at the back, pulling a few other chairs away so they could sit comfortably. "What with those ruins out there. But our brew is as good as it was back then, if not better. Same recipe, same rich flavor. I'll bring some right out."

Sage leaned forward with a grin. "Oh, and Tae — some of the Arrowmount Special?"

The gnome winked and a mischievous look crossed her face, much like Cobb's from earlier. "You boys will not believe your taste buds. You've come to the *only* place in Arrowmount worth eating the Special at — don't listen to anyone who says otherwise, especially Corwek. He and I need to have words."

Tae bustled off back behind the bar as Ari glanced at Sage, lifting an eyebrow in question.

"Corwek is the cook for the Old'n Narrow," she explained. "The bar on Fetterly Place. Honestly, I'm surprised she didn't go after Cobb today, usually they're always at each other's throats. They're siblings."

The inn was built sturdily with large old stones colored by time and smoke. Wooden beams ran along the ceiling, from which hung old relics, trinkets, and pots that looked as though they were coated in at least a hundred years of rust.

Notches and burns and old ale stains from years of service pockmarked the chairs and tables around them. The Bronze Bee smelled like dust and stone until Tae began to cook behind the bar, out of sight, and suddenly they were bathed in the rich, nutty scent of cooking butter.

Tae brought over their plates and drinks a while later, setting them on the table with a clatter before reaching above her head and giving each a strong push, the plates spinning right to each person with practiced precision.

Tae tapped Sage amiably on her thigh before she walked off to the bar once more. "Enjoy."

"Dig in, I know you'll love it," said Sage, taking a hearty bite of the food in front of her, butter dripping down her chin. As Finn reached for some utensils, Sage slapped his hand away. "Without any utensils, it's the proper Arrowmount way."

The Arrowmount Special turned out to be an incredibly large plate of herb-and-butter fried fish slices, accompanied by a delicious smelling mix of hearty vegetables and glistening potato cakes bathed in cheese. He sunk his teeth into a bit of fish, the buttery outside bursting with flavor. Inside was perfectly flaky and so utterly delicious that Ari had to close his eyes for a moment, savoring it.

"This is perfection," groaned Finn, digging in with both hands.

Tae, from the behind the bar, let out a snort. "You bet your handsome ass it is."

17

FRECKLES

Finnean

Finn thought that he would become tired of the little seaside town by the fifth or sixth day of their stay. But, as he woke in the same inn bed a week in, with the morning sunlight casting Ari in a soft halo of light, the call of seabirds outside their windows mingling with the waves beyond, he found that he was actually excited to still be in Arrowmount.

He also began to recognize the faces of the townsfolk, which is something that he had not done in years. When he had taken on the title of the Shade, he became a shadow at court, only noticing faces he was told to notice by the king. Even then, they slipped from his mind as soon as the job was done. Those at court became the same faceless people swirling around him, so what was the point in remembering them?

Here, though, Finn began to remember. Sometimes even faster than Ari did. Next to May and old Chervil, they had become familiar with Bertie and Helen Cobb, and knew, by sight, some of the people that worked along Fetterly Place. He was even beginning to create a mental list of those who lived along the cobblestones. There was a set of apartments built behind Cobb's Down-By-The-Beach in a block of four — two up, two down — facing Fetterly Place that housed a number of people and families, including the old gnomish couple, Della and Neema.

They hadn't met the Lord of Arrowmount, Lord Wymarc, since he was apparently visiting the Kingdom of Pralon for some of the summer season. That didn't bother Finn much, since the idea of meeting someone who was attached to royal life in some way was more anxiety inducing than he would like to admit. He had never met a Lord Wymarc during his time as the Shade, but the idea of having a lord around did set him on edge.

Besides the people and the sea, Finn found himself smiling as he walked along the cobbles. He couldn't really tell why, but whenever he walked up or down the street, his feet felt like they were treading well-loved places that were entirely familiar to him. He often didn't have to look where he was going, too. His feet and instincts guided him around unsteady stones and townsfolk with ease, hardly interrupting his stride.

The best part of it all was Ari. He was always the best part of Finn's day, even before they had arrived in Arrowmount, but here? Ari simply flourished. Finn had never seen Ari this happy in the months they had been travelling together. It honestly made Finn not want to leave, which was an entirely foreign feeling.

"Ari." Finn leaned against the door jamb to their small inn bathroom on the seventh morning. Ari was angled over the basin of fresh water, hair pulled back with a small piece of leather, shirtless and dripping water as he looked up between his fingers. "You've gotten some color. And is that a freckle I see?"

"What?"

"Your cheeks, my love. They're all rosy from the sun."

Ari peered at himself in the mirror before glancing back at Finn. "You have too. You were golden before, but now?"

Finn laughed. "We should have a beach day. We've been here a week and have yet to actually have a proper beach day."

"A day with the sand between my toes, my love at my side…" Ari smiled warmly at Finn and reached over, threading his fingers over the waist band of Finn's trousers to pull him closer.

"Agh, you're all wet and cold." Finn cringed away as Ari slapped his arms around Finn's shoulders, clammy as a fish.

"I like the sound of a beach day," said Ari into Finn's ear, holding him fast. "Let's do it."

Before making their way to the beach, they headed through Arrow-mount to grab a few things from the market in the town center. Finn stopped to take a peek at the notice board in case news had come about the Shade as Ari walked around the market. Finn scanned the notices, glancing at a few new ones from locals, one advertising new puppies that had been born on a farm just outside of town and another advertising the start of strawberry season. Nothing from the king.

Ari picked up a few fresh pieces of fruit, including the now-in-season strawberries, and bread for lunch later, nodding to the half-orc woman running the fruit stall.

They decided to stop by May's for a late breakfast on their way back, lounging on some of her outside tables with delicious iced beverages as May prepared their food. Finn sipped at his iced coffee as he watched Ari braid his hair back in multiple sections. His white hair had gotten quite long over the months they had been travelling, and now it took Ari a while to do anything intricate with it. Finn appreciated every time he got to witness it. There was something about the way that Ari's thin, strong fingers weaved expertly, reaching back over his head to gather and create.

Ari quirked an eyebrow when he noticed Finn watching, a playful smile curling on his lips. "What?"

"You really are getting freckles, Ari. I didn't know elves could get them."

Ari let out a soft laugh and fastened off the end of his final braid, wrapping all four sections into one thick rope over his shoulder. "Most of the elves I know wouldn't even recognize what a freckle was, so you wouldn't be the only one. But I suppose anything is possible."

"Now, don't you two look absolutely at home," said May as she came over, placing two plates down in front of them.

"Your cafe is incredibly comfortable," said Finn, smiling up at her.

She twinkled down at them both. Today, she wore thin round glasses and had her curls tied up in a massive, messy knot at the nape of her neck. "Not only that, but there's an air about you two now. You no longer look like travelers here for a visit."

Ari reached for a bit of toast on his plate. "Oh?"

"Something about you two fits in our little town. I feel rather like Chervil," said May with a laugh before patting Ari on the shoulder. "He said the same thing to me all those years ago. You two let me know if you need anything else."

She turned and reached up toward some of the plants that blanketed the overhang on her cafe, poking them up and back into place as they began to twist down toward her. Ari made a soft sound, and Finn noticed him looking off after May with a sort of far off look.

"Gosh, this looks good," said Finn, turning toward his breakfast. "May is a true genius with her eggs and bacon, is she not?"

"She really is," answered Ari, turning back to his plate. Finn found Ari less talkative than usual over breakfast, as though he was stewing over something in his mind.

"You alright, my love?" Finn asked as they left May's hand in hand. "You've been quiet."

"Oh, yes, of course," said Ari, kissing him on the cheek. "I was simply enjoying May's delicious food. Let's go have our beach day, shall we?"

18

SEA CURLS AND SAND

Finnean

U nder the bright midday sunshine, Finn spread a blanket across the sand and set down his and Ari's boots along the edges to keep it down in the breeze. Ari plopped himself down on it, eyes squinting against the sun, book in hand, and smiled up at Finn as he slid out of his shirt.

"You look good like that."

"Half naked and sandy?"

Ari grinned. "Yes."

The hours melted by as the sun remained hot and high, slowly inching its way across the perfectly cloudless sky. One of the local elderly gnomes — she introduced herself as Della — came by with a bottle of lotion that she insisted Ari and Finn slather on regularly. To ensure that the sun wouldn't burn them to crisps, she said.

She was dressed head to toe in what appeared to be layers of linen cloth sewn to be the loosest possible shape that could still be considered

102

clothing. She looked like a walking cloud, skating over the sand.

"Make sure you keep reapplying it every hour. The sun can be quite nasty on skin if you're not well protected," she had said, leaving them the bottle and tottering away in her billowy white clothing, "If you need more, I can put you in contact with one of the stall keepers who keeps these potions stocked."

Ari and Finn thanked her, bemused smiles on their faces, before taking turns lathering the creamy lotion over each other's shoulders.

By the time the sun was beginning its descent into late afternoon, Finn and Ari had made a nest of clothes, boots, books, and leftover lunch bits on their blanket. Their hair had dried into salted sea curls, sand lining every inch of their bodies. Finn lay back on the blanket, a genuine bliss practically oozing out of him.

"We should vacation like this more often," he sighed, peering at Ari through one eye. "Honestly, my love, I wish this vacation could last forever."

Ari propped himself up on one elbow to look at Finn.

"How long should we stay here, do you think?" Finn asked, stretching both arms above his head. "Perhaps a better question is how long do you think these lovely folks will take until they want to throw us out?"

Ari chuckled, but the sound wasn't quite his usual laugh. Finn blinked up at him, narrowing his eyes against the sun. A tiny furrow between Ari's eyebrows that Finn only saw when he was puzzling something over was there. Finn reached up and gently ran a thumb over it, trying to smooth it out.

"Love, what's on your mind?"

"Do you really like it here?"

"What isn't there to love? Sunshine, incredible beaches, lovely people."

Ari nodded and looked out over the water for a moment before turning back to him. "Have you ever thought about settling down? Stopping all of what we... what we do?"

Finn felt his stomach drop slightly and the smile slip from his face before he forced it back on with a laugh. "Ari, we're adventurers. It's kind of what we do, travelling. We don't have anywhere to settle down."

"What if we *did* find a place?"

"It's something to think about," said Finn slowly, sitting up now so he could look at Ari properly. The strangest stillness had taken over Finn in the last thirty seconds as he thought about this. What would that be like, having a place to call home? Even back at the palace, it was hard to call the place home. It was more just his place of work, really. "But we still have the king on our backs, love."

"Right," breathed Ari. "But do we, really?"

Finn blinked at him in response.

"We have been on the run for eight months as a precautionary measure, sure," said Ari, tilting his head slightly to the side as the little crease reappeared between his eyebrows. "But we also haven't stayed anywhere long enough to know if we even are being chased or not. And I'm... I'm so tired. The constant movement, the constant travelling and unknown, darling, it's a lot."

He wasn't wrong, Finn too found a lot of it exhausting sometimes. But stopping it entirely... Finn breathed in long and slow, biting his lip. "Where would we —"

"Here. Arrowmount." Ari looked at Finn, concern pulling his eyebrows together.

"If we stayed here," said Finn, thoughts spinning. "What would we do, exactly?"

"Well, I'm not entirely sure," said Ari, looking away from Finn like he usually did when he was trying to pass a small fib under Finn's detection. It never worked, though it was cute that he tried.

Finn lifted an eyebrow, waiting, as a soft pink blush rose up into Ari's cheeks. He definitely knew what he wanted to do, if they stayed.

"Gods, you know me too well."

Finn let out a small laugh.

"The bookstore," said Ari, clasping both his hands together in his lap. "What if we bought it?"

"You want to *buy the bookstore*?"

"It's not like we don't have the funds," said Ari quickly. "We have the gold from when we raided that wyvern hoard, and I have the money from my job with the king I can send for."

"I'm not worried about the funds, Ari." Finn hesitated, trying to organize his thoughts. "I'm thinking about the change in our lives. How exactly are we going to go from being adventurers, travelers of the realm, to running a store? Neither of our skills really apply here."

Ari shook his head. "You're right. I should never have mentioned it."

Finn's chest constricted at the softly crestfallen look crossing Ari's face. "No, I — Okay," he reached between them and grabbed Ari's hands into his, "let's think about this realistically."

"Realistically."

"Yes, funnily enough, I too can be realistic sometimes," said Finn. He let out a long sigh that turned into a laugh. He glanced up and down the beach, noting a few people dotted here and there, though none were close enough to hear their conversation. "What of the Shade? What of the king? We can't just ignore that."

"Do we worry about him for the rest of our lives, darling?" Ari looked at Finn with a softly sad look. "I'm sure that word will come through of an official death declaration soon. We could wait here, instead of running."

Finn swallowed hard. The idea of staying still, of baiting the possibility of danger onto them here, swelled the panic inside of him. He began to twist his fingers into the blanket beneath him furiously and pushed out a laugh. "You know, I never thought I would even be contemplating a future, let alone settling down somewhere."

"I know. But it's possible, isn't it? To settle down somewhere?" Ari turned Finn's hands over and linked their fingers together, stopping his furious worrying of the blanket.

"These past few months have felt like I'm living someone else's life."

"It's *our* life, Finn. We should be able to do what we want with it. Wasn't that what we set out to do in the first place? Why should we let the Shade and some king dictate our life, still?"

"What if he does keep up the hunt?"

Ari's face pinched with worry. "Then... then we go."

Finn looked back toward the town, at the fluttering multicolored flags of Arrowmount. He thought about the town, the way the cobbles felt like home beneath his feet. The sun and the warmth. "This bookstore idea. Do you think that's really something we could do?"

"It would breathe new life into the town," said Ari, his eyes brightening. "Bring back that sad shop, free the books inside."

Finn could picture Ari standing amongst the shelves of Arrowmount Books, his fingers tracing the spines carefully. It wasn't much of a stretch to see him behind the front desk, helping customers. Gods, it wasn't much of a stretch at all.

"The more I think about it, the less I can come up with ideas as to why we shouldn't stay," said Finn after a while, looking down at their entwined fingers. "Staying here. This place really has a certain feel to it, doesn't it?"

"Even without the bookstore, is this something we could do? Finding a place to settle. It doesn't have to be here, it can be anywhere you want, darling. I'll follow you anywhere, you know that."

Was there anywhere else in this entire world that he would like more than this? He honestly didn't know. Could he really stay in one place? Is that something that he was allowed to do? He never once thought about doing that, even when he was planning a new life for himself back in Pralon. Every dreamt-up reality of his involved constantly moving around, seeing the empire.

Yet another addition to this life, this new life with Ari, that felt entirely like a dream. Why not live in it a little longer?

That thought alone let him push the anxiety down. Finn sucked in a breath and reached for Ari, drawing their heads together, resting both hands on either side of Ari's face. "I want to live this dream life with you, Arileas. I want to. Here. It'll be a new adventure."

"Truly?"

"This place has felt more like home than anywhere else we've been. Besides — forget the Shade. That title controlled my life long enough. And I can see how this place makes you incandescently happy, my love."

Of course, there is still the possibility that your old life will come calling, said a tiny voice in his head. *You would have to run, then.*

Finn pushed the thought away and reveled in the idea that this dream, this new life that Ari was giving him, was possible at all.

Ari's face twitched into look of pure disbelieving joy before he kissed Finn so fiercely that Finn lost the thread of his thoughts. When they finally resurfaced, both of them were laughing.

"We'll talk to Dew," said Ari after they gathered themselves.

"I have half a mind to run right down there and offer him all of our gold, if you're going to kiss me like that," said Finn, feeling slightly drunk on Ari and the salty sea air. "I don't even care that I have sand in places I will never be able to reach."

Ari snorted and pulled Finn to his feet, running off toward the sea. The water glittered like a perfect pot of gold in the late afternoon sunlight, the rhythmic waves washing over them as they crashed into the water. Finn reached out for Ari as they threw themselves in, the two of them falling back into the brilliantly blue water.

Maybe this *adventure will be a good one,* thought Finn. For however long it lasts.

PART THREE

Plans and Changes

19

MR. DEW'S FAREWELL

Arileas

Once they had settled into the idea of staying, Ari and Finn sought out Dew. His eyes widened in awe, as though they had handed him an entire kingdom of wealth. Sage stood off to the side, both hands over her mouth, eyes so wide and brimming with excitement that Ari thought she might explode.

"You're serious?" Dew squinted at the two of them, repeating himself for the third time. He shook his head. "You want to buy this place from me? It's falling apart at the seams."

"Weirdly enough, yes," said Finn, chuckling. "If you're interested of course. You still haven't exactly said yes or no."

Dew sputtered and wiped his hand over his forehead as Sage danced back and forth on the spot, making a sound like a boiling kettle.

"Mighty Maigsir," Dew cursed, his curmudgeonly, aged face completely transformed. He looked almost twenty years younger as he held a hand to his forehead in disbelief, the sputtering, surprised laughter still pouring out of him. "Yes. *Yes.* You two have just dropped a golden egg into my lap, lads. You've got a damn deal."

Sage finally couldn't contain herself anymore and threw her arms out in glee, knocking a tower of books over, and screamed. "I *knew* you would be the perfect fit!"

They left Dew and Sage to work through whatever they needed to before handing over the keys, and began to walk around Arrowmount, taking in the town they were now going to live in. Ari didn't really know why, but there was a new level of shine to the town now that he knew they were staying. A shine and a soft, churning anxiety, but that was held back for the moment.

They returned to Arrowmount Books a few days later, meeting the old dwarf outside of the shop. Dew was finishing up the process of tying his belongings into a heavily laden cart, two horses tied at the front ready for a journey.

"Thank you, boys, for this," he said, a grin sliding across his face. Dew's hands rested in his pockets as he nodded up at Finn and Ari. "A weight has been lifted from my shoulders."

Ari extended his hand to shake. "Where are you off to now?"

"Off to Claymore, to visit some family there. I haven't seen my sister in ages."

"That sounds lovely. I hope we can do the store justice."

The old dwarf took Ari's hand warmly, enveloping his hand in a worn, roughened handshake, and barked out a laugh. "You will, without a doubt. You'll have it better than I ever could in a few days, I bet. Don't know what I was ever doing, thinking I could take on a place like this."

"Are you *trying* to convince us not to buy this place?" Finn shook hands with the dwarf as they both laughed.

They waved goodbye to Dew as he hopped up into the front of the cart with a fresh spring in his step and drove off toward the front gates. Ari linked his fingers with Finn's and squeezed, anticipation shooting through every nerve of his body. It still didn't quite feel real, but now that they were here, standing in front of the shop, the anticipation and anxiety he had been feeling for the past few days danced in his stomach.

"This is it," said Finn, looking up at the crumbling facade.

They walked to the door together, only to take a surprised step back as Sage pushed the door open from the inside. Today, she wore what Ari could only describe as a party dress. It was made of a heavier, smoother material than the usual casual linen dresses that she wore, lined with a chiffon underskirt that helped it keep its shape. She swished lightly as she moved, the material flowing around her like a silken flower petal.

"I was watching at the window," she said, a grin bursting on her face, eyes watery. She withdrew a decently weighty brass key from a pocket and turned, locking the bookshop behind her. "I almost cried when Mr. Dew rode off. Well, I did cry a little, but that's because I'm so excited for you two to move in."

"Sage?" Finn pointed to the locked door. "You locked it."

"I want to make it feel special." She handed Ari the key, the cool weight of it settling into his palm. "It's officially yours."

Ari looked down at the key and turned it over a few times, feeling as though the entire world had narrowed right to this moment here. He felt Finn move next to him, the slightest of squeezes to his hand, and looked up. Sage beamed at him excitedly and stepped aside, leaving the door in full view.

This is it.

He stepped forward, pulling Finn along in his wake, and slid the key into the lock. He hesitated a couple of heartbeats before he turned it with a satisfying click, the door opening a breath in his hand. Finn smiled at him encouragingly as Ari looked back at him, and finally, Ari opened the door to their bookshop.

Finn and Ari walked in, followed by Sage, to see that the front of the store had been covered in decorations. Sage had set up a display of ribbons and flowers with a hand-painted sign sitting on the desk that read WELCOME HOME in bright blue lettering.

Ari's heart leapt up into his throat. He tried to swallow it down, but as he looked around at the rainbow of ribbon that was draped over the dusty book-packed shelves, he couldn't.

"Sage, this is absolutely wonderful."

She beamed at them before diving behind the front counter and pulling out a tray of cupcakes decorated with spiraling rainbow frosting. At that moment, the door opened and in spilled a few townsfolk, wearing fine clothes and holding various foods and drinks to celebrate. There seemed to be many more than just the few that had come in, the clustered front area of the shop instantly feeling overly packed.

Sage cringed. "Oh no, this place is far too small for all of us."

"Let's bring this down to the Old'n Narrow," suggested Chervil, adjusting his jaunty sailors' hat, which was the only new accoutrement that he had added to his regular worn clothing.

Ari held back slightly as the townsfolk cheered and began to file out of the store, Sage following them with the platter of cupcakes and her welcome sign, trailing bits of ribbon out the door.

In a heartbeat, the store was silent again, all the noise ending with the soft closure of the door. Finn let out an audible breath next to him. "We're actually doing this."

"Yes, yes we are." Ari's eyes skated around the shop, and for moment couldn't speak as more tears pooled in his eyes. "I didn't think I would get this emotional over this. It's a bookstore."

"It's you and me, Ari," said Finn quietly. "Can you believe that not even a year ago, you and I first kissed in that meadow?"

Ari laughed, wiping his cheeks. "I remember something involving a dagger at my throat, which is much more harrowing than us kissing in a meadow."

"Come on," said Finn with a snort. "Let's join them before Sage notices us missing."

20

LISTS AND DUST

Arileas

As the sun began its afternoon descent above them, Ari and Finn made their way back to the bookstore hand in hand, a touch tipsy after being plied with ale and mead and something that Chervil had said would turn Ari's hair even whiter, which had burned like pure acid. Sage walked down the street ahead of them with a bounce in her step, her dress twirling out around her.

Ari opened the bookstore once again. A beam of sunlight cut across the dank floors, highlighting the dust dancing through the air. He let out a long breath, taking in the shop, as the euphoria of the day began to fade. Slowly, his eyes started to snag on the different parts of the shop that they would need to address.

He took a step forward and pulled a bit on a shelf, the soft wood crumbling under his fingers. Both Sage and Finn, who had been chatting quietly behind him, stopped to watch.

Finn cleared his throat carefully. "Ari?"

Ari ignored him. "Sage, can you take notes?"

"Sure thing, boss," she said, fishing a bit of scrap paper out from behind the desk. "What for?"

"Let's start a list of what we need to do to this place."

"Ari, we literally just got in," said Finn with a soft laugh. "Maybe we can start in the morning?"

Ari looked at him.

"Right yes, okay." Finn nodded fast. "Let's say, uh, cleaning number one."

"Proper shelving," added Ari.

"Clean out the old books that are too damaged to sell."

"Reorganize the store's flow." Ari walked further into the store, Sage coming in behind as she scribbled. "Paint, too. Inside and out."

"Should we consider replacing the windows?" Finn motioned with a thumb backward the grime covered windows at the front. "And definitely the door. Maybe replace it with some nice double doors?"

Sage paused in her scribbling to peer at him curiously. "Why double doors?"

"Well, so we can..." Finn walked forward and made a motion with both hands, showing two doors being opened at once with flare. "Could create a wider entrance, much more welcoming than this cramped space."

"There is also the tiny matter of you getting the deed signed by Lord Wymarc," said Sage, tapping her chin with her pen. "He wasn't home in time to see Mr. Dew off, but I'm sure he'll be back soon."

Right. The lord of the town. Ari looked at Finn, who had stiffened ever so slightly at the mention of the lord. Something they were going to have to talk about later, without Sage around.

Finn cleared his throat and nodded at Sage. "On the list."

Ari tilted his head up and peered at the stairwell in the middle of the shop. He stuck out a hand and removed the cord still blocking entry. "What exactly should we expect from upstairs?'

Sage's smile faded slightly as she folded up their to-do list and pocketed it. She looked as though she was steeling herself to go to battle as she put a hand on one of the old railings. "I haven't seen this space in about a year since Mr. Dew stopped letting me go up. He used to store extra books up in his entrance."

"That's encouraging," said Finn dryly.

Ari sucked in a steadying breath and started up the stairs. The three of them ascended single file, poking their way around the books that clogged both sides of the treads. Sage tripped more than once over her own feet from the back, each time punctuated by the tiniest grunt of surprise as she caught herself with her tail, and the sound of falling books.

The rough, old door at the top creaked open under Ari's palm. The wooden trim around the door was slightly lopsided, having swollen open through the years of salty air.

"Ugh," said Finn as Ari pushed the door open fully. They were both assaulted with the scent of stale, moldering books and years of unmoved dust. Finn placed both hands on Ari's shoulders to steady him as Ari took an involuntary step back. "This is worse than the store."

In the light from the bookstore, the entrance of the apartment was opened to them. Ari stuck his head in, peering around. The scent of unused air and old belongings packed in too tightly greeted them, musty and stagnant. Ari had to squint to see beyond most of the entrance light, his eyes focusing to the dark shadowy interior. Between the mess of books and ruined papers and furniture there were perfect holes from where Mr. Dew had taken belongings from.

"This is *much* worse than I remember," whispered Sage, looking between Finn and Ari's arms. The gentle ridges of her horns pressed against his arm as she let out a long, worried breath.

They took it all in for a solid few heartbeats, neither of them saying anything. Finally, Finn cleared his throat and stepped in as far as he could before his path was obscured.

"I think I can see a window back there," he said, starting to shift things out of the way. Nimbly, he hopped his way around the room, finding a path through the mess, motes of dust billowing up behind him in gross clouds.

"Careful, darling."

There was a pause, then, a bit of light appeared in a far corner, illuminating the back of the place and Finn's head poking over a few things.

Ari winced at the newly displayed mess. "I think that made it worse."

"At least we'll get a bit of air moving in here. This place might benefit best from a well-placed fireball, love." Finn stepped lightly back into the entrance way and frowned at the place. "Ari, I love you, but there's no way I'm sleeping up here. We've slept in some terrible places, but this — *this* — is where I draw the line."

"We'll think of something. Sage, where was the bedroom last time you were up here?"

Sage pointed mutely toward the left, a gentle look of astonished disgust on her face. Finn stared through the mess once more, finding a path that Ari followed carefully to not disturb any of the mess. Along the back wall, there were innumerable piles of books that looked nearly destroyed.

Ari picked one up and held it up to show Sage. "I think I found out where Dew hid those water damaged books."

Sage looked deeply saddened. "I was wondering what he did with those."

Finn shoved open a door, revealing a bedroom behind. Ari and Finn stopped, their mouths slightly agape, at the space. It was completely bare except for a couple choice pieces of furniture, as though Dew had kept every bit of mess away from where he slept.

Ari peered at the bed, running a careful hand along the quilt. No dust at all. Even the pillows at the top looked fresh and entirely out of place. He looked at Finn and lifted his eyebrows.

"I think we can work with this."

Finn lifted a pillow, looking unimpressed. "Despite the bedding being well cared for, I'm still not staying up here until this place is clean, Ari. *It smells.*"

Ari took a couple pillows in his arms and withdrew his Bag of Space from his belt, sliding them inside. "I've got an idea."

21

Tiny Arcane Lights

Finnean

Ari held his bag open with one hand and began to clear space in one of the back rooms of the bookstore with his other, books spiraling up in a steady stream of magically moving objects. He flicked his wrist so that the mouth of the maroon bag sagged open further, large enough to fit a large watermelon as they disappeared into it, silently adjusting themselves inside.

Finn moved alongside Ari, sweat starting to bead along his collarbone and down his back as he hauled the heavy shelves out of the way, straightening a few of them along the walls. Finn took a step back and looked at his work, marveling at how a bit of cleaning and reorganizing could transform a space.

"That's an easy way to clean," commented Sage, walking into the room carrying a small cabinet. "I wish I knew how to do something like that. All I've got is tiny little druid powers, and most of the time I can just grow flowers out of things."

"That's more than I can do," grunted Finn, stepping back from the monster of a shelf that he had managed to shift into place. "There's nothing like feeling slightly useless than watching your partner magic something in two seconds that would've taken you an hour. What exactly is your plan here, Ari?"

"Awe, darling, you're incredibly useful," said Ari smirking at him as he made quick work of the books. "I figured we could do something with this room until we tackle the apartment. A little room, just for us."

"That's not a bad idea."

"I have them occasionally."

Finn furrowed his brow, peering around the room. "We need more, though."

Sage placed a small cabinet down in the middle of the room and wiped her forehead. "What else could a room need?"

"Besides a bed, of course, but that's upstairs," said Finn, "a room needs personality. Otherwise it feels like just a room with four walls."

She frowned at him.

"Come on, little fiendling. I will show you exactly what I mean. Ari, love, we'll be back."

"Oh, that's alright," said Ari from behind them dryly. "I'll just move the bed on my own, then."

"Don't forget, you have incredibly useful magic," said Finn over his shoulder with a wink.

Finn and Sage walked out into the golden sunlit street, the heat of the day coalescing in a soft orange haze over Arrowmount. Buildings bathed in a glow as shoppers circled around in the late hours of the day, getting last minute bits of shopping done. Shadows stretched as Finn guided Sage to the center of town.

Finn found himself drawn toward the crowd of market stalls in the middle of the town center. As they walked through it, he scanned the notice board quickly as Sage ducked down to greet a neighborhood dog. He frowned slightly, again noting the distinct lack of royal missives pinned there. Perhaps the return of the lord would bring with it more concrete word of what was going on.

What kind of lord are you, Lord Wymarc? Finn thought to himself, turning away from the board. The idea of having a lord nearby still wasn't entirely comfortable to Finn, but he had to keep reminding himself that no one except for King Zoren knew what he looked like. Sure, there was always the slim possibility that Wymarc would report word of new bookstore owners back to the crown, and that Zoren would then find interest in a name listed as Finnean and recognize him as the currently missing assassin from his court, but what were the odds of that?

Finn didn't want to dwell on it. Besides, the lord in question was currently not in town, and Finn had shopping to do.

One of the stall's owners was in the process of drawing a set of string with baubles hanging off of it around the top of the stall.

"Hello," said Finn, walking up and giving her a warm smile.

The stall owner turned in a soft swirl of greenery. She had greenish brown skin with whorls of bark on her cheeks and arms. Her hair was shaved on one side and spiraled down to her waist on the other in waves of green that shifted in color as she moved, much like a forest in the wind. "Hello. I'm Cecily, welcome to Ceci's Magic Goods."

"Finn," he answered. "Pleasure. What're these delightful baubles you've got hanging up?"

"Oh!" She turned and help up the end of the string. "They're not just baubles. Watch this."

Cecily reached a hand up toward the baubles delicately, gesturing in the air. Finn, who had seen Ari perform magic many times, watched, intrigued by the slower, smooth gesture. It reminded him of May's gestures toward her plants, something natural and caressing. The tiny stall alit with soft, white arcane light.

"How many of these do you think would be needed to strung around a room?"

"You're decorating?" Cecily ducked beside her stall, drawing out a box filled with the bauble lights. "Does that mean you and your partner are sticking around?"

Finn blinked at her. "How —"

"Small towns," she said with a chuckle. "We know things."

Sage leaned over, beaming. "They just bought the bookstore!"

"Wonderful!" Cecily smiled. "I don't necessarily have many things that work as decor, but I'm sure the rest of us around here have a few things that you might like."

Cecily helped Finn pick out a few things from her stall before walking him over to a few of her neighbor's stalls, finding the best pieces to go with the original bauble lights. He stuck to a neutral palette with a few warm touches, though Sage did sneak in a few more quirky items, like a strange twisted statue that looked as though it came out of a cave.

"Looks a bit like you," she said, holding it up so that she could compare both Finn and the statue's faces. Finn lifted his eyebrows, expression deadpan, as she let out a peal of laughter. His arms were now laden with boxes and a bag stuffed with a few choice pillows he had found amongst the stalls. "It has a weird face at some angles. I think Mr. Damaris would like it."

"Add it to the pile," said Finn with a sigh.

As dusk fell outside, Finn and Sage made their way back into the bookshop to find that Ari had indeed moved the bed on his own — thanks to help from magic — and had set up the room for them. Some of the smaller shelves and the one cabinet that Sage had brought in were positioned next to the bed as bedside tables, their mismatched shapes rather charming.

Ari himself was on the floor, scrubbing at a stain with large green gloves on, a determined look on his face. A light, clean, lemony scent filled the room, completely combatting the dust from the bookstore.

"Wow," breathed Sage, stepping into the space. "I don't think I've ever seen this place so clean."

"It's rather bare," said Ari, standing and stretching out his neck before eyeing their arms full of things. "But I don't think it will be for long."

Finn set his bundle of things down on the bed and took in the space. *This could work*, he thought. *Once we have our touch on it all, this is rather cozy.*

"Why don't you take a seat, my love, and we'll do the rest?"

Ari smiled at Finn and opened his hands in a *go ahead* gesture, sinking back on the bed to watch.

Sage and Finn spun around the room like a couple of worker bees, pulling their purchases out of their packages to be placed in their new homes. They adorned the bed in a warm terracotta color and added a few jewel-toned pillows that instantly richened the space. Finn let Sage have fun with positioning the trinkets and a couple art pieces around the room and on shelves as he himself got to work on hanging the arcane baubles around the room.

"What exactly are those, darling?"

"You'll see."

After about a half hour of stringing lights and decorating, Finn stepped back and admired their handiwork.

"I don't exactly know how these work," he said, motioning to the lights around them. "I think they need a magic user to get them going."

"Get them..." Ari frowned at them before reaching up with a long arm to touch one, realization dawning on his face. A small flick of his wrist, something much sharper and concise than the motion that Cecily had done, and the lights came to life.

"I know I talked a bit about castles and endless spaces," said Finn, moving to stand next to Ari, "but this is quite nice."

"Are you sure?" said Ari under his breath, looking at Finn. "I know we discussed it before, but I just want to ensure that you're still okay with all of this."

Finn smiled softly, looking up at the lights. He hadn't really let himself dive too deep into his feelings once they had decided to buy the shop and stay here, in Arrowmount. He knew he wanted a future with Ari, that was for certain — he wanted to be entirely detached from the life of the Shade, to have the freedom to do exactly what he wanted and not be beholden to a king dictating his life.

And he *was* doing that. He had been doing that with Ari for months now — despite the endless waiting period to see if word would get back to the kingdom, that the Shade had been felled. Here, with Ari surrounded by soft light and a cozy space, he felt at peace.

"Yes," he said softly, turning to Ari to place a kiss on his cheek. "I am sure."

There is still the chance of being found out, of there never being word, said a little voice in his head. Then it would be back on the road, running from all of this.

Something inside of him awoke and sniffed at the air, at the possibility of being back on the road. Some part of him still wanted that thrill of the true freedom of being only dependent on what he carried on his back, of planning and executing a job, and at the end of it all to be rewarded with treasure or gold.

The image of being on the road was replaced with the movement of

Ari's hand across one of the blankets he had purchased at the market, feeling the soft knitted weave.

Finn watched as Ari took in the room quietly, smiling bemusedly at the art and the trinkets Sage had put up. She had slipped out of the room at some point, leaving the two of them to their newly found room and life. She had even shut a sliding door behind them — one that had been hidden in the wall — and tacked a piece of paper to the back.

Finn started to laugh as he leaned in closer, reading it.

"What, darling?"

"Sage left her to-do list behind," Finn answered. "At the end, she wrote *make sure to lock the front* at the end. We probably should." He peered at the list, the middle one jumping out at him. "Ari, what are we going to do about that Lord Wymarc?"

"I've been thinking about that. You said you've never dealt with a Wymarc before?"

Finn shook his head.

"Well, then, if that's the case, to just be careful, I'll handle Lord Wymarc when he comes back into town," said Ari with a soft nod. "And when we sign the deed, then —"

"I'll sign under Goldmark. I should go by Goldmark anyway, no matter where I am. It worked enough for the party, so why not keep using it?" It wasn't as though he had been using *Shademark* for the past eight months with Ari — in fact, he hadn't ever given a last name to anyone, he just went by Finn — but the need for precaution tingled in his bones.

"Good, good." Ari leaned against the bed and yawned, his face relaxing into a tired expression. "I am absolutely exhausted, darling. And today was only the start. Look at the length of that to-do list."

Finn groaned. "Let's just stay right here forever. Lock the door, never to see the light of day. I don't even want to think of *cleaning* or *organizing* or *double doors* or —"

"Tomorrow's problem, darling. For now, let's sleep. In a *bed*," Ari said as Finn began to crumple to the floor. The two of them laughed as Ari went and pulled Finn up like a rag doll, guiding him up to the bed.

22

SIMPLE GESTURES AND FALLING SIGNS

Arileas

Late morning sunshine beamed down onto the cobblestones, hot air rising in a shimmer above them. Heat thrummed through the shop, oppressively thick. Ari watched as Finn dragged the sixth mangled shelf out from the shop, sweat beading down his face and sticking his shirt to his back.

"Need some help?"

Ari turned, momentarily jolted from his admiration of his partner to find a young wiry gnome standing with his hands in his pockets just beside the door. His short cropped dusty brown hair shone bright in the sunshine, and as he smiled carefully up at Ari, soft brown eyes squinted in the sun. Though Ari wasn't the best at guessing ages having grown up around elves, he supposed Andrew was around Sage's age.

The gnome extended a hand to Ari, shaking firmly. "I'm Andrew."

"Ari," said Ari, before gesturing over to Finn. "And that's my partner, Finn. Sorry, did you offer to help?"

"Yeah, I saw him out here struggling a bit when I was on my way to May's for work, and figured I'd offer help."

Finn walked over, wiping his hand across his forehead. "I'd love your help, if you have the time. Is May waiting for you?"

Andrew shrugged. "I don't really have set shifts; I just help when I want to. I guess you're the two who bought this place from Dew?"

"And regretting it a little more with every bookshelf," commented Finn, twisting to crack his back.

Andrew chuckled and peered into the shop behind them, at the half empty shelves and crumbling bookshelves. Ari led both Finn and Andrew into the shop. With a low whistle, Andrew thumbed a bit of a nearby shelf and it came lose in his hand. "Ah, yeah. I can see. I never realized how damaged the actual shelves were in here. It was literally being held up by books."

"Nor did we," said Ari with a sigh.

"Let's see how two pairs of hands works better than one," said Finn, nodding over to an empty shelf.

Ari lifted his hand once more and began to guide the books off the shelves with a neat flick of his hand, guiding them into his Bag of Space. He let the rhythm of the task and the heat soothe, numbing the regular noise of his mind into a calm. He didn't even notice Sage come into the shop until she was standing right next to him.

She smiled as he did a double take, the train of books crashing to the floor. "Hiya, Mr. Damaris."

"It's Ari, please." Today, Sage had laced thin strands of gold around her horns and had pulled her hair back into large, silky green curls that tumbled down to her waist. There was a distinct lack of frizz around her head from the heat, which made Ari frown slightly.

"Your — your hair," said Ari, reaching up to pat down his own which had grown a sizeable frizz halo from the heat. "How?"

"Magic."

"You're a druid, though."

Sage shook her head at him and plucked his bag from his hands. "Magic doesn't have to be *magic*, Mr. Damaris. I have powers that lie outside of my druidic magic, and one of them is style."

Ari blinked at her. *The young people of today,* he thought. *They scare me, sometimes.* "Alright."

"Speaking of druidic magic," she said, wiping a hand over her forehead. Today, she was wearing a thin, sleeveless linen dress, baring a shining collarbone, sweat gathering along her skin. "I need to air this place out, it is *hot.*"

She lifted her hands and closed her eyes, a small crease appearing between her eyebrows. Sage gestured with tiny waving motions until energy began to build between both hands. Ari felt a delightful breeze pick up around them, swirling playfully around their feet and up around his head, tossing bits of hair around his face. Sage's forehead creased in concentration as she gestured wide and arcing, sending the gust of wind through the place.

"Well, that's something," she breathed, dropping her hands as the gust of wind flew through the shop, momentarily dropping the temperature inside. "I've been working on my cantrips with May."

"It looks like you're getting the hang of it," Ari said encouragingly, mentally making a note to research spells that would help with temperature control. "I can't imagine learning something that is not written down in a book, so you're already leagues ahead of me."

Sage's already darker green, slightly sweaty face blushed deeper green with pleasure. "What's on the to-do list for today?"

"Cleaning, mostly," said Ari, turning back to the task at hand, looking at the now half-empty main room. "We've got to clear out this shop of books so we can assess the job ahead of us."

Sage nodded and held open the bag in his wake, a determined look on her face. The two of them worked in tandem inside the shop as Finn and Andrew methodically removed the shelving, the four of them slowly clearing out the space.

"Thank the gods for magic," said Sage a couple hours later as she sank onto a small stool they had unearthed from the piles of books. They had found a few bits and pieces, lost to the years of books collected on top and around them. Stools, old plant pots, a broken step ladder, and a bunch of old jewelry, all lost from patrons and Dew long ago. Sage collected the smaller bits in an old vase carefully, placing it on the front counter in case anyone came looking.

Ari and Sage took in the now empty main area of the shop, including a few skeletons of shelves that were still structurally sound. All of the books that had been piled up over the years had vanished into Ari's Bag of Space — which he was now thinking of calling the Library of Holding, since it only contained books.

Thousands and thousands of them.

Even with magic, though, Ari felt as though he had run for hours straight. His body shook slightly, and he dreamed of his comfy bed, tucked in the back of the shop.

"Iluinn's mercy, that was a lot," groaned Finn as he walked in from outside, wiping his brow. Both him and Andrew were dripping with sweat.

Ari turned to look around the main room, nodding along, not truly paying attention as he took in the state of the shop. Now that it was ripped down to the bones of shelves and entirely emptied of books, he could see every imperfection that they would need to fix. The paint job was worse than he thought, and the floors looked as though they were going to need replacing along the outside walls from water damage.

The heat in the room contracted, pushing into him, making him feel slightly nauseous. His heart squeezed with panic as he kept adding to a mental list.

"We've not even half of the shelves remaining," he murmured to himself. "Why — *why* Dew didn't replace them, I don't — they were — so dangerous."

"Mr. Damaris?"

"The flooring there has to be replaced, it's all moldy — and this is just the first room. It looks like that entire wall has been eaten through with some kind of bug." His eyes snagged on the now empty front desk, standing forlornly to the side of the shop. He barely registered the three people there, all looking at him. "This whole front room should be changed around to that the desk is in the second room, more front and center — we can't do this on our own, we're going to have to find carpenters who want to do the job, and then we have the —"

"Ari." Finn came to stand right in front of him and put both of his hands on either side of Ari's face and held him still, holding his gaze. Ari instantly grabbed hold of his wrists and held on tight. "Hey, breathe. We're going to be fine."

"Are we?" Ari squeaked, his heart in his throat pounding so loud that he could barely hear Finn.

"Of course we are," said Finn gently. "It's only the beginning. That's always the worst bit, starting. We're revealing how bad this place really is — we're pulling it down to the bones so that we can build it up even better. And it's not just you, my love, it's myself, and Sage, and now

Andrew too, all together. We're all here."

Ari started nodding, trying to breathe long and slow. Everything hurt, like he was breathing around a fist-sized rock in his chest. "Okay. Okay?"

"We're going to get coffee," said Sage quietly, pulling Andrew from the shop.

"Breathe, Ari."

Ari closed his eyes, focusing on the gentle pressure of Finn's hands on either side of his jaw, fingers threading into his hair. They stood together, Finn simply holding Ari as he breathed.

"I'm sorry," whispered Ari when he finally could focus again, the panic subsiding. He realized, then, that his cheeks were wet with tears. "I don't know what happened."

"There's nothing to apologize for," said Finn, kissing Ari on the forehead. "Take your time. I've got you, no matter what."

"You're too good for me, you know that?" Ari laughed, wiping the tears from his face and trying to pull himself together. He let his head fall into the crook of Finn's shoulder and neck, wrapping his arms around Finn's waist.

Finn hugged him close. "We're exactly right for each other, Ari."

By the time Sage and Andrew returned, laden with food and iced drinks, Finn and Ari were parked outside on a couple stools where it was marginally cooler, surrounded by the skeletons of the bookshelves.

The four of them settled into soft, meaningless chatter as they dug into their lunches. Ari sipped at his drink and let his eyes travel across the cracked and crumbling blueish grey facade of the bookshop until they snagged on the Arrowmount Books sign. It, too, was halfway crumbled and damaged beyond repair. The longer he looked at it, too, the worse it looked. It hung at a slight angle, as though barely holding on the left side.

Ari gestured with a free hand and pulled telekinetically at the edge of the sign. It creaked dangerously, alerting the others, who jumped out of the way as the sign came crashing down. The Arrowmount Books sign crumpled in half as it hit the ground, producing a tiny, sad plume of dust.

"Well," said Sage once the bits of dust settled. "That settles that."

"It was one strong wind from falling," said Finn, pointing up to where the sign was hanging. One of the rusting chains swayed there forlornly. "The chains are rusted through."

Andrew chuckled and held up a half of the sign, the wood crumbling like bread under his hand.

"I'll grab a broom." Sage carefully tiptoed around the wreckage and slipped into the shop.

Ari slipped his hand into Finn's and peered at the sign, staring at the name. "Perhaps, darling, we should also consider a new name for the shop as well."

Finn tilted his head to the side, eyebrows slightly raised in contemplation.

"Something a bit more us," said Ari.

"What about naming it Finn and Ari's?" suggested Andrew as Sage came back out with a broom. They started picking up the pieces of the sign and piling the bigger ones on top of the broken shelves nearby.

"That's a bit on the nose."

Sage began to sweep some of the dust away from the front of the shop. "Seaside Books?"

"Hmm...." Finn tilted his head back and forth, pondering. "Maybe? Let's think on it a little while longer."

Ari squeezed Finn's fingers once, letting out a small steadying breath. "We'll add it to the list."

23

A TINY BROWN CAT

Moonlight filtered through the shop's windows as Ari padded barefoot back and forth from room to room, humming tunelessly under his breath. The day's anxiety bubbled under his skin and shuddered in his chest, making him entirely too restless to sit still.

He paced the empty shop, trying to figure out the best way to organize the store, keeping his mind on things he could figure out and do. He ran through other bookstores he had visited in his mind to compare the spaces, a hand drawn map of the shop clutched in his fingers.

Upon entering the store, popular fiction and new releases should be shelved so casual shoppers might find something that caught their eye if they happened to wander in. Then, the favorite genres further in: romance, adventure, mysteries. But which ones would go where?

I have a few options, he thought. *Perhaps once we move the front desk to the middle room, we will have the more popular pulp crime novels nearby, catchy titles drawing the eye of people in line? Or maybe romances would be better?*

Ari groaned and walked back to the front, going over it for the hundredth time.

"Love, what are you doing?" A pool of warm arcane light appeared in the corner of Ari's eye as their bedroom door slid open, revealing Finn's sleepy form. "Come back to bed."

"I don't actually have to sleep," said Ari, looking at the paper in his hand and scratching out 'mysteries: back wall' and changing it to 'mysteries: middle wall across from desk.' "Meditating is enough."

"I'm aware, but this isn't meditating either."

Ari frowned down at his store map and sighed. "I can't relax. My brain is spinning around trying to put this place together. I have no idea what to do with the haphazard layout of the rooms along the back. And then there's the damaged room, too."

"Ari, it's three in the morning." Finn walked over and gently rubbed both of Ari's arms, keeping him still. "We don't have to figure this out right now. We have all the time in the world."

Ari rubbed a hand over his face, realizing how exhausted he was. "My brain won't let it go. I can't figure out which room the books should go in, where we should organize them, or..." He let his voice trail away, shrugging helplessly.

"Okay." Finn yawned wide before blinking a few times, waking himself up. He looked at the map and notes in Ari's hand. "Two minds are better than one. Tell me what you've got so far."

The two of them spent a good half hour walking back and forth together, treading over and over the worn wooden floors. After a while, they settled on having the middle room be an extension of fiction into crime and mystery, leaving romance a room of its own along the back, and adventure to follow that. The water damage at the back could be dealt with on a different day, once it was actually fixed and ready to be used.

"What about the books themselves?" asked Ari as Finn steered him through the sliding door to their room. "I need to look at them, start organizing them too."

"We can't do any organizing without proper shelving to put them on, my love," said Finn through a yawn. "Tomorrow, we will continue to deal with the rest of it. For now, I need sleep."

Ari opened his mouth to object.

"With you, in bed," Finn interrupted, "where it's *so* soft and comfortable." Ari made a sound of protest as Finn's fingers pushed carefully into his chest and knocked him gently back onto the bed and mountain of pillows there. The moment that Ari's body fell into the softness, all the fight left him, and exhaustion pulled him down.

"Hey Mr. Damaris."

Sage walked in through the front door as Ari looked up from the pile of papers around him, a tiny brown cat trotting in behind like she owned the place. The cat wasted no time in coming over to sniff at Ari's hands, letting him scratch her between the ears.

"Morning, Sage." Ari accepted a cup from her, taking a tentative sip and finding a gloriously sweet and milky iced coffee inside. "Is this your cat? I met her up around the neighboring hills the first week we were here."

"Nope, I don't think I've seen her before." Sage bent down and scooped the little brown tabby in one smooth movement, nuzzling close as the cat gently placed a paw on her face. She deposited her on one of the front windowsills where she promptly laid down in a cloudy sunbeam. "She's very friendly though. Mr. D., are you alright?"

"I'm a mess, aren't I?" He wiped a hand over his face and pushed himself to standing with a soft groan, muscles aching in his legs. He looked down at his crumpled linen trousers and shirt that he had fallen asleep in. "I've been trying to sort out the paperwork left behind the desk, and it's an absolute disaster."

Sage nodded and took a long drag of her own coffee. "Where's Mr. Finn today?"

"He said something about going off to find inspiration," said Ari, waving at the front door. "I was going to start in on my Library of Holding, but Finn told me last night that we shouldn't start organizing books until the space itself is clean and ready for them. So instead, here I am, sorting papers."

"Huh, alright. Let's see what I can help with."

Sage recognized most of the paperwork, which made things a lot easier as they sorted out what was important to the shop and what was old notes or other miscellaneous papers that had made their way behind the desk. Soon, they had multiple piles of organized, dated, and identified papers, and a mostly clean front desk.

"It is *disgustingly* dusty under here," commented Sage, brushing at her crinkled nose, looking as though she was going to sneeze. "How have I never caught this? We are definitely going to have to do a deep clean of the shop before anything more happens. Do you think your magic can help?" She added hopefully.

"It may," said Ari standing up and wiping his hands on the front of his thighs. "Though there is nothing better than elbow grease and a ton of hot water and soap."

"Speaking of cleaning." Sage pointed up to the ceiling above them.

Ari's insides recoiled at the thought of tackling the apartment and sighed. "We should probably clear it like we have the shop, shouldn't we? To comb through what's what."

The two of them made their way upstairs to the mess of an apartment, the little brown cat following in behind with her tail held high. It had not gotten any better in the couple days they had been here, despite Ari wishing it all to fix itself in the middle of the night. Finn and Ari had only come up to use the washroom off the side, which was much better stocked than the room they had at Cobb's Down-By-The-Beach. They avoided the rest of the apartment at all costs.

"Alright," said Sage, rolling up her sleeves. Ari cracked his neck, handed Sage his bag of holding, and began to magically sweep all of the books left up in the apartment inside. The cat batted playfully at the books and mess as they swirled through the air, her eyes alight with mischief. Once or twice, after Sage put the bag on the floor to clean out the kitchen by hand, Ari had to stop the cat from trying to jump into the bag after the magicked goods.

Within a couple of hours, they had managed to clear the mess from the room, leaving nothing but bones of furniture behind and layers of dust.

"There's a donation bin at the port we can take everything to." Sage wiped sweat off her forehead, leaving a streak of dust behind. Ari and she stared around at the apartment, taking in the interior now that it was mostly empty of clutter.

"Another man's treasure, and all that," said Ari, massaging and stretching his hands, which had started to cramp from the continuous motion of casting magic. The little brown cat padded up to him and sat on his feet, looking straight up.

"She seems to like it here," commented Sage.

"You do, don't you?" Ari bent down and scooped up the tiny cat into his hands, nuzzling her face. There was a beat before Ari sneezed fiercely, having inhaled a layer of dust that was on her fur. She meowed, irritated at the noise. "Sorry. You're incredibly dusty, little one. This might not be the place for you to stay quite yet."

He put her down, wiping the rest of the dust that was tickling his nose. She trotted off toward the door and vanished beyond, back down to the bookshop ahead of them.

24

MOONBEAMS

Finnean

Finn found himself neck deep in various textiles, having ventured into the back-storage room to a shop he couldn't remember the name of, blinking away mites of dust in the low light. All he could see was rich, multicolored fabric and mismatched home decor piled so high in the space that he had to wade through it to get out.

"How're ya faring, Finn?" Called the shop clerk from the door. They pushed a shock of bright blue hair out of their face, only for it to flop back down again. "Haven't gone and lost yourself, eh?"

"Not yet," Finn called back. "I don't really even know what I'm looking for."

They chuckled and waved at Finn, calling over their shoulder as they ducked back into their main shop. "Take your time!"

Finn slowly dug his way out of the pile of textiles he was in, hands and fingers feeling through the various fabrics and materials around him. Every so often he would pull out something that felt nice to look at, accumulating a small little pile of things.

That's all he could really call the miscellaneous selection of pieces he had found: a pile of things. There were a couple small mats, two decorative pillows, and a lamp without a shade that he decided to take with him as he climbed out of the back room, arms laden with his choices.

"Your hair is all stuck through with feathers," commented the shop clerk when Finn had emerged. They were up one a ladder, adjusting a few lamps on a high shelf.

"Ah, is it?" Finn looked upward, as though he would be able to see the top of his head. Finn caught a small name tag pinned to their chest that read SELKE. "I think I might have gotten attacked by a pillow at one point in there."

Selke laughed, waving him over to a desk that was surprisingly clean and organized, compared to the back room. In fact, their whole shop was rather organized and sparsely laid out, with only choice pieces on display. Finn looked around, slightly overwhelmed.

"That back room is a reflection of my own hoarding habits," said Selke, noticing Finn's expression. "Out here is what I like to present to the public. Clean, organized, and a total lie."

Finn paid for his finds and stood outside the shop for a moment, wondering why he had gone in in the first place. In looping script, the sign of the door read RUNES & RELICS. *Not at all what that place is,* mused Finn. He hadn't once seen a single thing inside that suggested runic magics.

He wound his way back through Arrowmount toward Ari and the bookshop, humming a tuneless song under his breath. There was something in the air today. He smiled at passing shoppers and locals, the summer sunshine beaming down on his head. At one point, a tiny brown cat passed through his feet, nearly making him trip, before continuing on her way through the town off to who knew where.

He found Ari standing behind the front desk when he returned, bits of hair coming out of its tie in long strands around his face, appearing as though he was somewhere between uproarious laughter and a nervous breakdown.

"Ari, my love, are you alright?"

Ari narrowed his eyes at Finn as he walked in through the door. "Why do people keep asking me that today?"

"It's probably because you don't look like yourself, Mr. Damaris," commented Sage, walking in from one of the back rooms, her arms laden with water damaged books. "Where have you been, Mr. Finn?"

"Perusing the town for the best things gold and gems can buy."

Ari moved out from behind the desk and walked over, eyes trailing the goods in Finn's hands. "Which includes a lamp without a shade, a variety of fabrics, and a... is that a feather stuck in your hair, darling?"

"Ah, yes. There might be a few. A pillow exploded when I was in the back of Runes and Relics."

Slowly nodding, Ari peeled a mat away from the pillows to get a better look. "What are these for, exactly?"

"Well, I'm not entirely sure," said Finn, pursing his lips in thought. "They simply called to me."

"Maybe they'll look good in the apartment upstairs," said Sage.

"The apartment!" Finn felt as though he had been struck by a bolt of lightning. "You're a genius, Sage. Yes, that's exactly where these will go."

He started toward the stairs, a soft, bubbly feeling in the pit of his stomach. Taking them two by two, he was up in the apartment in a flash, before coming to a dead stop in the middle of the room, where he dropped his purchases unceremoniously.

"Ari?"

"Yes?"

"You cleaned."

"Yes."

"Without me?"

"Yes, well, it's mostly just tidied of the insane amount of *stuff* that was up here," said Ari, coming up the stairs behind him. He leaned against the doorjamb and crossed his arms casually, totally at odds with his slightly over-extended expression. "There's a lot of actual cleaning left to do."

Finn frowned and spun on his heel, an idea forming in his mind. "Why don't I take over this part of the project?"

"Darling, I couldn't expect that of you."

"Yes, well." Finn set his finds down on the now visible kitchen counter. "We've got the shop on our hands — I mean we're not even a few days into this and the place is nearly cleaned out thanks to your magic, which is incredibly fast, love — so why don't I focus on making this space livable for us? One less thing for you to worry about."

Ari raised an eyebrow. "You really want to take this on?"

Finn nodded to himself as he took in the space, now clear of Dew's mess. The room was scrubbed clean, yes, but it was also scrubbed of any kind of personality now that there was nothing left behind but stains.

It feels right, he thought to himself. Someone living a life like this would want to put in the time, put in the effort, to create a space to live in. If they were really going to stay and live this life, well, then he would have to play the part. "Yes, I'm sure."

"Alright." Ari smiled softly at Finn before looking down at the bundle of things Finn had bought. "They do weirdly go together, though they aren't a matching set. And, I think there is a lamp shade in the bedroom for that base."

Finn grinned and began to usher Ari out. "Don't worry, my love. I've got this. You go handle the bookshop affairs and before you know it, we'll be living like kings up here."

Ari stopped at the door to their apartment and kissed Finn, long and slow. Finn's mind spun slightly as he pulled away, trying to focus on what he was last thinking about.

"Right. Yes." He cleared his throat and grinned, a little lopsided.

"Living like kings, with a dungeon full of books. Just like you said."

"I am always right, aren't I?"

Ari snorted and left down the stairs, leaving Finn alone in the now empty apartment.

"Right," he repeated to himself, turning on his heel and rolling up his sleeves, fingers itching for movement. "Time to crack on. This whole cleaning business should be easy enough."

It was in fact, not easy at all.

Hours later, long after the sun had cast warm golden streaks on the floor and the sky had turned to inky black, Finn tumbled down the stairs feeling as though his entire body had been scrubbed by a Blackshell Forest giant. His hands were so dry it felt as though the skin would start to flake away at the slightest touch.

"Ari?"

The shop was empty, save for a couple neat stacks of paper set along behind the front desk. Finn walked over and picked up the top paper of one, passing a glance over it to see something akin to an expenses page, though Dew had written notes for other things along the bottom, obscuring some of the final numbers.

We'll have to fix this, thought Finn, frowning at the next page. For the next couple down, he saw much of the same thing — page after page of well kept, neatly done expense tracking, only for the same scrawled notes to pass over parts of the page, bits of absent-minded thoughts jotted down.

Finn sighed and set the papers down, making sure to keep them in a neat stack. At least Dew was careful about his numbers.

Ari walked back in through the front door then, letting in a waft of humid night air, carrying a brown paper bag in his hand. "Ah, darling, there you are. You —" Ari blinked a few times, as though none quite recognizing him. "You look a bit…"

"Like I've been chasing the hag through that bog again? Yes, that about covers it."

"Did you scrub the floors with your face?" Ari walked over and reached toward something on Finn's cheek, wiping it away. "You need a wash, desperately."

"I should smell clean," complained Finn. "I have just been scrubbing for hours."

Ari smiled and leaned in, kissing him gently on the cheek where he had just run his thumb across, not touching him anywhere else. "I brought a late dinner from May's."

Finn poked at the bag in Ari's hands as Ari moved to set it down. The heavenly scent of butter, garlic, and various herbs wafted toward him, instantly making his mouth water. "What did she cook up tonight?"

"A bit of the Arrowmount Special," smiled Ari, taking out two small boxes of food that immediately filled the bookshop with the scent of butter. "She swore it would be just as good as the Bronze Bee's, if not better."

"Absolutely glorious."

"You're not touching this until you wash, Finnean."

After he spent a long while scrubbing himself rid of grime, the two of them sat on the floor in the front room of their shop, food between them, talking about everything and nothing as the moonlight filtered through the window. The world had fallen away in the hours that Finn had been working, melting off into the ether until all that was left was him and the apartment.

Now, sitting with Ari, the world shrunk again, to just them and the moonbeam they sat in. For all Finn could care, the world beyond the door of Arrowmount Books had entirely vanished. He was content to sit there, with butter and garlic running down his arms, his love across from him.

25

THE ALDERIDGES

Arileas

Arrowmount passed Ari by the following day in a gentle spin of warmth and color, a soft smile playing on his lips as he passed the now-familiar buildings. He headed toward a spot just off the center of town, as per Sage's directions. His shirt billowed open slightly in the hot breeze, the top few buttons undone. Years ago, he wouldn't have been caught with so much as a button out of place. Maybe Finn was rubbing off on him.

Businesses and apartments lined the streets between Fetterly Place and the town center. Sounds of children's laughter and games twined around corners of open alleyways, mingling with the haggling of shoppers down below. The butchers sat detached from others, a distinctly irony smell wafting from it, and a blacksmith off to Ari's right that filled the air with loud metal clanging as he walked.

Numerous stalls were set up with goods in the town center, everything from vegetables and fruits to trinkets and familiar arcane baubles as Ari passed. Townsfolk smiled at him no matter where he went, a few waving hello. He caught glimpses of all sorts of folk milling about, from orcs to elves to gnomes, and even a couple of towering giantkin and various catfolk. Everyone was dressed in light linen garb to beat the heat, sleeves of billowing shirts rolled back to bare forearms shining with sweat.

Soon enough, after consulting Sage's directions a few times in his head, Ari found his way to the Alderidges' Wood Working shop. A large shop front that sat on the end of a street, with what should have been an alley stretching along next to it. Instead of a typical alleyway, however, this one was full to the brim with wood of all kinds and covered with a roof to protect it from the elements.

Rough scraping and sawing buzzed from inside the building. Ari ducked to peer inside one of the windows, curious. Two figures moved about inside, in the process of building something, Ari couldn't quite tell. He pushed open the door and found himself surrounded by the scent of freshly cut wood and the taste of lingering sawdust in the air. The sound of a saw going in the back stopped the second the door closed behind Ari.

Ari looked around, taking in the beautiful woodwork that lined the walls and front of the shop, including a built-in desk made from a rich maple that made Ari's heart skip a beat. Something like that would be absolutely gorgeous in their shop. Various wood samples were bolted to the wall, all treated with some kind of oil and sealant, making them shine enticingly.

"Hello!" A pair of incredibly tall, muscly beings approached from the back. He could instantly see the resemblance between the two goliaths, from the sharp structure of their cheek bones and their warm stone-grey skin, to their angular noses and slightly crooked smiles. The one that had spoken had her dark, greyish-black hair chopped close to her jaw. She reached up and drew a hand through it, revealing one side had been shorn down to her scalp.

"I'm Arileas Damaris, my partner and I just bought the store on Fetterly Place."

"Ah, yes, old Arrowmount Books," she said with a laugh. "You can't be in this town long before word starts to spread about you like wildfire. Is it true that you and your partner are ex-adventurers?"

"Yes, you could say that," said Ari, chuckling.

"How can we help you today?"

"We have a fair bit of water damage in the shop, along one of the back rooms. I was wondering if you could come take a look at it, and see if it's fixable?"

"Huh," grunted the other goliath, an entirely bald man with a tattoo that ran up the back of his neck and onto his skull in strong, geometric lines. "I didn't know Dew had had damage to the shop. I'm surprised he didn't come and see us."

"I'm Di, by the way," said his sister, extending a hand. "Diana Alderidge."

Her brother nodded to Ari. "Dorian. We'd be more than happy to come and take a look at the shop."

"Great. When are you available?"

The siblings looked at one another and shrugged. "Now, if that works."

When they arrived back at the bookshop, Ari caught Di's shocked expression as she took in the carnage of old, swollen wood piles of broken shelves they had piled outside.

"It's a mess, I know," he said. "We don't really know what to do with all that old, rotted wood."

"There's an old mill on the other side of Arrowmount, they'll take any scrap and grind it down into something useable," said Dorian, picking up a piece to inspect. "Even as rotted as this."

Ari led them inside, showing them each of the emptied-out rooms. The siblings took in every inch of the shop without saying much, just nodding along to Ari's explanations as to what he envisioned for the interior.

When they got to the back room, Di sucked in a breath between her teeth as Dorian reached out and thumbed a bit of the wall. "This is more than just a bit of water damage," she said. "Have you gone out around back to see what it looks like?"

Ari hesitated. "I hadn't really thought of it."

"There might be a bit more of a story back there," said Dorian, who turned to head back through the shop and out the front. In a few moments Ari could hear his knuckles rapping on the outside of the damaged wall.

"We had a massive storm about half a year back," said Di, crouching to inspect the worst of the damage. Ari conjured three floating globes of light with a sharp flick of his wrists to illuminate the space. "It did a lot of damage to many of the waterfront buildings, as one would expect, but I didn't realize that it had reached this far back from the sea."

"Hi Diana!" Sage came bustling in, a smile on her face.

"Hiya Sage," said Diana, smiling. "How's your granddad doing?"

"Oh, you know, still mumbling about how many steps there are in the lighthouse, and that Captain Day who always leaves at the worst times. Whenever he sees her name on the port list coming or going, he gets into a blusteringly bad mood for days, knowing he'll have to man the lighthouse at specific times for her."

Diana made a pained sound of sympathy.

"Have any of you seen a tiny brown cat?"

"She hasn't been around all day," answered Ari.

"Oh, thought she'd be around, I picked up some treats this morning I thought she'd like." Sage poked her head around them to survey the damage. "What do you think, Di?"

Diana sucked in air through her teeth and frowned, arms crossed over her chest. "It's not great, but we'll have to see how far it goes exactly. Only way to do that is open up the wall. Why didn't you tell me the shop had damage, Sage?"

Sage dropped her gaze and fiddled absently with a teeny vine that appeared between her fingers. "Mr. Dew didn't want anyone to know."

"Arileas, do you mind?" Diana motioned to the globules of light as she ducked her head into the wall further, pulling away rotted wall as she went. Ari raised the lights to aid her, sliding a few in between the wall panels to illuminate the damage further. "Ah, yep, just as I feared."

Ari swallowed down the gentle seed of panic that had sprouted in his throat.

"Looks like the water has affected a fair bit of the back of your place, eating into the structure of the wall itself," said Diana, her voice coming out a little muffled by the wall. "You're lucky that it's isolated to this corner — the weight of your apartment above looks mostly supported by the other, unaffected walls. We're going to have to tear this bit back down to the bones to get a good look at it."

"Good thing Mr. Damaris was planning on painting the whole store anyway," said Sage, nodding with a soft smile on her face.

Paint, thought Ari. *This is going to need so much more than paint to fix.*

Dorian walked back in then, clapping Sage amiably on the shoulder in greeting. "The outside isn't too badly damaged, but we are going to have to dig behind it all to see how bad it is on the inside."

"It's all coming down anyway," answered Di, before launching into an explanation on the state of the wall. She stood, brushed her hands off on her trousers, and moved so Dorian could get a look, his stoic face nodding along to her descriptions.

Ari took an involuntary step away from the two woodworkers and their discussions, feeling slightly ill. He hated when things went wrong, especially when he didn't quite know the way to fix it.

"Don't you worry, Mr. Damaris," said Sage quietly, putting a hand on his arm, catching his expression. "The Alderidges are great. They've helped Granddad a few times with bits around the lighthouse. They'll fix up the shop better than we had it before."

"Right you are, Sage," said Diana. "It shouldn't be too much construction. Just this back room is affected, so it won't even get in the way of whatever else you want done in your place. Everything will be shored up stronger than before."

"I also noticed that you were in severe need of some proper shelving," commented Dorian, standing up once again.

"I am," said Ari, swallowing the nerves climbing up his throat. "Is that something you could also do, along with the back wall?"

"Sir, we are woodworking professionals," said Dorian with a soft chuckle. The smile that alit his face changed it entirely, softening the edges. "Of course, that's something we can do."

"What about a beautiful front desk, too, like the one you two have in your shop?"

Dorian and Diana walked back to the main room with Ari. Dorian drew a little bound paper pad and a pen from his pocket to jot down notes as they scanned the rooms.

"How about that door, too, Mr. Damaris?" Sage pointed to the front. "Like Mr. Finn suggested."

Dorian raised his eyebrows curiously. "New doors?"

"My partner was thinking double doors, but I'm not sure if there's enough room."

"That would add so much more to the front," said Diana, peering at the old windows and door. "We might be able to fix it up and leave these old ones. There might be just enough room to work with."

"I think leaving them would be probably best," said Ari, feeling the weight of the jobs piling on top of him once again. "They simply need a good cleaning."

"*Magical* cleaning," murmured Sage, raising her eyebrows at Ari. She was probably right — he had seen her scrubbing away at them previously. The grime seemed to be baked in with something stronger than sea breeze.

After a while longer discussing plans, Ari waved off the sibling duo and watched them walk down the street, heads tilted toward one another as they talked, towering over some of the townsfolk they passed.

"Sage, I'm about to lock up. You can head out, if you like, I don't see much for you to do in here."

Sage jumped off of the windowsill, where she had been seated for the past few minutes and nodded. "I should go help out Granddad anyway. He said something this morning about trying to clean the eavestroughs — I don't even think the lighthouse *has* them, but if they do..." She pulled a face that caused Ari to laugh sympathetically.

The two of them exited the shop, Sage waving to Ari as she went home, her tail swirling behind her. Ari wondered momentarily where Finn had gotten to before he set off into Arrowmount, his brain full to bursting off plans of shelving and changes to the shop.

His shop. *Their* shop.

26

LIKE A MUG OF HOT COCOA

Ari spent most of his day running errands, from finding a courier to run off to the Kingdom of Zidien for him to properly begin the process of transferring all of his goods and money from his old place, to walking through the market stalls and picking up groceries for the week. The town center bustled with activity as he walked through, shouts of hawkers mingling with haggling from the market stall owners and the scent of fresh food from the stalls surrounded Ari.

He strolled by the notice board to check it over, but there were no new notices pinned from any royal households. If he did need a chimney cleaned, there was an advertising for that. Unfortunately, though, the bookshop did not have one.

That could be quite cozy, he thought to himself. *A warm fire to settle down by.*

"Ari!"

Ari looked up, shifting a wooden box of fresh oranges onto his hip so as to better slide a fresh loaf of bread under his arm without dislodging the rest of the groceries he had gathered. Finn waved to him from a way down the cobbles and they met halfway, each of them laden with supplies. The multicolored flags above them flicked and tossed about merrily.

Finn immediately started to laugh as Ari walked up.

"What's so funny, darling?"

"Looks like we'll be eating for ten." He tilted the bags in his arms toward Ari, who was greeted with the sight of fresh produce and bread, just like he had in his own.

"We should really coordinate these trips," laughed Ari, feeling lighter than he had all day at the sight of his partner. "Then we won't overload the tiny kitchen with things. Where have you been all day?"

"Here and there," said Finn evasively. "I came back to the shop a little while ago and found it all closed up, though there were a couple nosy townsfolk looking in through the windows — did the meeting with the woodworkers go well?"

Ari filled him in on the Alderidges' plans as they wound their way back to their shop, the two of them moving inside with their doubly large haul of groceries. Finn winked at Ari as he grabbed the boxes in Ari's arms and peeled upstairs before Ari could stop him, sliding into the apartment.

"Finn?"

"Ah — nope!" Finn poked his head out of the upstairs apartment as Ari started to ascend the stairs. "This apartment is now off limits to you, my love. Besides the facilities of course, but you're not allowed to look anywhere else inside."

"Oh really?"

"I want to keep the goings on in here a secret," said Finn, a soft twinkle in his eye. "Don't give me that look, I promise everything is going okay.

Trust me."

"Alright," said Ari, drawing out the word suspiciously. He stepped down off the stairs and shook his head with a chuckle, the sounds of Finn moving around upstairs soothing him slightly. He didn't know what he would do without Finn around.

What if you do have to run?

The thought came fast and terrible through his head, unsteadying him. Ari clutched at the front desk, taking in the bookshop around him. He didn't want to run from this life. He wanted this to *be* his life, not the old one where they kept moving from town to town in fear of the name of the Shade. Ari wanted to live in this life fully and honestly — with Finn at his side. Nevertheless, that spike of anxiety dug itself into his chest.

Ari went to bed that night uneasily, despite how good the day had been, despite not seeing any new postings on the notice board. He couldn't shake the idea of them finding out that King Zoren had once again re-upped his missive, requesting adventurers to find and root out the Shade from wherever he was hiding. The idea that, if that were to happen, how fast they would have to get out of town, leaving everything here behind.

Ari, restless and overheated from the hot summer night found himself back out in the shop a while later. He pulled out a few of his old spell books from the confines of his Library of Holding and began to leaf through them, hunting for a spell that might help them regulate the interior temperature. He paced the length of the shop over and over as though his feet were trying to memorize the feeling of the floorboards, Finn snoring away in their bed behind him, and read.

The following morning, the anxiety had abated somewhat, but Ari's exhaustion remained. He couldn't do much about it, though, since they had a day of cleaning and planning ahead of them. Finn escaped at one point with Andrew, heading off into Arrowmount doing who knows what.

Ari found himself back at the front desk sorting through more papers that he had found in the depths of his Library of Holding, frowning at the notes Dew had left behind. They were entirely non-sensical to what was actually written on the paper — it looked as though Dew was using these rather important ledgers as note pads to himself to jot down any random thought that came his way.

"Hello?"

Ari stopped and looked up, surprised. Standing in the open front door of the shop was a slightly hunched over shape. A lanky giantkin with a pair of spectacles perched on their nose and a jaunty bright yellow bowtie around their neck smiled at Ari as they ducked into the shop.

"Hello," said Ari, clearing his throat of the dust he had unearthed from the paper. The whole shop seemed to be making dust at this point just to spite him. He realized with sudden clarity that he was wearing an old, wrinkled linen shirt that was in desperate need of a wash, and felt a flush of embarrassment creep over his cheeks. "Can I help you?"

"I'm Calian," said the giantkin, extending a hand. As they moved further into the shop, they stood up to their full height. Ari had to look up at them, which was something he rarely had to do, being quite tall himself. Calian must have been close to seven feet tall, if not more. The giantkin looked around the empty shop with a glint in their eye. "I must apologize, I've heard about the renovations and closure of the shop, due to it passing into your hands, however..."

Calian's voice floated away as they looked at Ari hopefully. Ari felt as though a firebug had alit in the back of his head. "Oh! You're here to shop! My apologies, I don't know where my brain is today. "

"I would be, yes, but I see you've already had a rather good clear out."

Ari laughed and looked around the shop himself, surrounded by the bones of a bookstore.

"Do you know when you'll be back in business? I'll spread word around, so that the other folks know." Calian scratched absently at a floppy ear. "I know many will miss walking around these shelves but will be all the more exited to come back when it's refreshed. It was rather crowded — I never noticed how large this store was before."

"One wrong move and the whole store would've come crashing down," said Ari with a chuckle. He leaned over the front desk and pulled his Library of Holding toward them. "I do still have all of the books in here, if you're looking for something in particular to pass the time?"

"Oh, I don't really ever look for anything in particular," answered Calian. "I usually walk around and see what calls to me from the shelves."

Ari began to pull books from the bag, laying them out on the top of the front desk. "Perhaps I can still be of help. Any genre in particular calling to you?"

Calian made a sound in the pit of their chest, contemplating. "Something easy today. Not romance, but I wouldn't say no to it being in the book. Perhaps something akin to sipping a delicious mug of hot cocoa."

"I know just the thing. Have you ever read anything by Baldree?"

"I have not." Calian stood a little straighter, a flash of interest crossing their face. "I am open to anything, of course, if you recommend it."

Ari dug around for a moment longer, sticking his entire arm into the bag, before he realized it was rather fruitless to do so when there were thousands of books at his fingertips. He closed his eyes and pictured his own copy of Baldree's book, calling it to his fingers.

"There is this one," he said, withdrawing the book. "That one felt like a warm cup of something delicious for sure. Slice of life, set in a town not unlike Arrowmount, and is perfectly happy. Or, if you're up for something a little bit more otherworldly, there is this one," he reached in again and pulled out another few books he loved, "or this one. It is a children's book, but I think anyone can read it, and this third one is a bit of a mix. These kinds of books are always my favorite to read — they warm you right through."

"Absolutely wonderful." Calian passed a hand over the covers, picking them up carefully to inspect. Their eyes sparkled behind their spectacles. "How much for all three?"

Ari quickly did the math, Calian handed over the gold, and the books were passed into their care.

"I really quite like that you are cleaning up the shop," said Calian, tucking their finds beneath their arm happily. "I have a good feeling about all of this."

"We had to get rid of a good seventy percent of the shelves, if not more," said Ari. "We're having the Alderidges come in and do some work and they're going to set us up rather nicely with fresh new shelves."

"I cannot wait to see the final result," said Calian, moving to the front door. "Are you expecting to open before the end of summer?"

"If all the renovations go to plan. Feel free to drop by any time between now and then, if you're ever in the need for a book, though. I've got my library at the ready."

Calian lifted their massive hand in farewell and ducked from the shop, leaving Ari with a rather breathless, anticipatory feeling. Though the visit had been rather short and sweet, it felt as though something had shifted inside Ari. As though now, standing in their empty bookshop having just served his very first customer, it felt like everything was a bit more real.

Part Four

Sun-soaked Cobblestones

27

FOR THE SAKE OF ADVENTURE

Finnean

Weeks passed as Finn and Ari continued to work on the shop and the apartment above it. Long days were spent with the sound of the Alderidges hammering away below Finn's feet as he cleaned and painted their apartment, organizing and working through the mess that still remained.

Evenings, though, were spent walking around Arrowmount, Finn and Ari hand in hand as they explored more of their little town and returned to familiar places. The Bronze Bee had become a regular spot alongside May's, and they had frequented the Old'n Narrow with a few of the other townsfolk on weekends, listening to the bard play.

They were slowly memorizing the cobblestones of their new home.

Finn lived for the moments where it was just Ari and him together, walking around town as the lazy golden summer sun sank below the horizon. It cast everything in a perfect romantic glow.

Calian the giantkin had returned a few times to see the repairs to the shop and to chat with Ari about the books they had bought previously, which made Finn's heart squeeze with pride. Calian, too, it turned out was a magic user, though not a wizard like Ari. The two of them had spent a few hours discussing spells in the back of the shop, and when Finn had come down from the apartment that evening, he found the interior cool and comfortable.

"Calian taught me a fantastic spell," Ari had explained as he sorted through some more paperwork that Dew had left behind the desk, a furrow between his eyebrows. "It should not only help keep the store comfortably cool in the summer, but warm and toasty when autumn and winter roll around."

Finn had nodded, impressed. "Is it ever lasting?"

"I will have to redo it every month when we need it, and my stash of dragon scale will probably drop a lot faster than usual. But that's a really small price to pay for a comfortable store."

"Lucky Calian knew something like that. They're beginning to become a regular of the store, and we're not even open yet."

Ari had laughed. He was already amassing a small group of regulars that popped in every so often to pull Ari away from whatever he was doing to fish around in his glorious Library of Holding for a new book or two.

A young elf named Branwen with long pointed ears adorned in an array of sparkling jewelry that shone against his dark midnight skin came looking for histories of the empire but remained rather quiet no matter how kind and coaxing Ari was. Finn wanted to step in and try to get this young boy to say something other than "yes" or "please" or "the histories, anything you have," but he stopped himself as Ari let the boy take his time with the collection. A gentle patience flickered across Ari's expression that Finn couldn't begin to fathom having.

Branwen accepted the books Ari had pulled out of his bag with a nod and a cautious smile. When he was done, he paid with a small mountain of gold before walking out with a slightly precarious pile of tomes in his arms.

The next day, a small red dragonkin child named Kaida and her mother, Zana, came into the shop. The little girl looked on the verge of tears when she saw all the shelves gone, despite her mother explaining to her over and over that she had known the shop was closed. Ari had swooped in and opened his Library of Holding for her, showing the innumerable books inside.

"Whatever you wish for," he had said, crouching on the ground next to her as she peered in, putting one careful red clawed hand on the edge of the maroon bag, "anything at all, I can pull from this."

"Like a *magic* bag?" Her eyes had gone wide, a bit of steam leaking from her nostrils.

Ari had nodded, looking amused. He had flicked his wrist, the bag expanding wide enough that she could probably hop in herself.

"*Exactly* like a magic bag."

Kaida had danced off down the street a little while later with two picture books about an adventuring princess in her arms, her mother's hand in hers. Ari had a funny little smile on his face for the rest of the day and had brought up Kaida a couple times in conversation.

"Do you think that Kaida enjoyed her books?"

"I'm sure she did. And everyone else will, when they come by." Finn placed a kiss on Ari's cheek, admiring him. "You have a gift with people, you know that?"

"It's you with the charm and the smiles," said Ari as they ate at the

Bronze Bee for the second time that week. Tae was absolutely knocking it out of the park with her food each time they returned.

"Not everyone is swayed by that," said Finn. "Like that Branwen boy. When he came into the shop, I would have badgered him with my smiles and chatter, whereas you just let him be in his element."

"He would've still liked you."

"He liked you much more, love."

Ari's expression turned contemplative as they finished their meal and returned home, walking hand in hand under the starry sky, the lanterns hanging on the outside of buildings lighting their way.

Arrowmount at night had a vaguely different feel than Arrowmount during the day, when life happily fluttered around the streets like the decorative flags above. Finn couldn't put his finger on it. Perhaps it was the cascading light from the lighthouse that streaked through the dark, over and over, guiding ships to shore. Perhaps it was the sea of stars above them, innumerable pinpricks of light swirling in a vast cosmos. Perhaps it was the change in atmosphere, as lanterns were lit, and folks headed home for the night.

The sky had looked similar over the countless nights that he and Ari had adventured across the empire — from between the branches of a forest, to the flats of a field as they made camp — but the feeling was different here in Arrowmount. Every time his eyes were drawn up to the stars, he felt a calm sense of comfort settle into his bones. Finn never tired of the night sky, but here with Ari in this tiny seaside town, he couldn't help but feel his wonder swell a little bit more.

What if you have to leave? asked the tiny voice in his head. He sighed, wondering that exact same thing as he and Ari made their way back to the shop, the sound of their shoes on the cobblestones clipping neatly under them. What if they *did* have to leave? He didn't entirely know what this town was doing to him, but the more he thought about it, the less he wanted to go.

He began to itch under his collar as they turned onto Fetterly Place, a bead of unease threading through his stomach. Perhaps he wasn't quite ready to say *forever* to this place, but that was alright, wasn't it? Even if they were now owners of a bookstore, and did have ties to the place, and...

You might have to run, still, said the voice. The possibility of having to run, though not a pleasant thought, did leave the door open to adventuring, which Finn did still love.

Ari's deft fingers unlatched the door and let them into the dark interior of the bookstore.

Why couldn't we still go on adventures? Finn thought. Would it hurt, to find something that could help them pay for the shop?

A soft sense of restlessness settled over him, an old familiar feeling that hadn't plagued him since he strode the halls of Pralon castle as the Shade. It was the tingling at the edges of his fingers for the familiar feel of his daggers, the anticipation of having a job on the horizon.

Ari sent for his goods and his money from Zidien, he thought reasonably, trying to calm the rising restlessness in his body. *Which would make going adventuring nothing more than a trip. You don't need the coin.*

They might not need the gold, no. But what about going for the sake of adventure?

The tiny monster inside Finn's chest growled in content at the thought as his fingers found one of the daggers he still kept at his belt.

Later, as the two of them lay tangled in their sheets, Finn felt Ari's eyes on him. Finn gazed up at the ceiling, pushing a small smile onto his face. The arcane lights around them glowed a soft white that cast everything around him into shades of coziness. Mingled with the scent of fresh wood from the Alderidges' work on the backroom and the softness of the bed around them, Finn relaxed and slowly shed the feeling that had been haunting him all night.

"Finn?" Ari's voice was gentle. His long, delicate fingers traced a haphazard pattern along Finn's chest, sending a pleasant buzzing through Finn's entire being.

"Mm?"

"What's on your mind?"

"I'm just thinking about us," he said, which wasn't an entire lie. "Do you remember when we came up to that little ramshackle town, the one with the broken-down windmill?"

"I thought I was going to lose you that day," murmured Ari, his hand stilling on Finn's chest. "When you were hit with whatever that hag had in that pouch of hers — you were just lying there."

"Thank goodness her tricks were mostly harmless," said Finn. "She only knocked me out."

"After cutting you to shreds. Why are you thinking of that day?"

"Mostly the after," he said letting a smile play across his lips. "It was so soon after the two of us had started off from Boarsrest, so we weren't entirely..."

"Comfortable?"

"Yeah, something like that. But then I remember waking up, my head against your chest as you carried me through that town, shouting for help."

"Gods," sighed Ari, closing his eyes and shaking his head. "I nearly lost it. I can't believe you heard all that."

"I did," said Finn, grinning. "It was that moment, you know, that I knew you loved me as much as I loved you."

"Finnean, you know I was head over heels for you basically the moment you walked into my life, right?"

"I know that now," said Finn, cupping Ari's gorgeous face in one hand, his thumb tracing one of Ari's sharp cheekbones. "Back then, that was the moment I could actually see it though."

"You silly man," breathed Ari, shifting to prop himself up on his elbow, looking down at Finn. "If you had only looked, you would have seen it long, long before."

"Would you ever want to go on the road again? I know we're here now, but if... if the opportunity came up?"

Ari shifted above him, his curtain of white hair glowing slightly in the light of the arcane baubles. "I don't know if I'm up for that adventuring business anymore. It was fun while we had it, but I was getting tired at the end."

"How come you never said anything?"

"Because I knew you loved it." Ari drew his fingers down Finn's chest and stomach, leaving a trail of goosebumps behind. "I will do anything you like, simply because I enjoy you enjoying it. But now we're here, making a life together. And we've been safe this whole time. No parties of adventurers coming to hunt us. No king breathing down our neck."

Finn couldn't help but add *yet* in his mind, letting out a deep sigh. The monster in his chest churned restlessly, but he tried to ignore it as he smiled softly at Ari. He still wanted the possibility of adventure hanging there, that they might one day go back out again.

With the chance that the Shade might not be declared dead, that King Zoren would continue to send out parties hunting him, who knew what would happen.

If it comes to it, thought Finn, *I can always run. Ari doesn't have to be tied up to my old life like I am. He belongs here.*

A deep pit of sadness spread in Finn's chest as Ari gestured to the arcane lights, plunging them into darkness. He desperately did not want to leave Ari. Ari was the love of his life. But he would if he had to, if his love didn't want to come with, in the end.

28

LITTLE COASTAL TOWN

Arileas

You actually fought a *hag?*" Sage spun in the crowded store, her dress and tail brushing dangerously against bits piled around them. Ari reached out and caught a tottering candlestick before it could fall.

"It didn't really go that well for us," said Ari, offering her an amused smile.

"Still," said Sage, breathless with interest. "I can only imagine the thrill that that kind of a battle would give. And then the joy and rush of winning? To realize you were heroes and had freed that small village from the hag's wrath?"

"I think you might be overlooking the danger that comes with things like that," said Ari, following her as she turned back around and continued on through the decor shop. The moment that Sage called a 'win' had been nothing more than a moment of unbridled fear so intense that had left Ari feeling totally unmoored. "It affects you, living in the constant fear that that day you're living might be the last."

"Isn't that what brings the thrill of it all, though? The danger? And with the ability to fight back — whether through magic or weapon — that's all you need. That's *power.*"

Ari sighed and chuckled quietly at Sage's innocence. He had never been quite like that, dreaming of adventure and running off after danger. He only wanted out of his home originally, to live a life where he wasn't crushed under someone's wishes, and then again to be free to live a life of his own means when he was under King Zoren's thumb.

Ari caught his reflection in an old antique mirror that was decorated with gold around the edges. The elf that stared back had tendrils of white hair falling into a face that was tinged pinker than it had ever been from the weeks of being in the sun. The sprinkling of freckles across his nose was more prominent than ever.

Mother would be appalled, he thought. A smile snuck onto his face at the realization that this was it. He was living the life he wanted: one of happiness and of freedom. And he was doing so with the love of his life at his side, which was the cherry on top.

"Ooh, that's cute," said Sage, her smiling face appearing in the mirror next to his shoulder a moment later. "I think it might go well in the shop, somewhere. Add a bit of something to an empty wall, if we have any left."

Ari nodded slowly, taking in the ornate gold filigree on it. "Let's loop around the shop and see if we find anything else before we go."

"You got it, Mr. D. Oh!" She lunged for a light green vase and held it up for Ari to see. "It would look so good on the new front desk. We should stop by the Alderidges' later to see if they have any bookshelf updates."

"You're really getting into this whole decor and renovation thing, Sage."

"What can I say, Mr. Finn has gotten into my head. He's got an eye for things that I could never see before. There was this — oop, never mind."

Ari blinked at her as she stiffened and bit her lip to stop herself from talking. "You're helping him with the apartment?"

She shot him a sheepish look. "Maaaaaybe."

"Then you can tell me what it's like," he said urgently. "He won't allow me up there, barring me using the bathroom. And even then, when I do go up, everything is hidden by hanging curtains. I swear, it kills me to not be able to see what he's doing."

"You'll see soon enough," she answered, tilting her head loftily and drifting off into the shop with a coy smile on her face. "Perhaps if you keep regaling me with stories, I will let you in on some secrets."

Ari spent the day entertaining Sage with stories of his and Finn's exploits across the empire, each of his stories embellished just enough to make her eyes shine. And she, of course, didn't let so much as a single detail slip about the apartment. He didn't mind, though. He rather enjoyed telling Sage these stories as they bustled around their little coastal town.

They passed through Arrowmount back toward Fetterly Place, stopping once at the local paint shop to check on their colors. It was meant to be ready in the next few days, which was exactly what Ari had been hoping for, since the Alderidges had nearly finished the back-room renovations. Soon, they would begin installing the shelving and the new double doored entrance.

"Mr. Finn!" Sage called, bounding ahead as they rounded onto Fetterly Place. Finn headed their way, a bag under his arm. He grinned at them.

"What have you two been up to today?" He eyed their wares and the rather large mirror Ari was carrying. "A bit early to decor shop for the store, no?"

"We wanted to be prepared," said Sage quickly, sneaking a peak into the bag under Finn's arm, her face breaking into a knowing smile. "I'm off to help Granddad with a bit of cleaning myself, so I'll leave you two to whatever new thing Mr. Damaris has decided needs to be cleaned."

"Good luck," chuckled Finn as she danced off down the road toward the lighthouse. "You know, I often wonder why she doesn't spend more time with friends. There have got to be other kids her age around here."

"She has Andrew, no?"

Finn tilted his head side to side, non-committal. "That's another kid that needs to have more fun. They both work too much."

Ari nodded in agreement, gazing off toward May's, where he could just make out the shape of Andrew coming out of the doorway under all that greenery to greet customers, an apron tied around his waist.

"They're both good kids. Much better than I was at that age."

"Yes, well, at that age you were running around a castle becoming well acquainted with shadows," Ari laughed, sliding his arm into Finn's. "What say you to a dip in the sea, darling? I haven't felt the sand beneath my feet in days."

The two of them dropped off their wares inside — Finn careful to deposit his upstairs, out of Ari's sight, despite him trying to sneak a peek — before heading down to the water as the sun sank lower in the afternoon sky.

Cool water tickled Ari's feet, splashing over his skin as they walked along the edge of it. At some point, Finn flicked a bit of sea foam at Ari with his toe, and suddenly they were off chasing each other around in the water, laughing.

Finn grabbed Ari around the waist and ran with him into the water, Ari yelling incoherently as he did. Before long, the two of them were soaked and neck deep in the ocean, the water mostly calm around them.

Ari floated on his back, letting his hair drift out around him, staring up at the sky as evening turned it a soft periwinkle. "We should really go sort out the shop a bit more, but I couldn't care less at the moment."

"You, Arileas Damaris, don't care about the shop?" Finn appeared next to him, looking perfectly sea-swept, hair curling around his face. He lifted Ari out of the water and pulled him to his chest.

Ari grinned and kissed Finn fiercely, tasting salt on his love's lips. "In this moment all I wish to do is float in the ocean."

"You know what is truly glorious about that statement, my love?" Finn wound his arms around Ari and spun them in the water. "We can do exactly that. Neither one of us are beholden to anyone telling us what we have to do, except ourselves."

"And Sage," said Ari, laughing. "I'm pretty sure, even though she's only eighteen, her punishments might be worse than any king's."

After drifting in the water for a while longer, the two of them made their way back up the beach and toward town, wringing their dripping clothes. With their hair drying in salted curls, they walked up the sun-soaked cobbles.

29

SOPHIE THE BOOKSTORE CAT

Arileas

A ri let the sun fall onto his upturned face a moment, basking in the warmth of the day. Today, Arrowmount fluttered with a delightful cool breeze, one that carried with it the sounds of seabirds that circled Chervil's lighthouse.

He walked back from the Alderidges' slowly, having found the shop closed up tight and windows dark, despite late morning sun beaming bright down on all of Arrowmount. He didn't mind, really, and instead of heading directly back to the shop, Ari wound his way through the cobblestone streets, taking in the sights of the town. He passed under the multicolored flags with a half-smile on his face, taking in the movement of the town around him.

A golden furred dog snuffed sleepily from his perch in a high window nearby. His head rested on his paws, the window framed with ivy and plants that wound up the wood and plaster. Ari passed by and reached

178

up to scratch him under his chin, eliciting the happiest, sleepiest groan.

Kaida, the little dragonkin girl, passed him in the street with her mom, handing him a slightly squashed yellow flower before waving happily at him as she skipped away down the street. He grinned after her, turning on his heel as he took in the street in a slow circle. *Arrowmount is wonderful,* he thought to himself, continuing on his way.

"Morning, Arileas," called a voice as Ari ducked back into the bookshop. Dorian came into view, clapping both hands together, creating a cloud of sawdust.

Diana came out from behind him and smiled, wiping back her fringe with her forearm. "We've got the backroom mostly finished — all that's left to do is wait until it's all dry before we come back to sand it smooth, and then you can paint."

Ari peeked his head in the back room and nodded, feeling as though a small weight had been lifted off his chest. The back wall looked newly built. Fresh plaster and stone hid any signs of damage, the room no longer reeking of decay and mold. "It looks fantastic."

Dorian smiled at him. "Have you given any thought to what you want to do with this back room?"

"I have a couple," said Ari. "Where you two here when Starla Waters owned the place?"

Both siblings nodded.

"Do you remember the circulating library she had? Chervil mentioned it to us when we first arrived in Arrowmount."

"It was nothing more than a little stand in the front of the shop," said Dorian slowly.

"Are you suggesting you make this back room a library?" Diana looked vaguely impressed. "That could work. I know lots of families around here would love that."

"Out of all the books that Dew had stocked the shop with, there's a surprising amount of them that aren't quite fit to sell but aren't quite done with their lives yet. It's something I was thinking about, you know. To give them a second life."

Di nodded and took in the room, a change coming over her face. Dorian withdrew his notebook and lifted an eyebrow at her, waiting. "We could make specialty lower shelves, for the kids, you know — and a reading bench, maybe? Along with matching shelves to the outside part of the shop along this wall."

Ari beamed at her as Dorian began to write.

The paint arrived two days later, after the Alderidges finished up the sanding and Ari had completely cleaned the shop of lingering dust. Finn walked in with two freshly brewed teas from May's cafe as Ari began sorting the cans of paint.

"You really think this color is a good choice for the walls, love?" Finn crouched down by one of the cans, which had been marked across the top with a smear of green.

"Trust me," answered Ari, picking up a brush.

Diana stopped by in the late afternoon, finding both Ari and Finn slightly dazed and covered in paint.

"Ah, just wanted to let you know that we're ready to go on the front door," she said as way of greeting. "I can see you two have been busy."

"Just a little bit." Finn gestured with his paint brush around at the space, speckling Ari with the rich green paint. They had gotten through one coat on one side of the shop, the change already shifting the mood of the shop.

Ari laughed, wiping his face. "We might have to wait a few days until the painting is done."

"Smart man," said Diana. "Dust and paint do *not* mix, and believe you me, there will be a ton of dust when we get going on the doors." She hesitated before looking down at her feet. "I think the two of you have a visitor."

The tiny brown tabby that had been frequenting the shop wound around Diana's legs and mewed softly up at them all. She had a tendency to appear whenever she liked.

"Once the doors are up, you two can start on the outside paint," said Diana. "Let us know if you need to borrow any ladders or anything for that, Dorian has a collection of all kinds. I'll leave you two to it."

"Thanks."

Finn bent down and scratched the cat between her ears with two paint splattered fingers. "Are you going to hang out here while we paint, little cat?"

The cat mewed thoughtfully up at him before strutting over to one of the windows. She leapt up with the softest sound and flopped lazily in what remained of the afternoon sunshine that shone in.

Ari felt something in his shoulders twinge with exhaustion. "We should take a break, darling."

"I think we can have this entire thing painted by tonight. At least the first coat." Finn grinned at Ari, wrinkling his nose. "Come on, my love. Once it's done, we can sleep for a week."

Ari pulled Finn in by the waist. "Fine. But, one more thing."

"Mm?"

Ari deftly took Finn's hand in his, the one holding the paint brush, and drew it up over the length of Finn's perfect face. It left a perfect streak of green behind, covering Finn from chin to forehead.

"You little —" Finn immediately launched a counterattack, a shining look in his eye as he easily disarmed Ari and coating his face and shirt in paint, the two of them laughing giddily.

Once the interior of the shop was painted and dry, the Alderidges began installing the new double front doors. It took a full day for them to remove the old one and frame in the space for the new ones, before they installed a set of beautifully crafted wooden doors that, when closed, looked like the open pages of a book. The dark, rich wood shone like honey in the late afternoon sunshine.

Ari welled up with tears when Dorian and Diana brought the two of them outside to see them fully for the first time.

"Would you look at that," said Finn, shaking his head slightly with awe. "It actually looks like something now."

"They're absolutely beautiful."

They drew the double doors ajar, the heft of them satisfyingly perfect as they swept across the cobblestones to reveal the shop. Though it was still unfinished, the effect was much the same as if the shop *had* been done. Ari felt a swell of emotion so thick he couldn't speak for a moment. The tiny brown cat jumped off her perch and circled around Ari's feet, meowing up at him.

Finn slid his arm around Ari's waist and pulled him close, their hips pressing together as they scanned the freshly painted interior. "It's nearly there."

"I still have to clean the floors and organize through the mountain of books.”

“Tomorrow.”

“Yes, tomorrow,” said Ari feeling a wave of exhaustion roll down his spine. “Not tonight. I wish for nothing more than blankets and your arms alone, darling.”

“We should do something about her.” Finn looked down between them at the little brown cat. He bent to scoop her up, gently lifting her up to look at her square in the face. She reached out with a paw and placed it on Finn’s cheek before peering at Ari with her bright eyes. “It seems as though we’ve been adopted, my love.”

“She needs a name.” Ari watched affectionately as the little cat reached the other paw toward Finn’s face as though saying *he’s mine.* Finn playfully bit at them with a smile on his face as she twitched her ears at him. “Cora?”

“I don’t know if that fits. Mable, maybe?”

Ari rocked his head from side to side and reached to scratch the cat between the ears. She looked at them both, her tail flicking impassively in the air. “Starla?”

“Hmm,” Finn said appreciatively. “Close. Definitely something with an S.”

“Sophie?”

The cat turned to look at Ari then, blinking.

“I think that’s her name, then,” said Finn, laughing. Ari plucked the cat from Finn’s hands and cradled her close to his chest, feeling the light rumble of her purrs as he scratched under her chin. “You know if a cat blinks at you, it means they’re totally in love with you.”

“Is that why you blink at me so, darling?”

Finn snorted and rolled his eyes, gazing at Ari and Sophie with a small smile on his face. “Sophie the bookstore cat. Welcome to the family.”

30

FIREWORKS AND MAGIC

Finnean

Fetterly Place buzzed with early morning shoppers and workers under a nearly seamless grey sky. The layer of cloud offered a respite to the heat of the past few days but promised a thick humidity by midday.

Finn's arms ached as he lugged the last few paint cans out of the shop. Ari came in behind with his arms laden with brushes and other supplies, using a bit of his magic to draw along a large ladder they had borrowed from Dorian.

"Happy painting morning," called a cheery voice. Sage and Andrew walked up, casting a lovely portrait of a green fiendling walking next to the small, strapping gnome. Both of them were dressed in old shabby clothes, Sage in a set of large salt-stained linen trousers tied around her waist with thick rope that Finn was sure she had stolen from Chervil. Sage handed both Ari and Finn coffees from May's with a smile.

"You two look like you're up to something," said Ari from behind Finn, brushing his hands as he walked up.

Andrew reached over and grabbed a paint can from Finn and raised his eyebrows. "We're helping you paint, of course."

Finn snorted and shook his head. *These two work too hard.* "Alright then, let's get to it."

The four of them began to paint, covering the front of the building in swaths of a bright, light yellow color, slowly eliminating the dulled grey-blue paint beneath it. Before long, Ari sent Andrew off to the Old'n Narrow bar to fetch the bard to keep them company. He returned a few minutes later with a tall half-orc woman walking along with him, her instrument in hand. The street outside the bookshop buzzed with activity as folks lingered to watch and help, the joyous music drawing a crowd.

Old Chervil and May came up a little while later to join in, May sporting a platter of food and drink for them all.

"Hey there," Chervil called up to Finn who was atop the ladder. "On days like this, the humidity tends to roll in around noon and brings with it a lethargy like none other. Best to get this done fast."

"Pick up a brush, Granddad!" said Sage as she skipped into view, paint speckling her face and arms in a smattering of yellow freckles as she gave him a swift kiss on his wizened cheek. "Don't just stand around, help!"

The townsfolk nearby took that as a missive to really get to work, and soon they had a crowd of people helping out. The energy of the morning filled Finn up to the brim with happiness as he looked down at the others from his perch on a ladder, spinning his paintbrush in his fingers. It was rather nice, having that small pliable handle in hand, rather than his familiar daggers that now rested upstairs, waiting for the next call to adventure.

Before long, as Finn stepped off the ladder to hand it off to Andrew and one of his friends to zip up and down, children began to play games around the cobbles, dancing to the lively music the bard played. A mother brought out a carton of colored chalk sticks to a raucous uproar of cheers, and as Finn watched, a mosaic of doodles exploded out around them.

"Oh!"

Finn turned to see Ari drop his paint brush onto a tarp and run off into the shop, a look of joy on his face.

"Where's he going?" asked Sage, coming around and picking up Ari's stray brush, wiping sweat from her forehead with the back of her arm.

Finn laughed bemusedly. "I have no idea."

They had their answer a few moments later when Ari came back out with a small, worn pouch the size of a coin purse that Finn hadn't seen since they were on the road. Ari dipped his fingers into it as he walked toward the gaggle of children, drawing out a glittering substance Finn knew was the rare magical component of dragon scale, sourced from the Nerian Empire.

Finn watched as Ari called out to the children, drinking in the sight of his love. All of them looked up at Ari excited at the prospect of something new. He began to weave patterns in the air, drawing on the dragon scale to trace glittering shapes that dissolved into magic. Small illusory fireworks popped around them, showering the now cheering and dancing children in multicolored glitter.

They began to circle around Ari as he continued to throw spell after spell into the air, combining smaller illusory cantrips with whatever he could cook up with dragon scale. This magic wasn't something Ari usually did — it deviated from the wizardry he was so attuned to — but it was lovely to watch. Plus, dragon scale was wickedly expensive when you could get your hands on it. But it was a potent and incredibly useful component to some spell casting, according to Ari.

"Gosh, Mr. Finn," said Sage, breaking Finn out of his reverie. "You look so sickly in love it almost hurts to look at. I want something like that."

Finn laughed and threw an arm over her shoulder, noticing that he had been dripping paint regularly down the front of his shirt and onto his shoe. "You'll find someone one day, Sage. Don't you worry about that. And when you do, it'll be all worth it."

"I know," she sighed.

"Besides — what's the rush? You're young, have so much of the world to see yet."

"The *rush* is the rush," she said shaking her head. "I want to know what it feels like to have someone I care about care about me so deeply, you know?"

"Oh, the shop looks wonderful," crooned a voice down behind him. Both Sage and Finn turned to find the pair of old gnomes, Neema and Della, behind them, gazing up at the shop. Neema patted Finn's arm affectionately. "Yellow was the exact color to choose."

"I never would have dared to go yellow," said Della, "but you boys are so much more daring and adventurous than us old folks."

Finn smiled as he took in the various townsfolk that had helped them all paint, the new facade of the bookshop quickly coming to a completion. Calian, the tall giantkin stood towering over a few of the shorter folk, a smile on their face. Chervil draped an arm over May's shoulders and cheered as Andrew finished the last bit of paint, stretching all the way up on his toes to reach. Sage beamed as though her whole face was going to split apart. Even little Kaida and her mom were there, Kaida's clawed hands covered in chalk and glittering magic.

A man Finn didn't recognize walked through the crowd then, a soft smile on his face. He was a little older than Finn himself, a bit of grey peppering the sides of his dark brown hair. Gentle smile lines traced his eyes as he turned to Sage, who walked up and greeted him.

"Well," said a voice as an arm slid around Finn's waist. "I guess that's it."

Finn winked at Ari and spun the two of them around to face the crowd. "I think we can officially call it there!"

The crowd cheered, the children dancing around them all to the bard's lively music.

"Thank you all for coming," said Finn, casting his voice up and over to be heard by everyone. "I'm so glad that this bookshop is becoming something that not only we have worked on —"

"It's a place that the whole town will have a hand in," finished Ari, beaming at them all.

"It'll be the Fetterly Place staple like it was meant to be!" someone in the crowd called. The rest of the townsfolk laughed and cheered, and soon the surrounding cobblestones were alit with what was quickly turning into a neighborhood party.

May winked at the two of them before she bustled off with Sage and Andrew, heading toward her cafe. They returned not long after bringing with them the scent of freshly brewed coffee, the clinking of ice, and even more food.

"Ari, do you mind?" called May, pointing behind her. "We might need a few tables."

"On it."

Finn let his love slip from his arms as he ran off toward the cafe, quickly magicking the tables outside into a trail of marching furniture. A few of the townsfolk swept in and helped set up the tables with ease.

Sage drew the stranger up to Finn, a slightly different smile on her face. It was one that reminded him of courtiers at the palace trying to be kind to those of higher station than them — a smile of politeness.

Finn stiffened slightly as he took in the man more thoroughly, catching the clean, well-made shirt and trousers he wore, and shining, brand new boots.

"Mr. Finn," said Sage, looking at him meaningfully, "this is Lord Wymarc, the lord that takes care of Arrowmount. Lord Wymarc, this is Mr. Finn, one of the new owners of the shop."

Finn's heart plummeted into his stomach. *The lord has returned.*

"Pleasure," said Lord Wymarc, extending a hand. Finn hesitated only a split second before accepting it, forcing a smile onto his face that he hoped was an approximation of what Sage was currently wearing. "I have to say, I wasn't expecting Arrowmount to have changed as much as it has since I left a few months ago, but here you are."

"Right," said Finn, clearing his throat. He looked over at Ari, who was busy helping put together the tables of food and drink, unaware of who was now in their midst. "Welcome home."

"I'm sure we have more business to chat about, but I'll leave that for another day," said Wymarc with what Finn assumed he thought was an affable chuckle. "You obviously have a lot going on here. I hope that Arrowmount can be your home for a long time, Finn."

Finn nodded, throat tight, as Wymarc winked at Sage before turning away again, bleeding back into the crowd of townsfolk. Those he passed stepped aside to let him pass with ease, nodding and smiling in the wake of the lord of the town.

Not long after, Chervil's earlier prediction came true as a rolling wave of humidity hit them all. They were thankful for the iced beverages as condensation ran down the sides of the glasses in earnest.

Finn held his own glass and sipped, taking it all in as he tried to ignore the rising sense of unease in his gut. He tried to remind himself that today had been good, had been *wonderful* with the town around them, everyone coming together to paint the store. He stayed slightly off to the side, slipping back into his role of watching.

I'm not apart, watching from the shadows this time, he said to himself. *I am simply observing this new life unfold. Our new life.*

Ari had somehow been coerced back into the bundle of children who were demanding more magical displays. He reached over and rubbed Kaida's little head, streams of smoke curling out of her nose happily.

Finn leaned against the open door of the shop, watching them dance. Ari was smiling so bright that it almost hurt to look at.

I wonder what Ari would be like if we had our own children.

The thought disoriented him so fiercely that he choked on his iced coffee, spraying it all down himself. He waved dismissively to a few of the nearby townsfolk who looked up in alarm, put his iced coffee down on a nearby surface, and ducked into the shop out of the heat.

Children? Was he really thinking of that? He had never once thought of wanting kids. As the royal assassin, that was never on the cards. Why was he thinking of this now?

His skin broke out into fresh goose pimples at the realization that he was standing in the middle of a bookshop that he owned with the love of his life, in a town where he was starting to feel more at home than anywhere else, he had ever stepped foot. The strangest mix of comfort, unease, and the feeling of being slowly drowned settled onto him, and he felt, very suddenly, like he couldn't breathe.

His feet took him into their bedroom, immediately reaching for his twin daggers settled next to his side of the bed. The moment the familiar weight was in his hands again, he felt a sharp relief pierce through the anxiety coursing through him, but not enough to tamp it down.

He needed out.

"Finn?"

He exited their room and saw Ari walking toward him, a smear of yellow paint on his cheek, glittering dragon scale coating his fingertips. Ari's usually perfectly done hair was loose around his shoulders, starting to frizz from the humidity. The sight of the pure joy on Ari's face made Finn suck in a pained breath, letting out a wheeze of laughter.

The joy quickly melted into concern as Ari stepped forward. "Are you okay?"

"Perfectly fine," said Finn in a voice that was much higher than usual.

"Finnean, do not lie to me. What's wrong?"

"I — I need some air," said Finn, walking back out of the shop as slowly as his panicking legs would let him. "Just a walk maybe. I'll be — yes. A walk."

31

WELCOME TO ARROWMOUNT

Finnean

Finn's rambled around Arrowmount in aimless loops, the panic in his chest solidifying into a knot. He avoided Fetterly Place like a plague to ensure that Ari wouldn't see him pass by the bookshop without entering. He couldn't take seeing what Ari's face would look like, or the cheer around the bookshop right then.

At a particularly annoyed look of a man hammering dust out of a rug as Finn passed him for the third time, his feet took him on a slightly different path and shot straight out of Arrowmount toward the grassy hills that surrounded the town. The moment that buildings no longer surrounded him, the knot in his chest loosened slightly. Before he knew what, he was doing, Finn took off running at top speed.

He hadn't realized how long it had been since he'd felt the wind in his hair like this, seen nothing but greenery around him, but as he ran a feral cry ripped out of him, and he lost himself to the hills.

A little while later, he found himself in a beautiful copse of trees looking out over Arrowmount and the ocean beyond. Aching, he let himself sink to his knees, chest heaving. From here, he could barely see the flickering flags that lined the streets of Arrowmount. The air flowed by him with a gentle breeze, silent except for the song of a distant bird.

If he squinted, he could make out the street that wound down to Chervil's lighthouse. About halfway up, the street crawled with folks still enjoying the impromptu party that they had started.

Guilt clawed up Finn's throat as he thought of Ari's concern and of how he had just run away from it all. He couldn't help it, though. Finn was terrified of what their life had become and was turning into. Sure, the anxiety had been there since Ari first suggested they stay, but Finn had kept himself busy with the store and the apartment. But today, today things felt like they were culminating in something *finished*. And then the appearance of Lord Wymarc, and the thought of maybe starting a family — all of it had been too much.

How was he supposed to adapt to a life of calm and peacefulness when his whole life had been balanced on the edge of a knife?

One of his daggers appeared in his hand and he started to fiddle with it, running it along his fingers and knuckles in smooth motions that started calming his heartbeat. A beautiful blue bird landed in a nearby tree, chirping at Finn cautiously.

"Feel free to join me," said Finn wheezily. "I'm just out here avoiding my problems."

The bird cocked his head at Finn.

"You know, I have this *perfect* life now. I never thought that leaving the kingdom would have led me here, to where I'm about to fully, officially, settle in with a glorious person that I can proudly call the love of my life. And that commitment terrifies me down to my core. Should it? Am I being cowardly?"

Blue feathers fluttered and twitched in what Finn approximated was a shrug.

"I know, I'm probably being ridiculous. Everything is working out so well. I don't want to leave Ari, gods no. I want this life, I do. But there's something..." he faded off, feeling the greenery around him like a balm to his soul. "There's something almost too perfect about a life like this, one of normalcy and calmness."

The bird chirped at him and set about preening itself in response.

As dusk began to settle in, Finn walked back through the town square toward the message board in the middle. He hadn't had a chance to look at the news for a number of days, with the business of the shop, but something burned inside of him now to see his old name in writing, even if it wasn't good news.

A group of odd people were gathered around it, peering at the board. Three of them were in armor, and all well-armed. Movement around the side of the message board caught Finn's eye as a fourth being with feathered arms appeared.

Oh, oh gods. *No.*

Not here, not them.

Finn's heart launched itself into his throat as he came to an abrupt stop, someone behind him colliding with his shoulder as they tried to walk around him. He took a half step sideways, glancing around the town center for ways out without them seeing him, before his eyes caught on a flash of jewelry on the shortest figure. Finn froze.

Instead of a gnome, a birdfolk, an orc, and a human from his past, a different adventuring party stood before him. Finn let out a long breath, tension unspooling from his neck and shoulders.

A woman that was nearly five inches taller than Ari with bright red curly hair bound in a tight crown of braids stood closest to the message board, with a burly dwarf at her side. The dwarf's beard was full of colorful beads that clinked as he turned to look up at the woman, the two of them debating something posted there. A third being shifted up into the air to peer over the dwarf's head as though they were floating above the ground, and as the sun hit them, it pierced through their opalescent, cloudy body. The birdfolk in full, shining plate armor, a large greatsword on his back in a travel scabbard, came fully into view. The sight of the feathers made Finn's stomach clench, but these were blue, not black.

These were just normal adventurers. Finn almost laughed out loud.

"Hello!" Finn walked forward before he could stop himself, waving at the adventuring party of four. They turned to him, the tall woman glaring down her nose. "Welcome to Arrowmount!"

"Hullo," answered the dwarf amiably, sticking out his thick hand for Finn to shake, beaded beard twinkling slightly. The dwarf's fingers were covered in rings of all sizes with various gemstones inlaid throughout them.

"What brings you to our little town?"

"We're currently searching for a good place with ale and a bed."

"And work, if you've heard of any," said the opalescent being, drifting closer with a slightly mischievous smile on their face.

"I know of just the place. I'm Finn, by the way."

"You look familiar," said the nearly transparent being, flickering out of sight for a moment as they spun around Finn, narrowing their eyes. Finn placed them then as an air elemental. He hadn't met many in his life, but the few he had —

Oh. The softest recognition flickered through Finn, as though the elemental's cocked head had locked something in place.

"Do I?" Finn forced out a laugh. In his mind's eye, he saw a small pearlescent child looking up at him with that same expression and head tilt in the halls of some distant nobleman's estate. *Shit.* "I myself was an adventurer, perhaps we crossed paths at some point."

"That must be it," said the elemental after a moment's hesitation, a smile breaking across their face. "I'm Drift, by the way. That grossly over-jeweled dwarf is Zantar, the tall scary woman is Laera, and the bird boy is Khu."

"I resent the term *bird boy*," muttered Khu, his feathers ruffling.

"It's a pleasure meeting you all." Finn clasped his hands together and smiled, feeling balanced on a dagger's edge as he said his next words. "You all must let me buy you a round — it's been so long since I've been on the road."

32

DAGGERS LIKE THOSE

Finnean

Finn led the party down toward the Old'n Narrow bar, motioning toward Cobb's as a place to stay for the night. They walked by the bookshop, still bustling with folks outside. Finn turned toward a flash of white as Ari spun toward them, but Finn didn't stop — he simply waved and continued on.

"That's the bookshop that my partner and I bought," he said, motioning back over his shoulder. "We're currently renovating it."

"You bought a *bookstore*?" breathed Drift, shooting a look over their shoulder at the newly yellow shop. "Why on earth would you do that?"

"It seemed right at the time," said Finn, forcing out a chuckle. "My partner was tired of adventuring and all that. We were looking for a place to settle down."

He saw the tall woman, Laera, mouth *tired of adventuring* with a look of disbelief on her face, looking down at Zantar. Finn heard the faintest

197

clink of beads as Zantar shrugged in response.

"I suppose you all wouldn't know the feeling — you're all still so young."

Zantar chuckled. He was probably much older than Finn himself was, though it was always hard to tell with dwarves.

"You're still pretty young," commented Khu casually. "Are *you* tired of adventuring, Finn?"

Finn opened his mouth to answer, then hesitated. *Was* he tired of adventuring? His recent panic over staying here and having a *future* here was probably telling enough. Drift smiled at his hesitation and looked sideways at Laera before throwing their arm over Finn's shoulder.

"That's malarkey," chuckled Zantar. "No one can be truly *tired* of adventuring. Sure, take a break, go on vacation — but when you get back on the scent of a job, when you start getting that hint of gold and treasure at the end of the road, that's when it all kicks back in, eh?"

"You're probably right," answered Finn, looking off toward the sea. The grey, cloudy sky above had parted at the horizon, a band of pinkish purple sky slicing through to reflect on the water like a hoard of gemstones. "Who knows, though. Maybe hearing your stories will be enough for me."

He and the party settled into at a table inside the Old'n Narrow and quickly were wrapped up in Zantar's telling of fighting both a hobgoblin and a bear. Finn slid himself easily into the table's energy, and before long, he even had Laera laughing along to his jokes.

"Finn?"

He turned toward the door to see Ari standing there, clean of paint, his hair smoothed back from his face. Sage appeared behind him, peering around the bar. Her eyes went wide as she took in the people that Finn was seated with, eyes tracing the armor and weapons that were sitting out on full display.

"Ari! Come and join us." Finn waved them over. "Everyone, this is my partner Arileas, and our wonderful bookstore clerk, Sage."

Sage's cheeks tinged a darker green as she nodded at them all. Laera looked up at Sage with a sly smile on her lips, eyes locked on Sage. "A bookstore clerk?"

"I — um — yes," stammered Sage, tucking a bit of hair behind one of her ears, knocking at a bit of the jewelry she had threaded over her horns.

Laera nodded slowly, eyeing her before dropping her voice and sliding over a large flagon of ale, making room for her at the table. "Seems like you could use some of that."

Finn chuckled as he turned toward Ari, reaching for him. "What brings you to the bar, my love?"

"I wanted to meet your new friends." Ari smiled, tight lipped. Finn sucked in the tiniest breath, straightening up a little. "When you walked by, I was curious."

"So, *you're* the partner who's tired of adventuring," said Drift, leaning slightly over the table to look directly at Ari as Ari sat down next to Finn. Finn could almost feel the bite in the look Ari shot him.

"You could say that."

"I probably explained it wrong," said Finn, handing Ari his flagon of ale with an apologetic smile. "We just happened to take a vacation here and fell in love with the town and couldn't really fathom leaving again."

Zantar snorted into his ale. "I cannot imagine what that would look like. Home is on the road for us adventurers."

Finn tried to ignore the way his heart lurched at that.

He, Ari, and Sage spent the evening and better part of the night in the Old'n Narrow, listening to the party's wild stories as the evening turned from amiable to downright entertaining. Throughout the night, though, Ari remained tense next to him.

Ari left long before Finn did, leaving a soft kiss on Finn's temple as Finn roared with laughter over Khu and Zantar pantomiming the dramatic part of a bar fight they had been in in Pralon. It felt as though there was the tiniest spark of energy between Ari's lips and his forehead, which jolted him ever so slightly out of the spell of the place.

Finn caught Sage and Laera looking at the two of them once Ari had left. Finn winked at them as Laera rolled her eyes and whispered something into Sage's ear, causing Sage to turn almost emerald with blush.

Drift appeared next to Finn, their cheeks tinged slightly purple with pleasure and drink. "I've figured it out."

"Figured what out?"

"You're that man," they said, peering at Finn through narrowed eyes as though they needed to focus a little harder to see him clearly. "The man I saw — he had daggers like those."

Finn let out a small huff of a laugh and looked down at the dagger in his hand. He hadn't even noticed he'd taken it out, flipping it between his fingers. "Really?"

"Yep, I'm sure of it. You're him."

With a surreptitious glance at the others to make sure they weren't listening; Finn turned his full attention to Drift.

"I saw you in a castle, once. You were so cool, standing there looking all dangerous in the shadows, trying to be —" Drift waved both hands mystically at him, "I don't know. Not seen and also okay with being seen? You were playing with your daggers, just as you are now."

"Ah," said Finn, forcing his voice to stay casual. He took a sip of his ale, trying to steady his now racing heartbeat. "I used to live in a castle, back in another life."

Drift's eyes went a little bit dreamy. "That must've been really something. All those riches around you? Why would you ever leave?"

"My, uh, employer and I didn't see eye to eye, you could say." Finn cleared his throat, eyeing Drift's face, wondering if the kid knew who Finn really was. It didn't seem like it as Drift looked at him with a slightly lop-sided grin. "I'm sorry to say I don't really remember you," he lied.

"Ah, that's okay," they answered. "I was just some kid. I knew I recognized you from somewhere. You were the one who made me absolutely obsessed with knives. You looked *so cool,* did you know that?"

Finn laughed, flipping his dagger across the top of his fingers, remembering the countless times he had done exactly as Drift explained, hiding off to the side of the great hall during whatever feast King Zoren was hosting at the time. Drift's eyes followed Finn's dagger before Zantar pulled them into another conversation, the thread to the past lost.

Finn, feeling as though he had just stepped up to a sharp precipice, downed the rest of his ale in two large gulps and raised his hand for another.

By the time the bar began to close, Nova, one of the owners of the Old'n Narrow, came over to have one last ale with their table. Finn could barely see straight. Sage slid under his arm to hold him upright as they ambled back down the road a few minutes later, sending off the equally as drunk party members toward Cobb's for a room to say in.

"Mr. Finn?"

"Mhmm?" He leaned on her heavily, settling his cheek on one of her horns. The tiny gold chain adorned there dug into his skin. "You're an incredibly lovely person, Sage, you know that?"

"I know it's probably not the time to mention this, but..." she let out a long sigh that sounded like rushing water. Finn's attention slipped for a moment, focusing on the sound of her sigh like it was a wave coming to gobble him up. "...know that you're serious about staying."

"I'm as serious as a sn-snake," he answered, slurring slightly.

"I saw the way Mr. Damaris looked at you when you left this afternoon. So, you better be."

Finn blinked slowly, feeling as though he should be having this conversation sober, but sometimes life is funny like that.

"If you ever leave, I will personally hunt you down," she said matter-of-factly as she deposited him outside of the bookshop. "Hunt you down and drag you back here by your sorry little human butt."

"My butt?"

"Yes, because you don't have horns, so I went for the next thing I could think of. Promise me."

"I promise."

33

CELEBRATORY DINNER

A ri walked through the town square the next morning, perusing some of the stalls. He gathered a delicious looking cheese, some fresh fruits, and a still-warm loaf of bread that smelled absolutely divine.

Finn had come home late the night before, rambling about how much he loved Sage and Ari — and he had mentioned something vague about the air elemental from the adventuring party — before he had crashed into the pillows with a snore. Ari figured he would be out for the count for a while.

He had been so worried when Finn had run off, a look of a caged animal in his eyes, that when he saw the adventuring party, Ari had thought the worst. One look at the plate armor and his heart rate had skyrocketed. But thankfully, this party was not their old one.

Ari knew that Finn was happy here. He could see it in the way Finn interacted with the townsfolk, how he spent so much time in the apartment above making sure things were straightened away. But there was

203

something that needled at Ari's heart when he remembered the way Finn's face glowed last night, surrounded by the party. Something that was rooted in the knowledge that Finn loved being out on the road, loved being free.

The threat of the Shade's name not being put to rest and the chance they would have to run still clung on as a possibility. As he stood above the vegetable stall, not really seeing the array of colors in front of him, a chill ran through his body. When was the last time he had checked the message board? He couldn't remember.

He spun on his heel and walked toward it, scanning the missives pinned there. The board had a few new papers pinned to it, a few notices about sales or listings for various jobs that people wanted done. Ari's eyes skated over the myriad of notes before his eyes snagged on a familiar king's seal in the shape of a Z, near the top center.

Oh?

Ari let out a steadying breath before he leaned in, taking in the words. Once — he blinked, having to refocus and read it a second time.

It is His Majesty's great pleasure —

The royal assassin known as the Shade —

Is proclaimed dead —

Ari's whole being stopped, restarted, and kicked into gear again in pins and needles as he reread it a third, then a fourth time.

Is proclaimed dead.

It had been a year. A *year*, but finally — here it was. In writing. He blinked at it a few times, feeling a sense of... he didn't quite know. Everything inside him came to a stop. For a moment, it felt insubstantial, standing there, reading these words that officially set them free.

He scanned it again. The other party members were mentioned in the notice, heralded as heroes for taking out this prolific foe that had "*plagued our kingdom for years.*" Seeing their names — Prim, Brennyn, Soren, Klea, and even his own — in print felt displaced, as though Ari was looking through the folds of the universe to a life, he had lived eons ago.

Finn is free.

The thought was so simple, so divine, that it took Ari's mind a full minute to wrap around as he stood there, staring at the message board, the sounds of the market around him dimmed and muted.

Someone jostled into him, apologizing under their breath as they continued on their way, jostling an unruly cart in front of them. The motion kicked Ari's brain back into gear as he looked around, mouth opening and closing like a fish. He wanted to yell the news out to anyone who would hear it, but no one knew. No one except him and Finn.

Finn is free. The magic worked.

The magic worked.

He tore the paper off the board and ran.

"Finn!" he shouted into the shop the second he burst through the door. Sophie the cat shot off the windowsill, disappearing into the empty shop with her tail raised in alert. Ari rushed through the shop, slamming open the sliding door to their bedroom and launched himself onto the bed. "Finn, get up!"

"Ari — oh, gods," groaned Finn, clutching his head.

Ari quickly summoned a hangover potion from a nearby drawer and shoved it into Finn's hands, waiting impatiently as Finn unstoppered it, eyes barely open, and swallowed down the contents. His warm brown face turned various shades of green before coming alive in a few heart-beats. After a few deep breaths, he opened his eyes fully and looked at Ari.

"Read."

Finn blinked slowly at the proffered piece of paper in Ari's hands, then up at Ari himself as the potion slowly worked. "What is it?"

"*Read it.*"

Finn's eyes skated across the page once, twice, then again as though his brain was finally processing it. His breath froze in his chest and his eyes widened, grabbing hold of the paper and bringing it closer to him as though not believing it was real.

"'... the royal assassin known as the Shade is proclaimed dead,'" he read.

"Yes."

"The — I'm — the Shade —"

"It's done, Finn," said Ari, feeling as though all of the panic and fear that he had been holding onto over the past year at the base of his stomach fizzled out of existence as he started to cry with happiness. "He's dead, darling. You're free. *We're free.*"

Finn looked up at Ari now, his face a picture of disbelief and shock as he started to breathe again. He blinked at Ari as though searching for the truth in his face. "It's done? Just like that. That's — that's it? It feels... so anticlimactic."

Ari tackled him with a laugh and began kissing him all over, relief pouring out of him as the reality fully hit him. Finn wrapped his arms around him and laughed, emotions bubbling out of him, too.

Finn burrowed his face into Ari's neck. "You can stop worrying now."

Ari pulled back, holding Finn's face in his hands. He looked at his partner's face, taking in the mess of black curls on his head that were stuck up on one side from sleep, to the swimming, wide blue eyes that were locked on his. Slowly, he placed a kiss between Finn's eyebrows and felt the man's arms cling on tighter.

They were finally free.

Once they had both composed themselves, Ari stood in the middle of their bookstore looking at the mass of wood that had been delivered earlier by the Alderidges in preparation for the shelving. He had his Library of Holding in hand, ready to begin the long task of sorting through books.

"I'm going out," called Finn as he walked down from the upstairs apartment, hair dripping from a wash. He looked particularly handsome today, dressed in one of his better shirts and a fresh pair of trousers. He ran his fingers through his hair once, looking around the shop, before doing it again, as though he had something stuck there.

"Where are you off to?"

"I feel like I can't sit still," he said, a slightly strained smile playing at the corners of his lips. Ari noticed movement at Finn's hip, his eyes drawn down toward Finn's fingers as they moved expertly, flipping a familiar dagger around and around. Ari frowned slightly. "And who knows, maybe I'll walk around our lovely town and find some inspiration for the finishing bits on the apartment."

"It's nearly done?"

"Nearly," said Finn as he kissed Ari in passing. "When I get back, we'll celebrate."

Hours later, Ari found himself surrounded by piles and piles of books, looking out at a darkening sky, his heart in his throat. Finn still had not returned. Ari opened up the double doors to let a bit of air throughout the shop, the scent of the sea rolling in with the breeze.

Ari had managed to sort through a good chunk of books and begun piling them in spots around the store where he wanted them to be shelved. Sophie snoozed in a window bed that Dorian had crafted for her on a whim, with a tiny little pillow Sage had brought over from the lighthouse. Ari leaned over and peered through the grimy window, wondering where Finn had gone.

"He's probably stuck talking to everyone he sees," he said to Sophie, scratching her little head, biting at the inside of his mouth.

A couple minutes later a knock came at the bookshop's door. Ari stood up from the sea of books he had found himself in. A man dressed in simple, cleanly starched shirt and trousers smiled warmly at Ari, peering in the open doors. "Hello."

"Can I help you?"

"I'm Lord Wymarc," said the man, extending a hand to Ari. "I met your partner yesterday, however —"

"Finn?"

"Yes, Mr. Finn, as Sage called him." The man let out a soft chuckle and settled comfortably on one foot, putting his hands in his pockets. Ari narrowed his eyes slightly. The lords that he had known throughout his life weren't ever this... casual.

"I wasn't aware that you had met him," said Ari. Finn had met Wymarc. *Maybe that's why he had run off.* "Please, come in. I'm Arileas

Damaris. I believe I have some papers that you have to sign, now that we own the store."

"Ah yes, the bane of all of our existences and yet the blood of our jobs. Paperwork."

Ari sputtered out a surprised laugh as he stepped back, letting Lord Wymarc in. Had the man just made a *joke?* Wymarc smiled at Ari with that same warm smile and walked into the shop, hands still in his pockets. He looked around at the space and the piles of books nodding, impressed.

"Much brighter than Dew had it," he commented. "I look forward to seeing what you do with the place once it's all pulled together."

Ari dug behind the front desk and withdrew the proper paperwork for the lord to sign and spent a couple seconds digging out a fresh pen. "It's been a fair bit more work than we were originally expecting," he said, handing over paper and pen. "The back's water damage was quite extensive."

"Water damage?" Wymarc looked momentarily taken aback. "Goodness, I hadn't known it had hit this far up from the sea. Dew never mentioned anything."

"No one but he and Sage seemed to know," said Ari, shaking his head.

Wymarc glanced at the paper before signing the bottom with a flourish, handing it back to Ari. "I assume that this paper is rather a bit less official feeling than all the work you've put in, but officially, the shop is yours."

"Thank you."

Wymarc took another look around the shop before kneeling down next to a stack of books nearby, picking up the top one and thumbing through. "You know, I've missed this shop. Even though Pralon has many wonderful bookshops, there's nothing like the one you have at home, eh?"

"You enjoy reading, sir?"

"Quite a bit. I have an extensive library of my own, most of it supplied by Dew." Wymarc stood, placing the book back atop the stack carefully. "I will definitely be making my way around to your shop in the future, Mr. Damaris."

"I look forward to it."

Wymarc sauntered off down Fetterly Place with a cheerful wave at Ari, leaving him feeling rather amused at the whole situation. Maybe this lord wasn't one they had to worry about after all.

To fill the time until Finn came back, Ari began to chip away at the windows, grabbing a bucket and some of the better cleaning supplies. He rolled up his sleeves and started scrubbing, throwing a well-placed prestidigitation in every so often to loosen the grime. At one point he hunted down a thin blade to help him scrape at the tougher spots.

It took him the better part of two hours to clean the one window alone, but when it was done, he was surprised at how much more light filtered through despite the late hour. Ari sat back, pleased with himself, hands raw.

And still, Finn had not returned.

Ari hesitated only a second before diving into tackling the second window, and once that one was done and night had properly fallen outside, he was sweating with panic. The sounds of townsfolk from the bar down the street drifted over to the shop through the open doors. He poured a bit of food into a small bowl for Sophie and set it up on the windowsill, entirely unable to sit still.

Still, Finn was not home.

What if he's hurt somewhere? Ari walked out of the shop and looked up and down the road for Finn, a heavy weight pressing on his chest. Ari tried to convince himself to calmly walk up and down Fetterly Place to see if he could find Finn, which was incredibly difficult to do. His limbs and mind demanded he pace and run frantically this way and that, but he knew that wouldn't make anything better.

The only thing that would fix things would be Finn.

A figure came stumbling out of the Old'n Narrow, carrying with them the noise and laughter from within. Finn's shining eyes fell onto Ari's as he beamed, clearly drunk off his ass.

"Finnean Shademark," Ari hissed at his partner, lunging forward to catch the stumbling man before he fell to the cobbles. Finn's arms flopped over Ari's shoulders as he placed a sloppy kiss on his cheek before fully passing out, dropping heavily into Ari's arms. "What in the nine hells are you doing?"

34

A State of Half Awareness

Arileas

Ari watched Finn's sleeping form all night, unable to rest. It wasn't like Finn to forget about an engagement of theirs, to run off into the streets twice in two days like wolven hunted him.

That was the point that stuck, too. There no longer were any wolven hunting him, metaphorical or literal. Ari got up and paced the store until Sophie the cat appeared and jumped onto the moonlit-covered windowsill, looking at him curiously.

"I don't know what to do with him," Ari said to her, feeling as though his brain was going to implode from the amount of thoughts swirling there.

Was buying the bookstore a mistake? Was that what Finn seemed to bothered by? Or had meeting the Lord of Arrowmount gotten to him that much? The fact they were settling down hadn't seemed to bother his partner before, but Ari couldn't get rid of the thought. Perhaps Finn was losing his affection for this life, for Ari himself, for —

The thought was so ludicrous and terrifying that Ari stopped mid stride, as though he walked into a solid surface. Finn had always loved adventuring. Perhaps this long respite from the road had made him realize that that was the life he wanted, just as the respite had made it clear to Ari that he could never go back to on the road life.

Was it Ari's fault, for wanting to stop?

Ari crumpled to the floor and put his head in his hands, trying to stop the thoughts from swirling, pain expanding in his chest. What if his fears weren't wrong? What if Finn really did want to leave?

Panic seized Ari's chest as his heart began to shatter at the thought. Anxiety and guilt twisted in his stomach until he felt physically sick. Tears burned at the back of his eyes, but he forced himself to not let them fall.

Finn hadn't left. Not yet, anyway.

Dorian and Diana interrupted Ari's spiraling not long after the sun crested the horizon and began to install the shelving. His heart pounded out a rhythm along with their hammers as he stood inside their makeshift bedroom, stomach still churning.

Once the shelves were up, there was very little else that they had to do. The old front desk was still stationed in the front room of the shop like a decrepit sentinel, soon to be swapped out once the shelving was up. The new one was ready and done, waiting at the Alderidges' shop to be installed.

Finn awoke not long after the noise began, a soft groan emitting from beneath a pile of blankets. Ari turned, kneading his hands together nervously.

"Finnean," he said in way of greeting as he watched his partner down yet another of their hangover potions. They would have to place an order soon to replenish their supply.

At the sound of Ari's tone, Finn turned and peered at him, a furrow in his brow. He looked about ten years older than usual this morning, his face haggard and sickly looking. "Morning."

"Are you going to explain yourself, or shall I just stand here and wait?"

It took Finn a moment to slide the pieces into place. Ari's heart thudded painfully as he saw *excitement* appear on Finn's face.

He cleared his throat and looked as though he was trying not to laugh. "Ari, oh — I completely apologize for last night, I don't know what came over me. I misplaced myself and time."

Ari frowned and waited for him to go on.

"I ran into that adventuring party from previous — yes of course you remember, right — and we got to talking again. I was swept up into their tales. Oh, I should have told you sooner, but I know one of them."

"*Excuse me?*"

"Or rather one of them knows me. The air elemental, Drift?"

"Hold on," said Ari, holding up a hand. "You're telling me that a kid saw you as —" he dropped his voice and mouthed *the Shade*, "— and you're not worried about that?"

Finn waved his hand dismissively. "They were a little kid and didn't know that I was the Shade, love. They still don't know. They only remember me as a noble with a couple of fancy daggers that caught their attention."

Ari crossed his arms, trying to hold himself back. "So, wonderful. They remember you. They recognize you from your past, when you were still *him,* and you're not worried about it at all."

"It's been well over a decade since they saw me, and they were probably so drunk that night that they don't remember our conversation anyways." Finn waved a dismissive hand in the air. "That's beside the point — you'll never guess our luck, my love. Last night, they told me about a glorious opportunity on the outskirts of Feycross. One with *treasure.*"

Ari sucked in a long, steadying breath, feeling as though he had run headlong into a wall.

"We can leave in the morning with them, and we would be completely free to adventure like we used to," continued Finn, riling himself up. The old, haggard look about his eyes had faded now, and he looked exactly like the man Ari had met in that tavern, months and months ago. Finn twirled his dagger over and over, the motion making Ari slightly nauseous. "There are rumors of a portal to the fey realm itself there, and there's this beast that's been plaguing the town for a big, hoarding all the jewels and gold and such. We —"

"I don't know who this 'we' is you're speaking of," said Ari, his voice low. Finn's face froze as he looked at Ari properly. Ari's emotions were spinning so deeply inside of him that he was having a hard time processing anything. "*We* cannot up and leave this place, Finn. *We* bought a *bookstore.* One that, if you haven't noticed, is days away from being complete. There is no *we* going on this ridiculous adventure."

"Ari, please, you're not listening," said Finn quickly. "This could be our chance to —"

"To do what exactly?"

Finn swallowed visibly and stood, putting his hands up in a soft placating gesture. Ari twisted his arms tighter and took a step back, stopping Finn from touching him.

"It's our chance to live like we wanted to," said Finn, his voice slipping into a low hiss of want. "Like the lords we were meant to be. Imagine the luxury we could have, Ari! Diamonds and rubies and —"

"That's a life *you* dreamed about, not me," said Ari, cutting him off. "It was nothing more than a frivolous dream, and never was a serious goal. I wanted to spend my life with you, freely."

"I know that," said Finn, irritation flashing across his brow. "Ari, I never joked about wanting a life of riches. I want to be able to live comfortably so that we don't ever have to rely on anything else! That's why I'm doing this."

"You don't think we have that already?" Ari's voice rose in volume now, last night's panic leaking in. "Finn. We've both amassed enough wealth in our lifetimes that we don't ever have to worry about anything like that."

"Sure, we have gold and jewels, but with having a bookshop you know we could always use more —"

"You want the adventure," said Ari, the realization hitting him square in the face. "You're chasing that danger. You *still* want that. Why didn't you say anything before, Finn?"

"I — I've been struggling to understand how I've felt, and you know I love it here."

"We decided this was going to be our life," said Ari, his voice wavering now. "I never wanted riches. I just wanted you, plain and simple."

"No," said Finn sharply, taking steps closer to Ari, close enough that he could grab him if he wanted, but he kept his hands to himself. "*You* decided to live this life. It was *your* dream to buy the bookstore, not mine."

Ari recoiled, Finn's words like a slap. He stared at Finn for a few heartbeats, the tension hanging in the air.

"That's why you've been different," Ari said quietly. "Work is coming to an end on the shop, so you're looking for the next thing. The next great adventure."

Finn looked down at his feet and sighed. "Ari —"

"Are you not tired?" Ari's voice broke as he took in his partner, the man he thought would stay by his side for days. "This life of running, of constantly being on the move because of what haunted you — haunted *us*. Did you not expect at some point that we would settle down together, or did you think we were going to run ourselves into early graves? I want a life where I can breathe, Finn, and not worry about whether we were going to see the next sunrise. I never felt like I could breathe properly until we came here."

Finn raked his fingers through his hair, leaving it standing up in a disarray, and opened his mouth to interrupt but Ari ploughed on anyway.

"But this isn't enough for you, is it? *I'm* not enough."

Finn froze. His expression fell as though he was about to be sick. Closing his eyes and turning away from Ari, he let out a long breath, his shoulders sagging.

He walked away from Ari and back to his side of the room, where he began tearing things out of drawers. He pulled on old leather pants that Ari hadn't seen him in since they were on the road — and slipped both of his daggers into his belt.

Ari felt his world melt away as he watched Finn grab everything that was his in minutes, shoving it into his riding bag, and left.

Finn didn't say a single word. He never even looked back.

Ari's heart fell into a million pieces as the love of his life walked out the door.

PART FIVE

The Heart of it All

35

BACK ON THE ROAD

Finnean

Finn became used to riding horseback again slowly, the gentle sway lulling him into a soft trance the longer they rode. The party kept a hard pace, travelling for most days well into the night, only stopping to swap horses if they could. At night, Finn's back and legs ached so fiercely that he hobbled stiffly to their camp and could barely get back up in the morning. But he kept at it, and by the morning of the fourth day, he finally started to feel comfortable again as he slid up into the saddle.

It took Finn about five days to feel anything other than a vague numbness when he thought about Arrowmount, and when that vanished, he was consumed by guilt. But, by then, it was far too late to turn around.

It was also about five days before he realized there was someone tailing them.

As the ex-royal assassin, he had once been honed to notice when eyes were on him. A weird sense of annoyance at himself settled around his shoulders when he finally realized they were being tailed. He should have noticed that ages ago.

He stiffened in his saddle and made eye contact with Laera, the person riding next to him. She gave him a curt nod, having noticed as well. Under her breath, she murmured, "Whoever they are, they've been following us since we left Arrowmount."

A stupid, absolutely ridiculous ray of hope bubbled up in Finn's chest at the thought that it might be Ari coming along after all. In his mind's eye, he could see the two of them, reunited, successfully overthrowing whatever fey beast they were about to face.

"I don't know who it could be," he said finally, brushing aside the vision of Ari's beaming face — it was too painful. "Let's keep on ahead and see if they decide to show their face."

The party settled in to make camp off the side of the road as dusk began to fall. Finn watched the road itself through a break in the trees, waiting for whomever it was that followed them. Laera was on alert, her greatsword in hand as she leaned against a tree, also listening.

"Ale, for our new adventuring partner," said Zantar, handing Finn a flagon of ale. "To celebrate what we are embarking on, eh?"

Finn accepted the flagon with a small grimace. He wasn't much in the mood to celebrate.

Laera burst into movement, lunging out of the trees toward the road. Finn launched himself onto his feet as a soft yelp of surprise sounded on the other side, followed by Laera's sharp laugh.

Could it be —

A crown of green hair and horns appeared instead, walking meekly in front of Laera's beaming face. Sage was dressed head to toe in one of her usual dresses, though this one was incredibly dusty from days on the road. Finn caught sight of riding leathers beneath her skirts as she walked up, and over her shoulder hung a stuffed travel bag. Tucked partway into a belt and small sheath, a rather ornate dagger hung at her hip.

"Sage," Finn said, shocked into soft laughter. "It was you following us?"

Her shoulders drooped. "You knew?"

"You're not the quietest, Tealeaf," Laera teased, reaching over to tweak the tip of Sage's horn.

"You shouldn't be here," said Finn, motioning for her to sit next to him on a downed tree. "It's not safe."

"I am quite aware of that, Mr. Finn," she said, trying to look braver as she sat up a bit straighter to look him and everyone else in the eye. "I *want* to be here."

"Bah, cut her some slack, old man," said Drift as they drifted over cross-legged in the air. "We're too far out from Arrowmount now anyway."

Sage bit her lip as though she was physically restraining herself from talking. Her eyes hardened as she looked at Finn. He heard her voice leaking through a drunken stupor in his mind. *If you ever leave, I will personally hunt you down.*

Finn shook his head and laughed resignedly. He hardly had the authority to send her back home, and since he wasn't really a part of this adventuring party, it was up to them whether Sage could tag along.

"I'm fine with it," said Laera with a shrug. "But, if we ask you to move, you move. If we ask you to run, duck, stay behind, save yourself — anything, you do so. Am I clear?"

Sage frowned at her. "I can take care of myself."

"I know you think you're capable," said Laera calmly. "But we all know what we're doing when it comes to beasts and creatures and battles for our lives. You, well-read though you are, are more definitely not. Right?"

"I am completely capable," Sage said, glaring at her.

Laera stopped and blinked at her slowly. A cocky, disbelieving smile spread across her face. The large barbarian crossed her arms, her muscles flexing, and jutted out her chin. "Prove it."

A muscle in Sage's jaw clenched as she looked over at the rest of them, eyes snagging on Finn, before she pulled the ornate dagger from her belt and held it out toward Laera, focusing on her. Finn immediately cringed at her grip and her stance. The way Sage's fingers grasped the hilt of the dagger too tightly and too high up for any kind of proper cutting reminded him immediately of the first time he had picked up a dagger.

That wouldn't do damage against a fly.

Let alone a barbarian who usually wielded a greatsword.

But Finn had to hand it to her. Sage set her jaw and narrowed her gaze, ready to at least try.

Laera raised an eyebrow at Sage before she took a step forward to close the space between them, leaving her greatsword sheathed leaning up against a tree.

Finn opened his mouth and started to rise, wanting to give Sage a couple pointers just to help her not get absolutely clobbered, but Laera was already launching into movement. Without any fear for the unsheathed blade, she stepped up to Sage as she tried to defend herself. With a few precise movements, Laera disarmed her, sending the ornate dagger flying. She snatched both of Sage's arms as Sage tried to get away and pinned her tight against her chest.

"So. Am I clear?" Laera tilted her head a little around one of Sage's horns to speak.

Sage's nostrils flared, but she didn't fight back. "Yes."

Finn took one look at Sage's downturned face and had to bite back a smile at the fierce expression there. Her fists clenched by her side before she forcibly relaxed them, and subtly lifted her chin. Laera let go, bending to pick up Sage's lost dagger. She turned it over and inspected it before handing it back to Sage, a neutral expression on her face.

"I will protect you, little bookstore clerk, as long as you listen to us. Got it?"

Sage nodded sharply before she turned away, her cheeks tinging slightly darker green.

Later that night, Sage found Finn sitting against a pine tree and plopped down beside him in the dirt. "Mr. Finn."

"Sage."

"What exactly do you think you're doing?"

He looked around him and shrugged. "Sitting."

"Don't be funny with me. You promised."

Guilt gnawed at the inside of his stomach. "Is that what you're doing out here then? Chasing me down?"

Her eyes flashed toward Laera, but she nodded. "I couldn't let you just run away from Mr. Damaris like this. I have to make sure you get home safe."

"I appreciate your concern, Sage, but please. This..."

"If you say this is an adult matter, I will fully bind you to a horse and send you back to Arrowmount," she hissed, waving a finger at him. "I've been practicing druidic magic with May, I know how."

He didn't doubt she would, either.

"I hope you know what you're doing to him," she said finally, her shoulders sagging. "At least I left a note. You walked out on him to chase after gold and treasure."

"You're too wise for your age, you know that?" Finn's heart ached so fiercely that he had to swallow a few times before he could speak again. "I know I've made a mistake, Sage. Possibly the largest one of my life."

"And what are you going to do about it?"

He shook his head and closed his eyes. "I have no idea."

That night Finn's spinning mind and aching heart kept him awake, his whole being threatening to implode. He kept replaying Ari's expression in his mind. The betrayal written on every inch of his perfect face pierced right through Finn's heart even here, miles and miles away.

He spent the sleepless night staring up at the stars, wondering what he was doing there at all. What did he want, really? Finn knew that he had to do this, if not to prove to Ari that this had been worth it, but because turning around now made his heart twist into knots. He had to —

He —

Fuck, he thought to himself, turning over on the ground. *What have I done?*

Ari's pained face swam in front of his eyes as dawn covered the world into gentle, dulled purples and blues. Exhaustion pulled him down as the party around him stirred, ready to start another day.

36

PARADE OF ONE

Arileas

F inn didn't come back.

Not that night, the next, or the next. Eventually, news filtered down to Ari that the adventuring party had left for a job, and his heart crumbled anew. He had hoped that Finn would come to his senses and would turn around and come back to him, but he was wrong.

On the second morning, he awoke to find a note pinned to the front desk in curling, cramped writing.

Mr. Damaris,

I am so, so sorry.

I won't be able to come and help you wrap up the finishing touches of the shop this week because — please please please don't hate me! — I'm going after the party. I saw Mr. Finn with them, as though he was going with them, which I thought was wrong, because why would he go adventuring without you? But I followed them out of the town, and I could not believe my eyes as he got on a horse, too!

I promise I'll be safe and okay.

227

I took Granddad's dagger that he keeps hanging on the wall, and I'm going to take the fastest horse from the stables to catch up to them. But most importantly, I promise I will find him and hunt him down.

- Sage

P.S. I'm so, so sorry again!

P.P.S. Please don't open the shop until I get back!

P.P.P.S I mean, you can, but I really hope you don't.

Ari found himself laughing sadly as he held the note, shaking his head at Sage. Of course, she had run off after the adventuring party — that didn't surprise him at all. He hoped, desperately, that they would keep her safe. She really didn't know what she was getting into.

He sank down to the floor behind the old front desk and his laughter dissolved into tears. Now he wouldn't even have Sage's brightness to cheer him up.

The gentlest touch of a whiskered nose alighted at the end of his fingertips before Sophie the cat began to rub her head along his hand. She mewed softly at him as he looked up at her through blurry eyes, sitting delicately by his knee. He scratched her between the ears as the tears continued to stream down his face, watching the way her little orange eyes inspected him. She pushed her way up onto his lap and curled there, a soft weight of reassurance, and began to purr quietly.

It took him a little while to pour everything out and pull himself back together, but he did it in the end. Or at least, he tried to.

May and Chervil had taken less than half a day once Sage had left to realize something was off. Chervil had also woken to a note from Sage, which had sent him off walking around the entirety of Arrowmount looking for the adventuring party even though they had already left. May had taken Chervil in arm and brought him and a bundle of food toward the bookshop, pushing their way inside.

"Andrew is watching the cafe for me," she had said to Ari, taking him gently by the hand and pulling him out of his room, where he'd been curled up in darkness. "Chervil and I wanted to make sure you were okay."

"So, the whole street knows?" Ari had said, his voice breaking.

Chervil had walked the length of the store, poking his head into every room, before settling himself on a chair next to them with a gruff sigh. "Folks either saw your Finn leaving with the adventurers or had heard from someone else. You know how news travels 'round here. But no one saw my Sage."

May reached out to gently tap the back of Chervil's deep blue hand reassuringly. "She's a smart one, Chervil. You know she won't be putting her nose into anything she shouldn't be."

They kept coming back, too, whether alone or together, to make sure Ari was still functioning. Every time Ari heard their knock on the bookshop's door, he stood up straighter and felt as though he could breathe a little easier.

He spent the remaining days working in the shop until every last bit of it shone and looked exactly right. The piles of books inside his Library of Holding dwindled as the books found their homes on shelves. For days, he kept himself in a state of half-awareness and his hands busy until there was nothing more to do.

On the sixth day that Finn had been gone, he felt something tighten and wind up inside of him, as though a tiny snake of iron had curled up his spine. As he stood in the shop scratching between Sophie's ears, he realized how exhausted he really was, but today, Dorian and Diana were expected with the new front desk.

So, Ari got to work.

He fed Sophie and spent the morning walking around the shop, touching books here and there, adjusting them where needed. The back room, too, needed only a few finishing touches. He would have asked Finn or Sage to help since they both liked decorating, but since neither of them were here, Ari would have to figure it out on his own.

Ari opened the front doors, letting in the sunshine, and walked out onto the cobbles in front of the shop. Warm sunlight bathed his face as he closed his eyes, tilting his head up toward the sky. Slowly, he felt himself filling up with the warmth, recharging again.

He reached up to pull his hair into a half-hearted ponytail and headed off into Arrowmount to pull himself and the shop together.

A few hours later, he returned with new decor items that he had sourced throughout Arrowmount for the backroom. He paraded a few chairs behind him with magic, their shapes bobbing a top the cobbles, garnering quite a few stares, he made his way back toward the shop like a solemn, determined parade of one.

37

BRIGHT CHERRY PIE

Arileas

Diana popped her head into the backroom as Ari fluffed the last pillow, startling him out of a reverie.

"She's ready."

He followed her from the room only to stop in his tracks the second he laid eyes on the piece of furniture that the Alderidges had brought in.

It was, in a word, *exquisite*.

"Skies," he swore faintly, moving toward it in a slight trance. The scent of freshly cut wood, lacquer, and stain lingered in the air of the bookshop as Dorian took a rag to the top, shining it up.

The honey-toned wooden desk fit perfectly in the middle room of the shop. Intricate flower details on the front curled around a wide, flat space centered in the middle of the desk, blank like the face of the moon. In behind, Diana had designed a set of matching wood shelves for inventory and any orders customers place within the shop. Shelving ran almost

231

edge to edge of the wall, leaving enough space on either side for someone to walk past.

"We left it blank for the name of the shop," said Diana, motioning to the space on the front. "I wasn't sure whether you wanted to keep it as Arrowmount Books, since the sign is gone outside."

"Neither Finn nor I —" he choked on Finn's name, heat burning at the back of his throat like acid. He shook his head and cleared his throat, running a hand along the surface of the desk. "We hadn't decided on a name yet, but when it happens, you'll be the first we call. We do need a sign, after all."

Diana showed Ari compartments and shelving they had built into the desk, including a secured built-in metal safe hidden away inside it, behind a clever door.

"You both are geniuses," he said, slightly at a loss for words. "It's perfect."

Dorian clapped him amiably on the shoulder. "No problem at all."

When they left, Ari spun slowly on his heel, taking in the shop.

The rich green walls around him soothed his soul as he took in all the brand-new shelving. Every bit of wood saturated the shop in the exact honey-warm tone that Ari loved and reminded him of every cozy corner of every bookstore he had ever walked into. With sunshine pouring in through the now clean windows and Sophie basking in the middle of the floor, eyes squinted closed, Ari felt as though he was exactly where he was supposed to be.

It was done. Every little thing that he had worried about, everything that kept him up at night wearing a path in the wooden floors, was complete. And it was all absolutely perfect, from the shelves and the books atop them, to the back room that no longer had a partial wall caved in and swollen from water damage.

Ari let out a long sigh, a knot of tension unwinding between his shoulder blades. A soft, aching happiness settled in his heart. He did a round of the shop once, twice, then, on the third time through, he finally came to a stop at the closed sliding door to his and Finn's bedroom. When the apartment upstairs was complete, he wasn't entirely sure what they would do with this extra room. Probably turn it into storage, or perhaps a room exclusively for sitting and reading with a few tables for those who wished to enjoy some of May's wares inside as they browsed or read.

Finn should be here, he thought, turning once more to the shop itself. *And Sage.* They had put just as much work into this space as Ari had, and deserved to revel in the perfection before he opened the door to the public.

His feet took him out of the shop then, toward May's. The sky was bright and the day hot, humidity clinging to the air like tension. A few townsfolk waved to him as he passed, smiling kindly at the man who now owned the bookshop on Fetterly Place.

He found Chervil seated outside at a table, a newspaper folded part way in one hand and a fizzing purple drink in the other. The old fiendling looked over the edge of his spectacles at Ari, eyebrows raising.

"You're out and about today, Arileas! How're things?"

"I — well." Ari cleared his throat and shrugged, a soft laugh escaping his lips. "I don't know. And that's okay, I guess. But I do know one thing. The shop is ready."

Chervil's eyes sparkled as his face cracked into a smile.

"I would love if you and May could come and see it," continued Ari, turning to peer inside the cafe for May. She walked out in that moment, bringing Chervil a slice of bright red cherry pie. "If you have a minute to spare, of course."

"I have as many minutes as you need," she said, reaching out a soft hand to pat his arm, sending a wave of warmth to Ari's chest. "What is it?"

"He says the shop is ready," said Chervil gruffly as he pushed himself out of his chair. "Leave that tasty pie right here on the table, I'll be back. And we'll need another slice or two, since we'll be celebrating with Arileas here when we return."

"Sounds like a plan." May ducked inside and waved at the lone patron — Ari was unsurprised to see Calian seated within — and threw the apron around her waist over a chair nearby. "I'll be right back; do you mind holding down the fort?"

Calian answered with a pleasant nod. "I'll keep everything under control."

Ari led the two of them back to the bookshop, feeling like he was riding on a large wave in the ocean, not knowing what was coming next.

He paused for a moment, taking a deep breath, before he pulled open the double doors of the bookshop and stepped inside, gesturing to a variety of arcane lights he had stationed around the shop. They bathed the shop interior in a soft, cozy yellow glow that matched the sunshine streaming through the now sparkling clean front windows.

Both Chervil and May gasped, their soft intakes of breath swelling Ari's pride up like a balloon.

"Oh, Ari," breathed May, taking his hand. The tiny plants that always curled out of her pocket and around her clothing started to grow. Flowers bloomed along a long vine that was curled around her hair, pops of purple appearing along the gold strands, as her eyes watered.

The image of the flowers inspired Ari then. "May, would you mind helping me out with a few plants for the shop? It feels like we need to fill everything out a little bit more, and not with just books."

"I would be more than happy to," she answered, her eyes sparkling. She squeezed his hand once before letting go, looking around the shop.

Ari stayed by the window to scratch Sophie's head as Chervil and May walked the shop, taking it in inch by inch. Sophie the cat purred happily leaning into his hand. An aching absence hummed inside of him, as though he could feel the ghost of Finn standing next to him wrapping an arm around Ari's waist and pulling him in.

Gods, I hope he's okay.

38

EMERALDS THE SIZE OF MANGOS

Finnean

Adrenaline and pain coursed through Finn as he lent down to Sage, helping her to her feet. The wound along his ribs throbbed painfully, and he gritted his teeth to stop gasping in pain. Sage was covered head to toe in rubble and grime from the fight, but thankfully, she was unharmed.

Her eyes sparkled with light as she laughed and threw her arms around him, saying something in his ear that he couldn't quite catch through the pounding in his ears. She let him go and rushed off toward the others, throwing her hands up in celebration. Tiny flowers burst into the air from the tips of her fingers, showering Laera and Drift in a mirage of petals.

All around him, the party cheered, filling the now dead fey beast's layer with noise, sound ricocheting off of the high stone walls of the cavern.

The beast itself lay dead in the corner, its massive corpse filling up the

236

space. It was the most obscenely wondrous creature Finn had ever come across. Both its head and stomach were a dusty purple, but the rest of its body down to its misshapen hind legs and long serpentine tail was a rich midnight blue. Two incredibly massive tusks the size of Finn grew from the snarled snout, which had proven incredibly dangerous in the fight. One had been chipped on the side, sharp as a blade's edge.

With one hand pressed against his ribs to staunch the blood from a particularly lucky dodge of his — if he hadn't dodged at that moment, he would have been bisected in half, eerily making the events of a year ago flash through his mind — Finn sank down amidst a mound of treasure. He watched as Zantar and Khu began to sort through a pile of jewels, a glow of joy on their faces that Finn himself once knew.

Finn could only scrape together pure relief that he was alive and a deep unending want to be back with Ari. All of this journey, he kept looking over his shoulder, expecting to see Ari's beautiful face framed with his glorious white hair, rocking side to side on his horse. It felt physically wrong, as though he was constantly wiping his skin with the slightest touch of acid, that Ari wasn't here with him.

Now, sitting amidst more jewels and gold than he had ever laid his eyes on, the realization hit him like a ton of bricks. All of this — the adventuring, the jewels, the success of a job done — meant nothing to him if Ari wasn't there to share it.

I should be gloriously happy, he thought, threading his fingers through a pile of gold coins next to him, letting them fall like a shower of rain. He dug a little deeper, his fingers finding an emerald the size of a mango. *I should be reveling in the adrenaline, the joy of a fight.*

He laughed sadly then winced, the motion shooting pain through his wound. It was always Ari. He couldn't remember ever loving a job when he was the Shade. It was only when he had joined the adventuring party and had shared the joy with Ari that he had seen what it could be to really be an adventurer — what it meant to be truly, incandescently happy.

"I'm a fool," he told the emerald, peering at it. It was flawless. "I'm a complete and utter fool."

He should never have left. He could have died here, died having not had a proper goodbye with the love of his life, leaving him stranded in their bookshop with betrayal writ all over his features.

All of this — for what? A taste of what he thought he wanted? Nothing in the world should have been able to take him away from Ari. As he sat amidst a hoard of treasure, holding that massive emerald, he realized how little he wanted any of it.

Khu drifted over at some point to help Finn wrap the wound in his side and handed him a healing draught. It sent rippling shivers over Finn's ribs and skin as its magic sealed the wound shut, his breathing a little easier as the pain subsided.

"Take whatever you like," said Zantar as he made his way over to Finn. "You deserve it — can you believe that beast had thorns, on top of the venomous bite? If you hadn't clocked that when you had, we would have all been dead."

Finn smiled at him tiredly and took a few handfuls of the treasure around him, including the massive emerald and an oddly light stone that shone like an oil slick despite being pitted like raw granite about the size of Sophie the bookstore cat.

A deep and powerful ache settled into his bones as he sat there, the adrenaline fully leaving his body. Every one of his bones screamed to be bathed in warmth and wrapped in a comfy cloud. He closed his eyes and thought of the comfy bed tucked into a room inside their shop, surrounded by soft arcane light.

Gods, he thought to himself as he let out a pained groan, pushing himself up off the mound of treasure. *I am really not meant to do this anymore, am I?*

Sage came over practically dancing on air. Finn noticed a new set of gold jewelry draped around her horns and through her hair, tiny rubies shining periodically around the chain like minuscule eyes. Her face was still flushed emerald with the thrill of the win.

"Isn't this just *everything*, Mr. Finn?"

"You've taken to it like chocolate on ice cream." Finn adjusted a bit of the gold chain caught on itself over one of her horns.

Her face flickered slightly, looking back over her shoulder toward Laera and the crew. "They were talking about going onward to Alieweth," she said softly. "There is a boat waiting for them there, and they plan to sail the Caspasian Sea. I know I should get back to Granddad, but does it make me horrible for wanting to go, too?"

"I think he would be heartbroken if you didn't at least go and see him before you decide on a life of adventuring."

"I should." Her shoulders sagged as she turned back to him, opening her travel bag to show him what she had found inside. "I do have a couple jewels for him, too. And a new dagger, so that he can keep his."

"Sage," said Finn, putting a hand on her shoulder. "If you really want to be an adventurer, I don't see why you shouldn't go. We have a port in Arrowmount — if these wonderful people wanted to sail by and pick you up on their way, then..." he shrugged gently, trying not to move too fast and hurt his body anymore.

Her eyes brightened, despite a frown crossing her face. "Granddad would never let me go, though."

"You won't know unless you ask," Finn answered quietly. "Sometimes that's all it takes. Chase what you want, Sage. That's what drives souls."

Sage grinned, wrapping her arms around him once more. The little rubies twinkled at him as he patted her back.

"You don't mind if I quit the bookstore?"

He laughed and let her go, winking at her. "We'll hold your place forever, if you ever decide to come home."

Sage laughed and let go, closing up her bag of gemstones. As she turned away to rejoin her party, she looked at him over her shoulder. "Where is your soul telling you to go, Mr. Finn?"

"If you're no longer working in the bookstore, you can at least call me just Finn."

"Fine, Just Finn," she said, giving him a cheeky smile.

He breathed in long and slow, a smile spreading on his face. He knew exactly where his soul was telling him to go.

39

HEAVY BURDENS

Finnean

T he sun cast a spray of gold across the ocean as it rippled and winked between the trees, welcoming them home. It had been a little over two weeks since he had last set foot along those cobblestones, and Finn's heart galloped toward home almost as fast as the horses did.

Finn's stomach twisted into knots as he and Sage drew ever closer, but despite the nerves, he couldn't help but smile. He stopped his horse momentarily to reach down and gather a bundle of wildflowers, tucking them into the space between his chest and his shirt beneath his outer, thicker leather vest to ensure they stayed safe as they rode.

The stables outside of Arrowmount welcomed their horses in, sending both Finn and Sage off down the streets with their bags of riches and travel worn bodies. Finn carefully transferred the bundle of wildflowers to one of his bags, the tiny bulbs peeking out in a burst of color.

Sage and he fell into a comfortable silence during the last stretch toward home, which continued throughout their walk to Fetterly Place.

Finn cast a sidelong glance at her, noting the pensive expression across her face as she took in her hometown with the fresh eyes of an adventurer. She'd bound her green curls in thick braid that ran between her ruby-and-gold adorned horns. And, rather than one of her usual dresses, she wore riding leathers and a simple, loose white linen shirt.

He left her to her musing as he looked around at the multicolored flags affixed above the streets. White, fluffy clouds floated behind them as they danced happily in the sea breeze, snapping gently above them. A light scent of salt clung to the air. Finn's boots clacked familiarly along the warm cobblestones.

Home.

The two of them continued onto Fetterly Place, the ocean and lighthouse coming into view at the end of the cobblestones. From here, Finn could see the bit of freshly painted yellow that was the bookshop.

A bloom of fresh excitement and nerves started in his stomach, nodding to the familiar faces around them. He could feel the double takes as townsfolk took in the two of them, ragged from travel and carrying heavy burdens.

"I take it that word got around," said Finn under his breath as they reached the outside of the bookstore. "I'd hurry to your granddad before he finds out you're home from someone else."

Sage's cheeks took on a darker green color as she looked up at the store. "Sage."

She sighed and nodded. "You're right. Of course, you're right."

She left his side as he took in the entrance of the shop, eyes tracing the open book carved into the doorway. The bright yellow paint along the facade of the shop reminded him of Ari's smile, and for a moment he stood frozen, trying to ignore the pounding in his heart. The windows shone in the sunshine, having been entirely scrubbed clean of the old sea grime. Through them, Sophie the little brown cat snoozed happily in the sun bathing the windowsill.

Everything was so entirely different than when he and Ari had first laid eyes on the place, with the peeling blue-grey paint, the grime covered windows, and the rickety shop sign.

Finn's throat tightened with emotion as he remembered that day, coming in with his love by his side. Now, he was staring at two closed doors, holding him off from Ari. A deep ache spread through his chest. *Why is it so difficult to take those steps, close the distance, and open the door?*

He couldn't tell whether the shop was open or closed, but he honestly couldn't see why Ari wouldn't have opened the shop to the public while he was gone. They had been just finishing up the renovations when he left, so by now, the store would be more than ready.

Finn sucked in a breath, still hesitating. What if Ari didn't want him back? He knew it was a ridiculous thought, but it brushed across his mind with a surge of anxiety all the same.

Before he could get too lost in his own head, though, the shop doors swung outward. Ari nearly walked headlong into him. His love's eyes went wide and he took a couple steps back, the doors closing behind him.

The tiniest bit of sound escaped Ari's lips, barely a gasp. "Finn?"

Finn drank in the sight of Ari, from the curling wisps of hair escaping from a haphazard bun atop his head to the freckles across his nose, down to the casually open neckline of his dark-blue linen shirt and brown trousers. Ari's mouth opened in surprise. An ache coursed through Finn's chest, a yearning to reach forward and hold Ari and never let go.

"Ari."

"You — you're back. You're alive."

Finn nodded, a crushing and entirely overwhelming feeling settling into his chest and throat. He swallowed and cleared his throat, looking down at the bags in his hands that held the treasure and his belongings, road weary and dusty. "I am."

Ari stood up a little straighter, setting his face into a steady held expression as he eyed Finn up and down. "You're absolutely filthy, darling."

40

DARLING

Finnean

That one word cracked Finn's heart in two. *Darling.* In all his years on this realm, he had never heard a word so glorious. He melted ever so slightly and took a tentative step forward.

"I am so sorry Ari," he said, the words soft. "I should never have left."

"No, you shouldn't have." Ari closed his eyes and tilted his head down with a soft laugh before peering up at Finn again, his eyes swimming with unshed tears. "But I also shouldn't have said the things I did when you left. I should have realized you weren't ready to settle yet."

"I was ready, and am ready, my love," said Finn urgently. "It wasn't only you that wanted this life. We decided to do this, together."

"You dream of adventure, darling."

"I dreamed and continue to dream only of you, Ari." Finn took another tiny step forward. They were so close now, close enough that they could reach out and touch each other, if they wanted to. His arms ached, wanting to hold Ari, to touch even just his hand — anything that would bring them closer. "I am so, so sorry that I didn't stay and talk this

245

through with you. It was rash, and foolish, to run."

Ari crossed his arms, eyes skating over Finn's face. "What about the adventure? The job?" He could almost hear Ari's unspoken words hanging in the air. *Did you love it? Will you leave again?*

"I hated it," said Finn, chuckling softly. "It never occurred to me that the actual jobs we did weren't what I loved about being on the road. I never once liked a job as — well, as my old self. Not *once*. But when I met you, and that party, things changed. You walked into my life and everything flipped upside down, my love. I no longer hated what I was, what I had been trained to do, because it helped us.

"It took until I was kneeling in the middle of a pile of jewels and gold to realize it, but I only liked the adventures we had together because, well, you were there. The way your face would light up at the end of a particularly taxing fight, turning toward me. When I was sitting with all that treasure around me, all I wanted was to come home to you."

"Me?"

"It has *always* been you. From the moment we met in that tavern, when you were sitting between a birdfolk and a tiny gnome looking incredibly miserable as the barmaid set down a flagon of ale in front of you, it's always been you."

"I was miserable," said Ari quietly, a small smile playing at the corner of his lips, "until an absolutely beautiful man with eyes as blue as the ocean walked in and smiled. Then I knew I was in for it."

"I'm here, Ari. I'm here until the end of my days. This is it. Arrow-mount, the shop, you — until we're both old and cranky and can no longer get up those stairs to our apartment."

Ari hesitated, his brow furrowing. "Is this going to be enough for you? Staying here, settling in. No more adventure."

"I want you, my love, more than anything else in the world. This is more than enough. *You* are more than enough, more than I could ever deserve. I know I've said that I've always wanted a life of luxury, but I would be happy with you in complete squalor, Ari. I was happier with you on a dusty road with nothing more than our bags as pillows than I ever was inside castle walls."

Ari's cheeks colored and he looked down and away, swallowing visibly. Finn bent and retrieved the bundle of wildflowers from his bags before reaching toward Ari, hesitating. With a soft nod from him, Finn threaded the flowers carefully through Ari's braids, just above his pointed left ear.

"Promise me something," whispered Ari, looking deep into Finn's eyes as Finn's fingers lingered along the side of his love's face. "The next time you feel anxious about something, promise me you'll talk to me about it first."

"I promise." Finn let out a shaky breath and brushed a careful hand along Ari's jaw, running his thumb against his cheekbone. "This is our new adventure, Ari. This is the start of our second story. No matter what we do —"

Ari drew him in with a sharp tug of his shirt and kissed him fiercely, like he was drowning, and Finn was air. Finn threaded his fingers into Ari's hair, gripping the back of his head tight. He ached for this proximity, to feel Ari close enough that he could hold him forever.

He never wanted to let go. Never again.

When they broke apart, Finn registered cheering. "I think we have an audience."

Ari laughed, the sound and feeling bubbling up against Finn's chest. They turned, seeing a small crowd around them. He caught sight of May and Andrew, old Neema and Della, Dorian and Diana, Calian the giantkin, and even Kaida and her mom, dotted between other townsfolk who had helped paint the outside of the bookstore.

Finn threaded his arm around Ari's hips, his fingers gripped into the material of Ari's shirt, keeping him close. "I'm glad you're all here, actually," Ari said, smiling out at all those gathered with the slightest pink tinge to his cheeks. "Spread the word — the store is going to have a grand reopening in three days!"

"You didn't open the store?" Finn turned to him as the crowd cheered again. "Were there some delays with the shelving or the desk?"

"It's all done, and I could have. But, I just…" Ari shook his head and leaned his forehead against Finn's. "I couldn't bring myself to without you here. And Sage, of course. She would kill me if I opened without her."

A few folks came up to them and shook their hands, welcoming Finn home and congratulating them on the bookshop. Ari threaded his fingers through Finn's, his soft unmarred skin warm against Finn's rougher, scarred hands. Finn looked up at the shop again as the crowd began to disperse, leaving the two of them be.

Finn smiled up at the old hook that still swung above their doorway, secured into the wall above their new front doors. "How about A Second Story?"

"Mmm?"

"For the shop name," he said, motioning to the shop with his free hand. "We need a new sign, and I still think Arrowmount Books isn't quite the right fit."

"A Second Story." Ari smiled wide. "That's perfect. I'll talk to the Alderidges tomorrow."

They stood there for a little while longer, the sea air twisting around them, hands clasped tight, neither one wanting to be the first to let go.

Finally, Ari said, his voice breathy and quiet. "Come and see."

Finn walked through their shop slowly, taking in the fresh, wooden shelves of organized books, the clean lines, and the richness of the paint. Here and there grew real, living greenery between the shelving and books, plants that had already wound their way around some of the shelves. The scent of newly cut and stained wood held on the air as he moved, erasing the memory of the musty old shop entirely.

Finn could see a bit of every single bookshop they had visited reflected in the space around them. Here, though, Finn wanted to hole up inside for hours to browse, which he had never felt before in a bookshop. For an avid book lover like Ari, this shop must be something straight out of a dream.

Ari himself waited by the front window, scratching Sophie the cat surreptitiously, watching Finn take in the shop. Sophie hadn't been very happy when Finn walked in, and even now, she sat glaring at him, her tail flicking back and forth. He would have to buy her a particularly tasty treat (or five) to get back in her good graces.

"It's perfect, Ari," said Finn, still taking in the shop.

"Really? You think so? I was still a little concerned about where the mystery novels are, but this is the only way the shop makes sense in my head, and well, I just..."

"Really."

Later that night, Finn studied Ari's face as gentle moonlight leaked through the window behind their bed, sheets tangled around them. He staved off sleep for a while, slowly running his fingers through Ari's unbound hair, gazing at the slopes and edges of his love's face.

Golden Evening Sunlight

Arileas

The night before the grand reopening of the shop, Finn took Ari's hand and lead him to the stairs that lead up to their apartment.

"It's finally ready," said Finn, slightly breathless. Ari's heart squeezed at the light in his eyes, and the gentle crease of his forehead. "I meant to have it done when I left — but, well, I left, so..."

"I bet it's wonderful," said Ari, squeezing Finn's fingers reassuringly before heading up to their apartment.

The small space had totally transformed. Both new and old furniture was arranged perfectly for entertaining, warm honey wood that matched the shelving down in the shop below. A long, cozy couch sat along the wall to the left, with a few squishy, mismatched armchairs angled around it, each of them adorned with a multitude of pillows. Most of the blankets and pillows were rich jewel tones that reminded Ari of the luxurious tapestries back in King Zoren's court, which added a level of depth to the bright, clean space.

Soft, blue-white walls were decorated with ephemera that reminded Ari of Arrowmount. From an old, slightly rusted anchor to a painting of Arrowmount beach with the lighthouse in the corner, to the multicolored blankets and pillows and the soft arcane lights positioned around the space, it was perfect.

As Ari moved into the space, taking it all in, he noticed the choice of end tables that had shelves built into them for storage, which made him smile even wider. They'd be perfect to fill with books. He turned on his heel and saw the long wooden shelves that were built into the wall along the side of the door, left mostly blank for Ari's personal library.

The kitchen and bathroom had been scrubbed top to bottom, countertops replaced with fresh, polished stone, and the cabinets had been repainted to a soft, muted green a few shades lighter than the shop's walls.

Finn leaned against the door, hands in his pockets, as Ari took the space in. Ari moved to the bedroom, noticing that it was already furnished with the bed from downstairs.

"When did you do this?"

"I had Andrew and Sage help me when you went to the market this morning," said Finn with a soft shrug.

"Sneaky."

Finn had strung the arcane bauble lights inside, illuminating the bed adorned with a fresh comforter and bright pillows, and the old shelves around the room had been replaced with freshly made ones that matched the store downstairs.

Ari turned back to look at his partner, his love, and beamed at him.

"Do you like it?"

"Like it?" Ari closed the distance and pulled Finn inside, wrapping him in his arms. "Darling, I love it."

The morning of the grand reopening shone bright and sunny with fluffy white clouds dotting the sky. Ari paced inside the shop, running a now familiar route between the shelves in front of their new desk — freshly carved with their new shop name — and the front of the shop, checking and double checking the snack tables they had assembled for the day.

Sage was fussing with a tiny green bow that she had tied around Sophie the cat's neck for the occasion, looking anxious herself. Sophie batted at the bow cautiously, wondering why it was staying around her neck.

When Finn walked into the shop, momentarily letting in a burst of sunlight and sound from townsfolk outside, Sage turned and looked at both of them, clasping her hands in front of her. "I have news."

Finn froze, a disbelieving smile growing on his face. "You're going?"

She nodded fervently, an anxious smile blooming across her face. "Granddad is *finally* okay with it."

Ari looked between the two of them, at a loss. Finn had filled him in on their adventure, but he hadn't really mentioned much about Sage's time there. Ari figured it was so Sage herself could tell everyone herself, but as of yet, she had been surprisingly quiet whenever they saw her.

"Going?"

"Oh, Mr. Damaris," said Sage, turning to him and looking simultaneously so happy she could burst and incredibly anxious. "I'm joining the adventuring party — you know, with Laera, Zantar, Drift, and Khu? They're coming to get me."

"Wow." Ari shook his head, impressed, but not entirely surprised. "I always knew that you were going to find yourself swept up in some kind of adventure, Sage."

Sage threw her arms around Ari's neck and laughed. "I'm so sorry to leave you so soon after the shop reopens, Mr. Damaris."

"No problem at all," he answered, beaming at her as she let go. "We'll find someone to help out, if we need."

"I got word from Laera this morning that they got their hands on a ship and crew and are coming down this way to get me. Laera —" she cleared her throat and Ari noted the darker tinge to her cheeks. "The *party* seems excited that I'm joining them. But — I don't want to wreck today. Today is about the bookstore. I just couldn't hold it in any longer."

"Today will be two celebrations in one, then." Finn walked over and threw an arm around her shoulder. "Ari, I dare say we'll have an experienced adventurer on our hands soon."

"Smart and capable. You're going to do great."

Sage gave Sophie the cat one last pat between her ears and spun on her heel to take in the shop one last time. She grinned under a wonderful flower crown that had been weaved in between braids and curls and horns, adorned with golden jewelry spotted with rubies. Today, her dress was bright and summery with thin sleeves and a corseted bodice that held in a plethora of skirts that positively bloomed when she moved.

"Whenever you're ready, Mr. Damaris."

"Please, Sage," said Ari, laughing. "You can call me Ari."

"As long as I work here, it's going to be Mr. Damaris and Mr. Finn," she answered with a smile. "Tomorrow, when I leave, it will be Ari and Finn, I promise."

Ari swallowed a small lump of emotion that rose suddenly in his throat, feeling watery and jittery all at once. He took a deep breath and straightened his shoulders, feeling Finn's arm loop around his waist.

"We've got this," said Finn softly, placing a kiss to Ari's cheek, careful not to jostle the tiny wildflowers woven through his braids.

"Let's do it."

They walked forward, reaching out and opening the double doors wide, letting in a cascade of warm, salty summer air and sunshine as a crowd of people outside cheered.

Finn beamed around at them all. "Welcome to the grand reopening!"

The same half-orc bard from the painting day kicked up a merry tune, smiling at the townsfolk. Ari had gone in search of her for today's grand reopening and found her covered in suds — Kirandir, as she had introduced herself, worked at the Old'n Narrow bar during the day so that she could entertain as bard at night. Today, she wore striking dark leather pants and a red shirt, buttons open to her breastbone as she sang along to her lute.

Some of the townsfolk moved into the store, helping Ari and Finn transport the tables of snacks out to the cobblestones outside, leaving room for people to walk freely amidst the newly built shelves inside.

"You'll find popular fiction here," said Ari, moving along with the small crowd into the store, "and romance there, adventure and crime further in. The back room is a small library of used books that we thought might be good for those who wish to borrow books instead."

"Sounds wonderful," said Zana, Kaida's mother, who stood holding onto the little girl's hand, keeping her from running amok in the shop. "We will definitely be interested in signing up."

"Fantastic, I have a tracking system to keep everything lined up and organized, if you'll come with me." Ari led them over to the front desk where he pulled out a couple cards he had designed with Sage, and a thick leger book, taking down Zana's information and which books she was taking out. He reached over the desk and handed Kaida one of the cards, where he had written her name along the back. "Bring that card back with the books if you wish to take out more, so that I know you're a trusted member."

"Ah, here we are." Ari turned toward an elegant older dark-skinned elf woman who held out her hand. Both of her long-pointed ears stretched out past a shaved head and were dotted with a host of gems and hanging charms. "Levana, pleased to meet you. I've heard all about you and your store from my son, Branwen."

"It's a pleasure," answered Ari with a smile.

The shop buzzed with life as patrons from all around Arrowmount came to see the renovated shop. Ari set up a few stacks of books to hold open the doors, keeping the flow of sunshine and shoppers easy and free. Without realizing it, the morning slid by. Ari alternated between standing behind the counter or swapping out with Sage as he visited with the townsfolk and Finn outside. He set a few of the quieter children up in the library with a few books, and soon they were crawling all over the soft chairs and blankets inside, finding the best spots to read.

Calian the giantkin arrived a little closer to noon in a nicely starched dress shirt and a rather jaunty bright blue and yellow bowtie. They nodded to Ari as they ducked inside the shop to peruse, quietly smiling at those around them.

Andrew and a couple other teenagers Ari had seen around Fetterly Place arrived around midday, all of them carting incredible amounts of food and drink from May's Cafe. May herself arrived soon after, Chervil's blue-horned head coming in behind.

During a moment of reprieve in the afternoon, Ari ducked out of the shop as the sun began to set beyond the rooftops of Arrowmount. He gasped, surprised, as he found himself swept up in Finn's arms. Finn spun the two of them around to Kirandir's music as the evening sunlight bathed the cobblestones in gold.

"We've done it," murmured Finn in Ari's ear, pulling their bodies closer together as they turned, the song slowing to a new one where the bard began to sing along, rich and melodic. The crowd had dwindled throughout the day, and now only a few townsfolk filtered in and out, checking out the shop and leaving with freshly purchased stories bundled under their arm, ready to whisk them off to new worlds.

"We have," answered Ari, leaning his forehead against Finn's with a smile, feeling absolutely, incandescently happy.

42

SAGE'S FAREWELL

Arileas

The Arrowmount port swelled with activity as Finn and Ari walked onto the wooden docks, joining the throng of workers, travelers, and sailors moving about. Brine and the slightest smell of fish lingered in the air. All manner of ships were docked today, from tiny row boats that were stocked up with goods ready to bring out to larger barges to larger ships that reminded Ari of pirate ships from adventure stories he read as a boy.

Shouts and hawkers filled the air, mingling with the cries of seabirds from above and the lapping waves beneath them.

"There," said Finn, pointing ahead to a large vessel crawling with a few figures off in the distance. It was anchored, waiting for its passengers to arrive. "That's the ship Sage described."

From top to bottom, the ship itself was fit for transporting goods and fighting off whatever one might find in the water. Though Ari himself

257

had never stepped aboard a ship, he knew of the stories of the various sea creatures and roving pirates that lived in the waters of the Caspasian Sea.

A collection of small row boats were moored nearby, with a few familiar figures transferring crates on board. A large woman with startling red hair stood and stretched, devoid of her usual plate amour. A light linen shirt strained over her muscles as she directed a few workers around her.

"Watch it, those are delicate!" She shouted at a dwarf moving a crate nearby. "They're peaches worth more than your life, Skism, and if I see so much as a single bruise —"

"Sorry miss," said the dwarf, nervously putting the crate down into the bottom of the boat.

"Laera!"

Ari turned toward the voice and noticed a light sage green figure cutting through the crowd, closely followed by an aged dark blue one. The red-haired woman turned with her hands on her hips toward the shout and let a brilliant smile break across her face as Sage threw herself into her strong arms, hugging her fiercely.

Finn and Ari walked up as Chervil and May joined them, smiling at the pair. Behind Laera fluttered Khu, who hopped out of a rowboat to greet them all.

"Are you all packed and ready?" Finn threw an arm over Sage's shoulders and gave her a squeeze. "You're off to be a proper pirate, you don't want to be stuck without rope."

"Adventurer," Sage corrected. "I don't think we'll be participating in any pirating."

"Not that I'm aware of," said Laera, shooting a quick wink in Sage's direction that made Ari smile.

"Just — be careful," said Chervil with a grimace, reaching to pull his granddaughter into a hug. "I know all of you really love chasing adventure, but there's also something to say about knowing when to run, alright?"

"Don't you worry, Mr. Tealeaf," said Laera, extending a hand to him. "We'll take good care of your granddaughter."

Ari wrapped his arms around Sage in a quick hug, the travel bag slung over her shoulder thudding against his hip. "If you need any replacement reads for your journey, feel free to send me a letter and let me know what port you'll be stopping at, and I'll have whatever's new shipped out your way."

"You'd do that?" Sage's eyes shone with unshed tears.

"Of course. Adventuring tends to get boring sometimes, with all that down time and nothing to do." He smiled and reached into his pocket, withdrawing a small, midnight blue velvet bag. "This is for you."

"Oh!" Sage lit up at the sight of it. "It'll be great to carry all my jewelry!"

"You'll find that it's quite a bit more spacious than it appears," he said. "Maybe your Library of Holding will rival my own one day."

Her mouth fell open. "A *Bag of Space*?"

"From both Finn and me, to thank you for all you've done to help us with the shop. Without you, we wouldn't have bought the shop and fallen in love with the town in the first place." He grinned at her. "There are a few of my favorites in there already, to get you started."

She threw her arms around him again and squealed with delight. "I will send you all as many letters as I can to keep you updated on our adventures, so you won't get bored of sitting around without me."

"Sage!" The group turned to see the crowd parting, a figure pushing their way through. Suddenly Andrew appeared, at hip height of most of the sailors around. He brandished a long, thin package about his height toward Sage. She bent down and gave him a big hug. "I thought I was going to miss you. This is for you."

Andrew handed her the package with a smile. She gasped unwrapping it fast, revealing a beautifully crafted longsword sheathed in a bundle of leather, balanced to Sage's height. The hilt of the blade was wrapped around with a beautiful dark blue grip, and the pommel was wrought into a bronzed head of a lion.

"Andrew," Sage breathed, looking at the length of it, drawing it slightly out of the sheath. "This is too much."

"It's from all of us. You'll learn how to use it, to stay safe?"

Sage glanced at Laera, who took the hilt of the blade and unsheathed it entirely. Everyone backed up a few feet to give her space. The brilliant gleaming metal shone in the sun as Laera inspected it, giving it a few twists in her hand before sheathing and handing it back to Sage with a smile. "I'll have you fighting like a master in no time, Tealeaf."

Sage blushed slightly green as she strapped the sheath around her waist and slid the sword in so that it rested comfortably by her hip, next to an ornate dagger. Finally, she let out a long sigh and smiled tearily around at them all.

"Oh, I didn't realize this would be so hard," she said, her voice coming out thick and watery.

"It's always hard, leaving those you love behind," said May, rubbing one of Sage's arms lovingly. Laera stepped back, leaving them to their goodbyes.

Chervil wrapped his granddaughter in one last crushing hug before she stepped away, standing next to Laera and Khu as the last of the crates were loaded on board their little group of rowboats. The crew settled in to take them back to the ship waiting patiently out in the water.

"Make sure you don't go up that creaky ladder without Andrew or someone else to watch you, Granddad," Sage called to Chervil as she stepped on board next to Laera. "And see Dorian and Di about getting a new one made. It's too dangerous to keep climbing up to check on the light."

"Yes, my dear," said Chervil, a watery smile on his face.

"Stay safe!" Finn called as Laera shoved the boat away from the dock with an oar, waving at them all. The other row boats quickly fell into line behind them, carting crew members and crates toward their ship. "Make sure to watch your back at all times, enemies will pop up when you least expect it!"

Ari found it hard to speak for a few minutes as they watched the little trail of row boats meet up with the ship. Finn squeezed Ari into him.

"She'll be okay," he whispered in Ari's ear. "She's more equipped than all of us ever were."

"Oh, I know," said Ari, chuckling and wiping a tear from his cheek. "She's going to love it out there."

Chervil, May, Andrew, Finn, and Ari waited until the row boats were all tied to the side of the ship and lifted out of the water, the crew officially on deck with their goods and passengers. A small figure stood at the edge of the deck waving at them as the sun began to set, casting the world in rich oranges, pinks, and purples.

As the ship raised anchor and set off, their small group turned and began to work their way back toward Fetterly Place, arm in arm, one member short. They walked up to the old lighthouse and stood, looking out at the ocean a while longer, away from the noise and business of the port. Sage's ship travelled out to open ocean, shrinking on the horizon.

Just before it vanished, May gasped and pointed out toward the ship. A beautiful burst of magic escaped from the deck of the ship, casting fireworks up into the sky in an explosion of color. Their group cheered and waved, even though the ship was much too far gone for Sage to see.

After

A few weeks later

Finn walked into the meadow, wildflowers brushing against his knees. The sun kissed his wild dark hair, illuminating a soft halo on his head. He had one of his favorite loose shirts on, the buttons open down to his breastbone to catch the late summer sun on his brown, bronzed skin. Both wrists of his shirt were cuffed with two pearl buttons, prizes that his partner had given him a few weeks ago to celebrate the anniversary of a couple magical beads used long ago, in another field of wildflowers.

He let his fingers trail along the tops of the plants, smiling with a funny sort of smile down at them.

"What is it, darling?"

He looked up toward the voice, his smile widening into a look of pure joy as his eyes met his partner's. A lithe, handsome elf with white hair that was currently braided back in three twisting braids that collected into one thick cord draped over his shoulder, sat leaning against a tree.

Ari sat amidst the wildflowers, shaded by heavily laden branches with brilliant green leaves. Golden yellow sunlight leaked through the canopy in swaths of color around him. In his hands lay a book, one finger carefully placed between the pages, holding his spot as he looked up at the man, an expression of pure happiness across every feature. Ari had a few flowers threaded them through his hair, dotting the braid with yellow.

"I am simply admiring the beauty."

"That look on your face is not one of just contemplation, Finn," he said, smiling. "It's one of mischief and planning."

"And is that so bad, that I am planning, Ari?"

Ari felt his heart swell as it always did as Finn walked over to him, a look on Finn's face so plainly in love that Ari couldn't help but melt.

He would risk it all to see that smile a million times over.

The man pulled out a familiar old dagger to slice free a perfect sprig of tiny white bulbs from a bundle of wildflowers near his hand. Twiddling it in his fingers, the tiny white flowers danced.

"For you," said Finn, walking up and sinking down to his knees in front of Ari, wildflowers tickling his face and throat. Finn reached up, and, much like he had back in the meadow at the beginning of this story, their story, he threaded the flowers right above Ari's long, pointed ear.

Ari smiled, looking into Finn's ocean blue eyes, noticing a sheen of joy there he hadn't seen before. It almost looked like he was about to cry with happiness. "What's got you all sappy, darling?"

"You," he answered simply.

"Oh?" Ari found himself slightly breathless, as though he was meeting this man for the first time. "Little old me?"

"You are the furthest thing from old, Arileas," he said, rolling Ari's full name around his mouth deliciously. Finn moved up until his lips were just a breath away from Ari's, pausing, holding the air there with the pure power he knew he had. "You're mine, my love."

"And you are mine," breathed Ari, closing the space and kissing his love deeply, perfectly, tasting the sun and sea air on his lips.

Finn moved to sit next to him, lacing his fingers with Ari's together in his lap. They sat together, gazing down over the seaside town that had become their home, the ocean glittering off in the distance like a tapestry of rippling gold.

"We should go back down to the shop," murmured Ari as Finn let his head drop onto Ari's shoulder. "I'm not entirely sure Andrew will be able to handle the mid-morning rush."

"You mean the rush of the three regulars who enjoy walking around the shop for hours?" Finn chuckled. "Andrew is more than capable. We can take a break, my love."

"Yes, well, if we're not careful, we might accidentally spend all day up here."

Finn moved so that he could take Ari's chin in his fingers, turning Ari's face toward his. "And would that be so bad?"

"No, but we have responsibilities."

"I remember coming to this town wanting no responsibilities at all," said Finn, letting his head fall back onto Ari's shoulder. "Remember that? When we were on vacation?"

"Instead we found a life here."

"A life among books and the sea."

"The most perfect life, don't you think?"

Finn let out an uproarious laugh, taking the book that Ari's other hand still held fast. He slid his thumb into it as he brought it over, making sure to keep Ari's page. "You and your books."

"It's a *good* life," said Ari, amending his earlier statement. "But what makes mine perfect is that I get to own my own bookstore with a rather curmudgeonly old man by my side."

Finn gasped dramatically. "When did Dew come back into town? I ought to have a word, stealing my love from me."

"Perhaps you can duel for my heart, like the heroes do in my book," said Ari, tapping the cover of the tome Finn now held. "Swords and everything."

"Would you accept daggers instead?" Finn chuckled. "Do you think the two heroes are in love?"

Ari tilted his head, thinking. "Yes, I believe they are. They have a way of talking to one another where they banter constantly, and end up rather close in conversations, and always have this drawn out pause before they pull away. One of them, in fact, is the other's manservant and has secret magic powers he must keep hidden away unless he wishes to find himself at the end of the hangman's noose. It's all very dramatic."

"Perhaps we ought to learn from them," said Finn, flipping the book open and inspecting the page he had held. "We don't have tension, do we?"

"We don't need tension, darling." Ari took Finn's face in hand and kissed him tenderly on the side of his forehead. "We have love. That's more than enough."

"'True, and deep, and lasting,'" recited Finn, pointing to a line on the page. "You know, I could get into this reading thing."

"That's halfway through the book, Finn. You can't get a sense reading one sentence partway through the story."

"Ah, you forget. The middle is my favorite part. That's where all the drama and action bits happen."

Ari deigned not to tell him that those bits usually happened near the end of a story, right before the big declarations or the climactic end battles. Instead, he smiled, shook his head and sat back once again, leaning into Finn's warm shoulder.

"Are you tired of this place yet, my love?"

"I could never become tired of the beauty of such a place," answered Ari, looking out at Arrowmount laid out below them. "That would be next to impossible, darling."

Wildflowers danced happily in the golden light, their brilliantly colored heads ducking and swaying throughout the meadow. Arileas and Finnean both sat together, hands entwined, contemplating the journey that had brought them together, and what would come next.

CHARACTERS

- **Andrew**: A young gnome who helps at May's cafe.

- *Arileas Damaris*: (pronounced: Arr-ih-lee-ass Dam-Ahr-iss) Our lovely elf wizard.

- **Ayla**: (pronounced: A-la) A Boarsrest inn owner.

- **Bertie Cobb**: The owner of Cobb's Down-By-The-Beach.

- **Branwen**: A young, studious elf.

- **Brennyn**: Original party member, human ranger.

- **Calian**: (pronounced: Cal-ee-an) Mysterious giantkin who seems to live around Arrowmount.

- **Cecily Little**: Magic Goods stall owner, earth elemental.

- **Chervil Tealeaf**: (pronounced: shh-er-vill) Lighthouse runner and owner, Sage's granddad, blue fiendling.

- **Dew**: The old owner of the store Arrowmount Books, dwarven.

- **Della**: An elderly gnome who lives on Fetterly Place.

- **Diana Alderidge**: One of the pair of siblings that own and operate Alderidge's Wood Working, goliath.

- **Dorian Alderidge**: One of the pair of siblings that own and operate Alderidge's Wood Working, goliath.

- **Drift**: Adventuring party member, air elemental sorcerer and rogue.

- ***Finnean Shademark/Goldmark***: (pronounced: Fin-ee-an) Our lovely human ex-assassin.

- **Kaida**: (pronounced: kai-dah) The little red dragonkin child who loves books.

- **Khu**: (pronounced: coo) Adventuring party member, birdfolk paladin.

- **King Tenan** (Pralon): The king and sovereign ruler of the Kingdom of Pralon. Finnean's employer, and, according to him, a distant relation.

- **King Zoren** (Zidien): The king and sovereign ruler of the Kingdom of Zidien. Arileas' employer, and the one who originally hired Ari and Finn's adventuring party to hunt and kill the notorious assassin, the Shade.

- **Kirandir**: Local bard, half-orc. Works at the Old'n Narrow.

- **Klea**: (pronounced: klay-uh) Original party member, orc paladin.

- **Laera**: (pronounced: lay-rah) Adventuring party member, barbarian.

- **Lord Wymarc**: The Lord of Arrowmount, human.

- **May Camire**: Owner of May's Cafe, half-elven druid.

- **Neema**: An elderly gnome who lives on Fetterly Place.

- **Ollie**: A magical accomplice from the Kingdom of Pralon that Finn purchased magic from to enact his freedom.

- **Prim**: Original party member, gnomish barbarian.

- **Sage Tealeaf**: Bookstore clerk turned adventurer, green fiendling druid.

- **Selke**: Ruins & Relics shop owner.

- **Soren**: Original party member, birdfolk cleric.

- **Taena Cobb**: Owner of the Bronzed Bee, gnome.

- **Zantar**: Adventuring party member, dwarven fighter.

GLOSSARY

- **Alieweth**: (pronounced: ah-lee-weth) A northern kingdom, part of the Nerian Empire.

- **Arrowmount**: A coastal town, where our story takes place.

- **Bag of Space**: a magical item that has an extra dimensional space held within it, which makes it a very handy tool for adventurers, because it holds a lot of stuff. The one Arileas Damaris uses is primarily for his books (he affectionately calls it his Library of Holding). Ari's is a bit special, much like a magic bag should be. He can adjust the size of the mouth of the bag with a flick of his wrist, to accommodate the size of things he puts inside.

- **Birdfolk**: Beings that are comfortable both in the sky and on the ground. They can have many different kinds of plumage, as birds do. They aren't overly tall as beings, and often are never taller than about five feet.

  - *Notable birdfolk:* Soren, the cleric from Finn and Ari's original adventuring party, is a black birdfolk, akin to a raven. Khu, the paladin from the adventuring party that Sage joins, is a blue birdfolk, akin to a bluebird.

- **Catfolk**: Feline humanoids who are covered in fur and have very cat-like features. They are mainly bipedal, however can get around very quickly on all fours. And, much like aarakockras, they range in many different variations and colorings.

- **Claymore**: A village in the Brenem Empire

- **Dragon Scale**: a magical component so potent that it acts as conduits to spells that need components to create. Dragon scale is mined out of the Nerian Empire's mountains, and is a highly sought after commodity in the northern empire. It is rarer to see in the Brenem Empire, but of course like all commodities, it makes its way where gold will take it.

- **Druids**: A class of magic users that are much more nature based, and find their magic through the force of nature itself or natural deities.

  - *Notable druids:* May, the half-elven cafe owner, and Sage, who is learning still.

- **Elementals**: Humanoids that take on aspects of their elemental lineage. Most commonly there are air, fire, water, and earth elementals, but as there are many different aspects to each element, you'd be hard pressed to find many elementals who resemble one another, even if they were of the same element.

- *Notable elementals:* Cecily Little and Lottie Luck, earth elementals.

- **Feycross**: A small village in the Brenem Empire, where Finn and Ari first meet. Rumoured to have a portal to the fey realm nearby, but that has yet to be confirmed.

- **Fiendling**: Humanoid beings that have fiendish blood running through their veins, which gives them their often unique colouring, horns, tails, and occasionally sharp teeth. Along with average humans, they can range from about five feet to just over six feet tall.

  - *Notable fiendling:* Our lovely Sage, the bookstore clerk, who is a druid-in-training sage green fiendling. And her granddad, Chervil, who is a dark blue aged fiendling with incredibly impressive horns.

- **Fireball/ball of fire**: A very powerful and slightly reckless fire-based spell, most often used by wizards, that originates as a bright streak of firelight from the spell caster's fingertip and explodes out in, funnily enough, a ball of flame.

- **Giantkin**: A broad term to refer to races of folk who loosely resemble humans, in a way, but are related to giants in a distant, second or third or tenth cousin fashion. In this work, this term is used to refer to giantfolk that occasionally have large drooping ears and wide faces with a slightly snout-like shaped nose. They're very tall, often reaching well over seven feet tall, and range from having tough, grey skin with no fur to slightly softer, more furry beings.

- *Notable giantkin:* Calian, the mysterious being that loves books and hot cocoas and often is seen wearing a jaunty bowtie.

- **Goliaths**: A half-giant race of tall humanoids, most often with varying grey-toned skin. They range from over six feet tall to well over seven feet.

- *Notable goliaths*: Diana and Dorian Alderidge.

- **Gust**: A druidic cantrip wherein a small gust of wind can be conjured. Sage uses a gust cantrip to help air out the store in the middle of cleaning, momentarily helping drop the temperature.

- **Hags**: Horrible, corrupted witches that are connected to the dark fey and primal magical forces. They often take the form of old women to fool passers by.

- **Illusory magic**: A school of magic that aims, usually, to deceive the senses and minds of others. Spells include the ability to go invisible and disguise one's self. There are some more lovely spells seen cast by Ari himself as he entertains the children outside of the bookshop with illusory fireworks.

- **Iluinn**: The God of Life and Endurance.

- 'Iluinn's Mercy' is but one of many curses throughout the Brenem Empire that uses the god's name, and probably one of the more tasteful ones, to be honest.

- **Maigsir**: The Goddess of the Sea.

    - Mighty Maigsir, or other creative expletives, have been often heard throughout Arrowmount as a favoured curse.

- **Mosfell**: A small village in the Brenem Empire

- **Ollie's Magic Memory Beads**: A magical invention invented by Ollie herself, though she doesn't advertise that very often. It is a memory charm condensed and held in a physical form for non-spell casters and spell casters alike to handle and cast said spell remotely and whenever they like. When used, the spell takes a few seconds to take effect — mainly so that the "caster" can get away from it and not be affected themselves — and is amplified to cast across an area, rather than the usual modify memory spell which is directed at a single person. This spell did work on Ari and would have continued to work on him if he had not seen Finn again, despite the brain fog bothering him. He had brain fog because he was on the edge of the range of the magic.

- **Prestidigitation**: A very minor cantrip that allows the caster to do something minor, such as snuffing out a campfire or cleaning dust off of clothing.

- **Radiant magic**: A branch of magic that is based in divine power, often seen used by clerics and paladins. It glows in a heavenly light.

- **Trolls**: Very large monsters that exist, really, in any climate in any part of the empire. They are very tall — on average nine feet tall — and are pretty brutal to come across. Trust me, you don't really want to.

- **Wisps**: Malicious creatures that appear as torches or lanterns to lure travellers off their path. They can shock any attackers that come nearby.

- **Wizards**: A class of magic users who learn to do magic through a spell book and lots and lots of practice.

  - *Notable wizard*: our very own Arileas Damaris, who is affectionately called a "silly wizard" by Finn at least once.

- **Wolven**: Very large wolf-like creatures that hunt in packs, and often live deep within the Blackshell Forest.

ACKNOWLEDGEMENTS

I think it would be remiss of me to not start this without acknowledging the person who began my obsession with cozy fantasy: Travis Baldree himself. Up until the moment I heard of *Legends and Lattes,* I had been unaware that my life was about to change irrevocably. Once that book was in my hands, my brain started to churn with possibilities, and two characters that I had once thought were going to have an action-packed adventure from kingdom to kingdom instead became two tired adventurers who really wanted to find a safe place to land. Thank you, Travis, for starting my own obsession with cozy fantasy, and launching much of the internet (or at least my side of it) into a deep love for all things soft and magical. With a side of coffee, of course.

Through the writing and creating process, it can be tricky to know whether or not your brain is going in the proper direction and that your story isn't absolutely unintelligible. Thankfully, though, I've been blessed by the universe to have found many people who have given their time and knowledge to help me make this story the best it can be. My lovely beta readers, you were all absolutely invaluable to this story, and I cannot thank you enough. Cat, especially – you have somehow become a beta reader for not only this project but every project that I've written in full since we met and have also become a wonderful friend as well. Thank you for your Taylor Swift love, the sharing of fox gifs and videos, and your championing of this book and its sequels.

To my lovely friends who have offered support, excitement, and endless help whenever I asked for it from day one. SJ, who was the first to know about Arileas (in a very different capacity than the one we see him in this book. I'm sorry for originally making him such a bastard, and I hope this book makes up for it); Yelani, Sophie, and Sofia, who, though they don't usually read fantasy, were excited about this project from day one; Hannah, Alexander, Tessa, Sarah, Luke, Ellie, Kas, Yoni, Nirmal, Tamsen, Danny, and Elliott, who all were incredibly enthusiastic and hyped this book up along the way; and Cass, who has been with me the longest, and has always been the best cheerleader to my creative endeavors. I love you all so, so much.

A specific thank you to my Dungeons and Dragons players who played in this world first — Tessa, Sarah, SJ, Yelani, Elliott, Alexander, and Hannah — I appreciate you all endlessly for allowing me to throw weird things at you and send you running around my world so I can have a reason to keep living in it, and for giving me secret bits of detail in the world that will one day make it into my written stories as well.

To Tessa Brenan, for being both an amazing friend and wonderfully talented artist who kept me updated with regular bursts of serotonin as she created *A Second Story*'s absolutely stunning cover — you are positively the best. Those sketches and the progress updates had me roiling with anticipation, and every time you sent me another update with progress, I couldn't help but spend the evening beaming and sharing the covers with everyone I could. You are so, so talented, and thank you endlessly for bringing Ari and Finn to life.

Thank you to all my lovely friends from my online life who were cheering me on from the moment I first talked about my idea to try to write a 70k-word cozy fantasy in a month, and every step of the way since. You all constantly fill me with so much joy when you express your excitement for and continue to support my content, and the way you immediately hopped on the Arrowmount Books train without having read a single word. My lovely friends, you are all the best, and I adore you all.

Thank you especially too to Sarah Sutton, Amy Prokopis, and Hannah Long, authors I've met through the internet that I can now happily call friends. The internet is so cool that way, isn't it? You guys are the best, and I am continuously inspired by you every day.

And of course, thank you to Sara Lubratt, my wonderful editor, who was incredibly thoughtful with her edits when I handed over this project and helped guide *A Second Story* to the final form you, dear reader, hold now.

There are so many more people in my life that have added fragments to my writing life and love of books, but I think the biggest contributors have to be my parents. Thank you, Mom and Dad, for building a love of reading in me from day one. Thank you for letting me buy innumerable books that I would read faster than you could keep up with or would stay sitting on my shelves collecting dust, for letting me create endlessly, and thank you for letting me use Mom's PC in the guest room to write *A Puppy Named Rudy* all those years ago. It was, quite honestly, the catalyst for all of the millions of words I've written since. I love you both so much.

And finally, thank *you* dear reader, for taking a chance on Ari and Finn's story. I hope it brought you comfort and a soft place to land for a little while.

About the Author

J. A. Collignon (AKA: Jenna, but you can call her Jenn) is a Canadian author based out of the prairies, who loves everything fantasy. You name it: fantasy books, movies, TV shows, TTRPG podcasts, and she even runs her own piratey Dungeons and Dragons campaign for her friends. Most often, she can be found on her couch with a thick fantasy book in hand.

With her first cozy fantasy book, *A Second Story*, the first in the Arrowmount Books series, you can rest assured that Jenn will be coming out with many more stories to cozy up with a mug of something warm soon!

Jenn is an avid member of the bookish internet community through her Youtube channel, Tiktok, Instagram, and Twitter. Follow her to keep up to date on future book releases.

Youtube: Jenn's Bookshelf
Tiktok: @jennsbookshelf
Instagram: @authorjacollignon
Twitter: @BookshelfJenn

9 781738 868209